The Dictionary of
Animal Languages

The Dictionary of Animal Languages

Heidi Sopinka

SCRIBE

Melbourne • London

Scribe Publications

18–20 Edward St, Brunswick, Victoria 3056, Australia
2 John Street, Clerkenwell, London, WC1N 2ES, United Kingdom
3754 Pleasant Ave, Suite 100, Minneapolis, Minnesota 55409 USA

This edition published by arrangement with
Penguin Random House Canada Limited

First published by Scribe 2018

Printed and bound in the UK by CPI Group (UK) Ltd, Croydon CR0 4YY

Scribe Publications is committed to the sustainable use of natural resources
and the use of paper products made responsibly from those resources.

9781947534520 (US hardback)
9781925322835 (ANZ paperback)
9781911617020 (UK hardback)
9781925548754 (e-book)

CiP records for this title are available from the National Library of Australia
and the British Library.

scribepublications.com
scribepublications.com.au
scribepublications.co.uk

For JL

When you dream of a savage bull, or a lion, or a wolf pursuing you, this means: it wants to come to you. You would like to split it off, you experience it as something alien—but it just becomes all the more dangerous.

—CARL JUNG, *CHILDREN'S DREAMS*

Pigeon

Columba livia domestica;
eating bread left by a homeless man
+ raw field recording of rain.

MY EYES BECAME HER EYES, the eyes of someone who died young. Which makes them hard to live with. But Skeet doesn't know this. Or Ondine. Or Valentina even. The only one left who knows is me.

Any eggs in the coop, Frame?

Yes, I tell him. But he hasn't heard. He's shaken out the coffee beans and ground out my voice.

The fork tines clink rhythmically against the steel bowl like the metallic call of a long-legged grassland bird I have transcribed. I am attuned to sounds. After all the animals I have recorded, read glyphic and elemental, like songs. He turns on the tap at the sink. He knows water works better than milk. It occurs to me we are a woman and a man in a stone house. The man making breakfast. It could be one of those tender moments that occur, the kind between sex and full-dressed protocol. But this isn't that. I haven't told him of the letter. It is a bit of a trick, this

1

timing between it and Skeet arriving out of nowhere by the same low sun.

We eat our food slowly, in comfortable silence. My legs dangle from the too-high chair like a child's. Skeet butters the bread in angular little lines, and says, This place is smaller than I thought.

I know, I say. It's intensely orchestrated, three-quarter size. She must have culled everything and photographed from cunning angles. What is that? High or low, I can never remember.

High.

He sips his coffee looking straight ahead. I am reminded of my fondness for him. How nothing between us is insincere.

You know this valley has been called the Playground of Kings, I say. The Garden of France. Which makes you think it should be those things, but all I see are these hot yellow fields of sunflowers that will soon be cut, gleaming and bristling like a big cat's pelt. They could be cornfields in middle America. I hold up my mug, feeling the steam on my skin. This coffee doesn't taste like anything. It has happened to food too.

He looks out the window and blinks at the sun.

I suppose it has a certain kind of beauty. He eats his toast. The beauty of death.

I've missed you, Skeet.

Anyway Frame, what does it matter? You're like an animal. Not even one percent changed by geography. He pauses. How are you?

Well you and I both know that isn't true. The leg is better, I tell him, but that is hardly an event. Aren't you going to ask me?

What?

About le grand projet.

Oh.

2

He is distracted. Normally this is his first line of inquiry. His eyes downcast, on the envelope with the letterpressed insignia and the same French font as all the graveurs on the table by the front door. A letter is pulled from a postbox and everything is pulled with it. Maybe it is me who is distracted.

Skeet gets up and paces the room, his fingers following the papers taped to the walls. I forgot this about him. He cannot sit for more than a few minutes. He goes quiet for a while and then turns to face me.

The photographs are everywhere, interlocking and branching patterns, extreme density interspersed with silences. All the data, the transcriptions in fieldbooks and papers with rubber bands in shopping bags on the floor. For a moment, I see the way someone else would see it. Not Skeet, but someone normal. How barking mad it all looks. As though I might have finally and definitely lost my mind. Despite feeling off-pitch, the project reassures me. I have always known myself in it.

After a long silence, Skeet sucks in air. Fuck.

Oh my god. What?

He stops dead. Frame.

What?

I don't know how to tell you this.

What? You look so worried. This look on your face, I've never seen it before.

He breathes out. He's not sure which thing to tell, there are so many.

What's going on? Is it about the project? I say, unsure.

Well— he hesitates. Yes and no.

Thud. We both startle at the sound. The bird again. It began hurling itself at the window before I left the house yesterday morning. I switched off the light and removed the keys and discs from the windowsill, all the deceptive things, to warn it off. *Thud.* It hit the glass again. The sun was bright and the wisp-white clouds passed above as I walked out to the car. In the country you are always driving. The glass is hot; the driver's seat swings wildly. I keep a breadboard wedged behind it, which allows my feet to touch the pedals and fixes the seat in position. The sky is vast and clear. There is only one road out. The fields blur, silvered by clouds that momentarily close over them. A relief from the gold sizzle that rattles the grasses dry and forces dogs to lie in shade, ribcages labouring. Everything grows from the cracks. Roses, ditches of poppies, trees bending with fruit. This time of year people come. They file into castles with conical spires. They pose in front of churches. I have no emotion for it. The beauty is general. The car radio crackles. What's-her-name is singing, *Yeah what have I got? / Nobody can take away.* And it suddenly strikes me as funny that we see ourselves as immortal. What I have got somebody *is* about to take away. Nobody gets out of here alive. The sun flickers in like a heartbeat through the evenly spaced plane trees that parallel the road, their wide calico trunks tessellate.

For months nothing arrived from the conservatory or the university, but today, in the small metal postbox, finally, a letter. I think of countless fieldbooks full of animal sounds shaped into images, webbed maps, rough chorales, thin silver frequencies. They all funnel into this single gesture, a woman swivelling on her heel, handing me a white rectangle, eyes fixed on the next person in line. Except they don't. I open it standing at the blue and yellow counter. Everything is bright and vibrating in the room. Pain swings and pits behind my eyes. Every little thing shoots off course, like looking up at the night sky of another hemisphere, not a single star you can name.

I drive home with the open letter on my lap, passing right by the short gravel lane to the house. It seems impossible that something that weighs almost nothing can contain such stunning facts. My breathing is panicked and sharp. The fields ripple and ride in waves from the wind. White cows all facing the same direction, lining up not as the farmers say to predict rain, but because the earth is one big magnet. The windows are down, open to birdsong and the thin layer of dust that bangs up from the cracked dirt road. These things I have seen a hundred times before I am now observing with total attention. The sky is saturated and smooth as stone, cut through with small grey wings. Cold perspiration films on my body, my clothes stuck to the leather seat. My hands are shaking. Of all the time it has taken between it and now. Facts never come soon enough. What is a fact? So much of life is lost vacant time of which you remember almost nothing. Memory is not a fact. But what is memory? *Billions of infinitesimal particles collected from outerspace, Edison said.*

Skeet moves his chair, the low timbre of wood dragging across the stone floor.

I first met Skeet years ago, at an airport, a kind of shack at the end of the tarmac where I was waiting for him in Whitehorse. He was tall with a good set of eyes, a bit of wildness in them. He looked serious, but had a part-grin that hid crooked teeth, the kind you don't see anymore. The first thing he said after looking around was, You get the feeling that this is a town where people arrive on horseback. He is friendly but remote. The fieldwork is such a welcome antidote to all the hours bent over laboratory recording equipment. We spend great swaths of time sitting in cold, dry snow, waiting. Our eyes darting, anticipating the flashes of grey that will appear against the blinding white. In town we see a raven kick snow off a roof that slides and lands on a man's head. It fits with the legend, where the Haida say they are the creator, but also the trickster. There is a white raven in legend too. Supposedly it brought the world into existence. It stole the sun and the moon and then flew through a smoke hole, turning black but also bringing light to the world.

Up there back then, Skeet was finishing his dissertation on lupine acoustic structures and had been sent to assist with field research. The conservatory said he was the brightest doctoral candidate they had ever seen. A Yukon winter. A cold-layered beauty. The sunlight through the icy air made the objects firelit. The truck skidded on its chains. I was struck by the feeling that all I wanted was to keep going. Everything felt safer sitting high up, looking out through chilled windows. I started to tell him things that I've told no one, and he talked too. His long limbs folded into the truck, eyes squinting at the sky.

He seems to have dropped out of nowhere. The name isn't his. He was born too early. Rangy, he was more mosquito than baby. Abbreviated and then stuck. He says his mother and father fought like cats and dogs until his father left for good. She was fifteen years old. Everyone admitted her beauty, but as self-destruction went, she was expert. Skeet says they lived above a shabby hair salon. Hairdresser found God, his mother told him. Closes shop at the wrong times. She had tried sleeping in rollers, but woke up feeling as though she'd been punched in the neck. She told him she couldn't think through the catpiss smell of ammonia from the perms. The one boy he brought home said filthy things about his mother the next day at school. She sat dead-eyed, smoking at the kitchen table in a see-through robe. She could get like that. He didn't know what was worse, that catatonic state or the frenzied one, when she said fantastical things he knew would never happen. He was always sent to school with his lunch in a narrow brown paper bag from the liquor store that ripped each time he pulled out its contents. Soon the teacher called his mother in. She wore a thin red leather belt with her tightest jeans she'd zipped up wet over hipbones with a metal hanger, lying on the floor. It made Skeet nervous. Whenever she wore them, a man would be in their kitchen the next morning. A child cannot grow, the teacher said, from eating potato chips and peaches from a can. The lunches are the starting point. His mother laughed, refusing to put out her cigarette. The teacher went further. He is a smart boy. She would help. His last vision of his mother before he was taken away was her standing in the doorway in nothing but a shiny, opaque pair of white underpants, clutching a bottle of rye. Black smudged raccoon eye makeup, the ends of her blond hair grazing her ribs. The smear of lipstick rubbed off from the bottle left her lips looking wounded. What are you looking at? His eyes going to the only clothed place. Godsakes, she laughed. It sounded like a crack. She looked down, then chopped her hands on either side of her pubic bone in a V. You sprang from these loins, she finally said.

When the woman had told him he could quickly go and collect his belongings he realized there was nothing he wanted to take. He was brought to a tall German couple, pastoralists who ran a self-sufficient farm and lived by Hermann Hesse's notion of the self. They adopted him. They tried to change his name to Hermann. They didn't like his name, which was tattooed above his birthmother's tailbone. He'd seen it sticking out from the top of her underpants, which he thought inane. What, is she going to forget his name? But they decided he'd already had too many things change. He grew up in the country. He watched nature programs with them, and they would quiz him energetically afterward. How many hearts does an octopus have! What's the lifespan of a housefly! Why do whales breathe air! It made him miss his mother. She liked to yell and laugh and slap the TV like it was a person. Except the show they saw about the opera singer. She got really quiet. All she said was, She's gotta voice like God is talking through.

The other children thought Skeet was cold, but inside a fire grew. He loved the start of school in fall. He loved fall. The scarlet leaves, he liked to think, were the minds of trees on fire. He liked the rows of glass cylinders in the science room at school. His favourite element from the periodic table was selenium. He grew to be surprisingly tall, like the German couple. And when he graduated from university, on a whim he bought a plane ticket from bursary money for his mother. He'd had a secret, but unpredictable, correspondence with her.

At his graduation, her seat remained empty long enough for him to think she wouldn't come. But she did come, oddly unaged. You've grown so handsome, she kept saying. She had her hands on him. If you squinted, they almost looked like a couple. She had unfocused eyes, a flask of whisky in her boot. She drained several plastic stemmed glasses of wine set out on a seminar table with a stiff white tablecloth glaring back under hot, two o'clock sun. As soon as he saw her, everything flooded back to him. Her need for attention. Her slurred speech. His longing for a mother whose face reflected something he recognized in himself. After the first prick of embarrassment, he always felt low. After all these years, after all the learning and travelling and studying, it occurred to him that she was still a child, whereas he no longer was.

Goddamn shit-hawks, she yelled, referring to the pigeons clotted on campus trees. She pulled out a pistol from her purse, steadied it, took aim, and then swivelled to face Skeet, saying, Okay, sugar, let's eat. Police were involved.

Skeet looked over at me in the truck. Something filled him

from the inside. His eyes pinned him to me with a feeling that neither of us yet knew. I felt his silent grief and a great wave of love for him, though all I managed to say was, They used to have a more exalted position in society, the pigeons.

He swallowed and nodded.

With their orange eyes and iridescent necks, I continued, they were brought to cities to be ornamental. Of course they are also vital messengers. They have been decorated in war.

Like a homeless man with a heroic past, he said, eyes fixed on an invisible mark.

The thing that his parents couldn't forgive was not what happened that day. Or that he'd contacted her. It's that he had done so without telling them. It's the trust, they said, that has been broken. The cardinal sin of the adoptee. When he left home to study and work, he was not sure if he would ever see them again. There were no letters.

A clatter of dishes, Skeet clearing breakfast. He takes out a pack of cigarettes, shakes two out, puts them both in his mouth, lights them, and passes one to me. Thing is, he exhales, what I'm trying to tell you— He pauses. Is that. Well. We're on the run.

The way he looks at me, I've no idea what to think. And I'm not sure what's more ridiculous. To have Skeet suddenly here out of nowhere or his using an expression like *on the run* as I sit here immovable.

Skeet, I'm ninety. I use the figure ninety, though in truth I am ninety-two. And still all this work left, I say, with an unintended quiver.

I see how close you are, Frame. You know that I do. I can help.

How, I say crossly, though immediately wish it had come out

more tenderly. I look at him, his hair sticking up in parts, and think there must be something left to do.

There's— we both say at the same time.

He says, You first, so loudly that I can tell he is surprised.

I received a letter yesterday, I say. I can hardly look in its direction. I take in air. It feels like burning. It's from a museum. I can't grasp. Skeet. My voice is tart, raspy. The letter says. I clear my throat. The letter says— It arrived, brief and reserved. I have read and reread it, as though some new information might appear. According to this letter—the sounds come out of my mouth, held in the air—I have a granddaughter. Suddenly I have to restrain myself from laughing, just as when you think of a word so long that it begins to sound comical. I start to shake a little. A function of dealing with cognitive anomalies, or so the evolutionary biologists would say. To think somebody had to go around zapping people's faces to come up with that. Skeet is silent.

But you know how—I search for the right word—*absurd* this is.

He looks down.

Seeing as I don't have any children.

The image of the nurses glints through. The stiff gown, the footprints in slush. Leaving alone. Everything half concealed. Skeet's eyes meet my eyes. I shake it off. It's not right. Memories are so primitive, they have so few witnesses.

The morning sun streams through the windows and brings warmth, and with it the low buzzing of the cluster flies that favour the windowpanes, drugged and slow. Skeet, I say again, as though he might not have heard. It is a torment of impossibility. A contradiction of things that are. Things that are not. *Thud.* The bird hits the glass again.

Maybe, he says, motioning toward the window, it's her.

Nautilus

The shell tricks you into thinking that what you hear
is the ocean, not the blood beating into your ears.

PARIS, YOU KNOW, is farther north than Newfoundland, Mother remarks coolly in a letter. There is no discussion of my returning home. They have found my behaviour disgraceful. When the nuns wrote to them of my latest expulsion, detailing my fractious behaviour and outlining their concerns for my future, I begged my parents to let me enrol in the art academy in Paris.

Father is exceedingly practical. He went into textiles and then there was a war. They needed uniforms, years of them. He became enormously wealthy. He thinks studying art is idiotic. It is only for the poor or homosexual, he said, believing both to be essentially the same crime. Mother, who knew the new money appeared crass, had an exacting brain. She hot-housed me in the areas she thought refined. She sent me books about Goya, Delacroix, and Turner's night paintings without referencing them. *Ivory. Do not forget the hairbrush I sent. Please use it at least twice a day. Sincerely, Mother.* She made it impossible to engage with her. She kept her distance, and seemed oblivious to what

11

was inside me. The books were confusing. It made me think she understood something fundamental in me.

They sent me away but nothing changed. At convent school the longing for my brothers, for the woods, was so pronounced it felt theatrical. When I'd left, my brother Arthur gave me a cigarette tin filled with pencils lined up like soldiers. Drawing, I'd learned, was one thing I was better at than my brothers. Mother had an art tutor come to the house every Wednesday afternoon. He said the reason famous artists have so many self-portraits is that it is a useful exercise to draw something you think you know. It is also the only view you have that is permanent. I look into the mirror. I have no idea how to transcribe this high-boned face full of angles. But he remarks, Very good, when he puts on his overcoat. More hatching here, he says, pointing to my cheekbone, and here at the hollow of the neck. If you use dark shading at the corners, it makes a mouth more alive. Draw, even if it is only for a quarter of an hour each day, and you will find yourself much improved. I began to carry a sketchbook with me, continually drawing my brothers' knightly faces, half blurred, in constant motion.

When I flip the lid to the tin at convent school it is like a detonator, sending a sharp longing through me, though drawing is the only way I feel better. The page glitters fresh each time. I draw portraits in the margins of my notebooks, which both comforts me and makes me more separate. I am expected to have no emotions. Do as I'm told. And though I understand this would be the easier course, I cannot help but do the opposite. It is a life of indoors full of silence, full of blame. Not unlike the precise attention of my parents, constantly obsessed with correcting my behaviour, my posture, my manners. I love being outside. What I miss is air. Cut off from sounds of my childhood,

I feel untethered and dull. When I arrive, the nuns' first words are, Rule number one.

The girls instantly hate me the way a fox hates a dog. And like most girls, they make a vocation out of exclusion. My grandmother Queenie once read to me that the first rule a geisha is taught, at age nine, is to be charming to other women. This is not my experience. My accent is wrong, my hair is wrong, and girls can be their most wicked when you don't look right. I am so unused to these mothered girls. Unfamiliar with their habits, their secret customs. They suck on pens, they roll the waistbands of their skirts. There is a moment of horror when I see emptiness in their eyes. Nothing is reflected back at all. Just empty, shining circles. They look like a small squadron in their pleated kilts and starched white blouses. The dorms like barracks, with rows of metal beds and one small side table each. I am unpopular because I am new, and not good at anything. I can't play field hockey. I am not good at religion. Drawing doesn't count. Though I am so deeply lonely, I don't make any effort to befriend them. I would rather be on my own than with people I don't like. When we file into the dining hall for meals, a group of girls gets up and moves their table far from wherever I sit down. She munches her food like a tomboy, they say. Just before we go to lunch, I see that someone has stolen my sketchbook and torn pages from it and taped them to the walls in the corridor. They've drawn over my brothers' faces. I blink, swallowing back tears. I cannot cry. No one here cries. It would show that they have broken you. Instead, I am shoved into the dining hall where there is silence, as we are not permitted to speak during meals. I sit straight-backed, listening to hundreds of girls chew their meat, swallow their soup. The *tink tink tink* of metal spoons against the bowls in unison becomes a dependable sound that feels like safety.

I start drawing maps of escape in black ink on small white sheets. The high stone walls surrounding the grounds, the gardens, the dormitories, the alley to the outside world, and a legend with numbers and routes below. The nuns write to my parents. *This child does not collaborate with work or play.*

Children are conformists. They sense my apartness a mile away. Even when I change schools, each time it is the same. There are almost no letters from home. And I wonder what it would be like, just once, to be met with something other than Mother's cool detachment when she sees what she regards as my needy, untamed eyes. I once saw a woman swing a small boy in wide arcs in the air to his shrieks of delight, a vast look of love in her eyes. The kind that galvanizes.

At the last school, I'd begun to have a recurring dream. It is always an island. A circular, spiralling shell. It is exotic and familiar. It is only when I land to attend the art academy, walking through the whorl of arrondissements, that I realize what my dreams have been about. They have been about Paris.

I grow my hair until it touches my waist, and wear it braided, pinning it up around my head. I decide to wear only white. My body is nervous, alert to everything. To chimes and clicks. The smell of chicory and Pernod, and the pervasive stale cigarette smoke from tabacs. The streets are unlike the unimaginative geometry I've known. There are no straight lines. I walk with purpose on the uneven cobblestones, along Boulevard Saint-Germain, the light spilling onto the stones, twisting away from the fragrant chestnut trees that line the street. I will never forget this light. Against the dove-grey rooftops it is a miracle.

Inside the gold-tipped fence of the Jardin du Luxembourg, gravel chews at my hard shoes. The park is populated with women—a stone angel with large sweeping wings, beautiful and precise, twenty French queens, the first statue of liberty. People sit in metal chairs and watch the octagon of water turn pink as the sun dips low. Autumn isn't about everything leaving. Here it is called *la rentrée*. The return. Through the park, on the other side of the cemetery, is Rue Froidevaux, the wide street with meticulously clipped trees where I have found a flat that will double as a studio. It was once a maid's room, and now sits above the atelier of Mme. Tissaud, a *rélieure* who makes, rebinds, and hand-sews books. Through the large front windows I can see a sewing loom, finishing presses, and wood-handled tools. When I walk through her door, Mme. Tissaud exclaims, Ivory!, embracing me so intensely I feel my lower vertebrae crack.

I am sorry, I offer. I am early.

She smiles slyly. Don't apologize. I don't like the word sorry. Besides, we count up the faults only of those who keep us waiting. I trust people who are early, she says, speaking in the direction of her bookcase. She marks a book with her eyes then takes a brown leather edition off the shelf. She is calm, deliberate. She wears a rough linen apron and has a face that is kind and wide, sackcloth hair. Kafka, she says, kept his watch an hour and a half fast.

I am thinking about how exactly that would work while I open the book, rich and coded, intrigued by a protagonist who has only a letter for a name. How nice K. looks on a page.

She draws the white thread through the eye of the needle and sits at the window sewing while we talk. She speaks in proverbs. I have five grown children, she says, holding up a hand with veins roped from age. They are my fingers. I cannot live without any one. When she looks at me, I feel naked. She seems sharply aware of how solitary I am. Fierce but unsure. All the things that match nothing in her. I see her tilt her head. As though she remembers something. Later she will look at me and tell me how hard it is to cope with youth, its moods, its intensities, everything we wish we could have access to later in life but never can. The great disparity, how there is so little of youth and so much of the other.

I was looking at a flat in the nineteenth. It was inexpensive, but it felt so far away.

I was born in the nineteenth arrondissement at the foot of Parc des Buttes Chaumont, she says.

Where I will later meet Lev, nocturnal wanderings through gypsum, fences of carved cement branches that I run my hand along to prove I am not in a dream.

After two months in Paris, I receive an invitation to dinner from the Hungarian-born architect Istvan Szalasi and his wife, Tacita, a friend I've met at school. Ours is a sistership I have never known. Our friendship, predicated on some oddly gratifying chocolate offered to me, our easels touching. Most women have problems with food, they are always trying to disappear, but like me, she thinks hunger is a mistake.

I see her three separate times the first day we meet. In three different arrondissements. In a city of three million people, this feels profound. Something passes between us, like an echo, a vibration. Whichever is deeper, harder to ignore.

When one of the instructors at the academy trips theatrically in mid-lecture in the first week, we both start laughing hysterically. I convulse, tears streaming.

Mademoiselle Frame, if you are unable to control your emotions, kindly leave the room.

Tacita and I are like magnets, the satisfying pull to the click. She notices that I use only one sheet of paper for notes, erasing the same page each time when it gets full. I know that I will like her when she doesn't ask why. Residue from the silent pacts I would set myself in childhood. If I can jump across the sidewalk without touching the crack, that will do it. If I can bounce the rubber ball one hundred times without dropping it, that will do it. Though I never stopped to ask—Do what?

Before she came to Paris, in Hungary, she spoke French for a living. She has a fine-tuned ability to interpret facial expressions of people whose languages she speaks, as though she has been born into their languages. She tells me that, like most things, it is a practice that relies on strategies. It is all in the tongue. You must be conscious of how the tongue moves in the mouths of the people whose language you wish to speak. She leans back and takes a sip of coffee. There is a lyric poet, she says, who calls translation a salutary gymnastics of the mind. When I look at her across the table, I realize that it has been years since I have actually spoken to someone I loved.

Where did your French come from? she asks.

Mother spoke it. She had a difficult time trying to find a French tutor for us. We had the same stern man teach us Latin, science, and mathematics. She eventually dredged up a plump ginger-haired teacher, named Mme. Plouffe, whose conjugation of irregular verbs sounded more like tragicomedy coming from her small pursed lips. *Bouche en cul-de-poule*. I had to will myself to attend to her shrill but oddly droning voice. *Asseoir. Courir. Devoir. Falloir. Mourir.* One of the first things she did was teach us Alouette, the children's song. *Alouette, gentille alouette. / Alouette, je te plumerai.* It sounded so jaunty until I realized that not only are they admiring the lovely skylark, but plucking its dead body of feathers systematically from its head to its feet. Whenever I hear that song I think of murder and Mme. Plouffe's puckered little mouth.

Tacita is ethereal and intense. Elfin. Someone who never spends money on haircuts. She cuts it herself, close to her scalp where it forms in thick dark waves. She tells me she first cut off all her hair as an experiment. It was coal-black, long enough to sit on.

I've always thought it an odd signifier of women's sexual powers, she says, given that it is actually dead. It is simply armour women wrap themselves in.

She is a *bricoleur*. She roams the junk shops looking for what most would consider rubbish. Her finds she then categorizes in her studio drawers. She collects everything. Flight maps, a doll's forearm, tiny glass jars, old photographs, watch springs, glass transparencies of the phases of the moon, stones the colour of midnight, loose red sand, children's blocks, plastic rose petals, butterfly wings sewn from linen, blue filaments, cutouts of birds and other creatures, satin stars stuffed thick with cotton, fragments of mirrors.

We drink café crème in one of the dim wood-and-mirror cafés beside the art academy. From childhood, she says, all I wanted was to be able to keep every object lined up on my shelves. I cannot collect fast enough to save them from ending up bloated on the river floor, decaying in back alleys, or buried deep below the ground. I love history that lives in the dirt and cracks and stains of things. With objects, perfection does not interest me, she says.

You explore by remaining open to everything.

And—she smiles into her thick white mug, she seems more here than anyone I've known—what about you? she presses. Where did the name come from?

Mother silently laboured for an hour and three-quarters, to the tick of a roman-numeralled grandfather clock outside the door, I tell her. She endured the delivery without a cry, her teeth clenched. I was almost blue, head jammed against pelvis so that there was a red mark on my forehead when I came out. My four older brothers filed in, their green eyes glinting, glancing at the baby wrapped in soft blankets. Albert, the oldest, three-quarters legs, said, She's as white as cigarette paper. Ivory suits her.

Mother shot him a silencing look.

Of course, once humans got involved, I say to Tacita, mythic qualities took a decidedly unbecoming turn. I think of the tragedy, harvested from elephants—assassinated and left to rot in the savannah, swarmed by flies—to make piano keys and billiard balls. I don't tell her that I was tormented because of it.

Where were you before you came here?

England. Convent school. I was expelled, I say, exhaling smoke. More than once.

Well done, she says, placing the cigarette back into the notch of the ashtray and resting her chin in her hand.

Well, I am not a blueblood like you, Tacita says teasingly. I am from a long line of black-haired women who come from drowsy farms. They lugged buckets of water through muddy villages. I didn't get to know my mother long enough. She was a diviner. She had the ability to find four-leaf clovers from anywhere. She once told me that to see them was like a bride looking through a veil. You don't look for them, you just soften your eyes to the shape. I turned to look at my mother, stunned, and said, I know about the veil. That was our closest moment. She died in childbirth. I was the oldest, so when I was twelve, I became the mother. And when I left to work in Paris, the next sister in line became the mother. We are like matryoshka, she says, Russian dolls. She drops her pack of cigarettes in her bag and says, We all have the same face. It is too expressive ever to be considered beautiful.

No, I counter. Like all charismatic women, you are beautiful. By conviction.

I look at Tacita, looking at me, emitting a certain steady warm intensity.

Paris is filled with fascinating objects in an infinite number of unlikely places, she explains to me. You'd be amazed at what I find in the trash, Ivory, her black eyes gleaming. She spends most of her time collecting. The ideas of art come later.

You know, I say carefully, the sadness is good. For your work.

She squints her eyes.

Happy people don't look down.

She takes me to some of her discoveries. A shop she's found by Canal Saint-Martin that sells doll eyeballs—rows of glass eyes in constant wobble, laid out on a wooden track, clicking as they touch like the silver boules tossed on the sand by grown men all over France. Tiny refracted Tacitas stare back at me.

We end up at the Muséum National d'Histoire Naturelle, where we sit for hours drawing the bones of animals assembled into perfect skeletons, and then smoke cigarettes in the adjacent garden that is also the Paris zoo. After being cut off from animals for so long, the sounds beat blood back into my ears. Velvet ruffling feathers and silences punctuated by thwacks, metallic chirps, grunts, and screeches, crisply defined against a faint wind—the incantatory rhythms of a live, twitching fugue. We discuss the effect of the Muséum and its contents, with its art nouveau metal flower railings, the dark winding staircases, the abandonment of bones. We discover, tucked in a dusty corner, a tiny skeleton of a two-month-old human fetus that has been propped up. A fetus is always seen half-curved and floating, a sickle moon. Upright it becomes utterly grotesque with its large skull, giant round eye sockets, stunted bird legs, and miniature ribs. It is displayed alongside the monkey ear in a jar of formaldehyde and the *monstre double*, the malformed twinned bat fetuses, in an odd democracy. We stare at it apprehensively, as though somehow we understand at the same moment that a baby will, for both of us, remain simply a collection of bones inappropriately assembled. I see my own reflection stare back.

Tacita leaves to roam the *brocantes* while I sit in the zoo where I spend hours observing the monkeys, gazelles, and hyenas. I often don't draw them there. I listen to them. I seek out the grassblades, the copse of trees, anything that will lead to a confluence of intimacy between the human and animal world. I practise for great swaths of time, always undisturbed. As in the cafés here, where everyone drinks and drinks and pays hours later.

I begin to keep a notebook of sounds.

Is it a diary? Tacita asks.

Diaries are just emotional weather reports, I tell her, writing and not looking up. They don't interest me.

I write in the notebook. *Nightingale: narcotic effect, lunar dust. Hyena: points of stars, cackle.* I add the word *dialects* with a question mark. Tacita writes in the margin: *Funny.*

I had hoped that I could paint my way into a pact I'd made in the woods years ago, a pact of saving. I haven't yet told Tacita about the animals. All the time in the forest, how I would hear their voices, shot like arrows through the silent trees. I heard their secrets and kept them to myself, huddled low in the mud, listening to the sounds issued from insects, animals, and birds at the roots and tops of trees. I took in all the silences as well as the sounds. The sounds around me and the ones inside of me. My inner life took shape around them. For the first time I was happy—was it happiness I felt? People always think that it's animals who are observed, but they observe us too. My brother Edgar liked to

21

tease me. Anyway, what's wrong with people? I remember looking at him concentratedly. People are noisy, I finally said.

This feels unrelated, I confide to Tacita. Capturing a living creature and then making it inanimate, deliberate brushstrokes, swirls of oil, seems so, inadequate. You can overwork it and it becomes stuffy and dull. You focus so much on the detail that you overlook the important things. All the little inaccuracies that make up the truth. A solemn and divine truth somewhere in their indifferent eyes that twists into you.

She doesn't ask about the pact. Instead she says, An unordinary life leads away from the past. Maybe it is something else. Maybe the creatures you seek to interpret are like starlight, or the moons of other planets. Maybe they need to be discovered.

Outside the Muséum, a roasted scent like fennel flowers saturates the air with its perfume, something that grows in one of the geometrical flowerbeds in Ménagerie du Jardin des Plantes that Tacita and I have become obsessed with. We pass perfumed women in silk stockings wrapped in furs with gold belts around their waists clicking along the streets, arms full of parcels. Despite looming threats, everything seems to be slowly growing more luxurious, more exaggerated. Eventually it will be complicated floorlength dresses, a retreat to safety, to something that is known. We comb the markets and bring everything back to Tacita's apartment. We decide the kitchen is a place of power. Alchemical. And though her art and that of the group mocks social conventions, still she finds herself wringing out Istvan's socks and hanging them out to dry over the balcony. We walk back to the kitchen.

I had never assumed they were married. But they were, eleven years, since Tacita was seventeen. They never met in Hungary, but she had stood inside a soaring building he designed in Budapest. She thought it an impossible feat, to make something that moved someone to the point where they felt a burning in their chest. She liked when he told her that he'd stayed awake on the site for twenty-four hours before making any sketches. He wanted to see the progression of light.

She says they have been with other people, like most of the artists in the group. But it has never interested them as much as each other. She says it so casually, with her big warm smile. I should feel self-conscious around her, having only just emerged from the high, thin world of girls. She seems so fully fledged, with her own kitchen, where she cooks and draws, and a studio filled with objects and photographs pinned to the walls. Her soft, low voice. Her bare feet. The exotic silk robe she wears with a thin tie around her waist. The way she runs her fingers through her short dark hair, the stacks of silver bracelets clattering on her wrist. I find I feel more like myself around her. She makes that part of me, with the secret shame of being so banished, into an artifact. But then I wonder, Am I right? Have I read her gestures correctly? More and more, we talk about what we want to make. We conspire together, our eyes electric.

When I watch couples resigned to their marriages, Tacita continues, the thing I cannot bear is the slackness underscored by bitterness. All the indignities they inflict upon each other, the little dropped remarks. How sometimes with married people you wonder whether what you're looking at is love or hate. Their lives drift so far from themselves that they spend them on nothing; they engage in banal domestic conversations like "It's time for a new sofa, don't you think?" She says she and Istvan live without routine in part because that is what clouds people's ability to see what they once loved about the person they are with.

I remember watching a famous Hungarian cellist play a

Elgar concerto, Tacita says, hands turning red from the cold sink water. For his encore he did something that caught everyone off guard. He played a line on the cello and then stopped. The hall was silent. Then he sang it back. Played a line and then sang it back. His voice and the voice of his cello overlapping until I had no idea what I was listening to. Which was more exceptional, his command over an instrument or a human voice becoming an instrument? I shut my eyes, Tacita says, and as an ordinary mortal accepted his superiority without question. Yet, while his genius filled every sliver of the recital hall, I thought, This person still needs to make toast. He still needs to feed his cat. He still requires his socks to be washed. She laughs. I'll never understand it.

Understand what?

Being human.

I find it hard to consider myself part of a category, I say. I know what it is to be myself but I'm not so sure what we are as a whole. We are a species, I suppose, like any other animal, just trying to find our place on the earth, except that we seem to need to discover the truth about the space we occupy.

I think that's why there is no such thing as wisdom. I don't believe in it. No one can tell you how to become who you are. You just have to live it to know it, she says.

Have you ever heard that recording of an English cellist who was broadcast playing Dvoák's Songs My Mother Taught Me in her garden? I ask.

She shakes her head.

The sounds of nightingales in the garden made it onto the recording. Singing the same four notes and then eventually adding a flourish, a fifth note. The broadcast was a sensation. They said it contained an element of ecstasy. But you know what

I always thought? The birds stole the show. The cellist must have been annoyed at this. Humans always want to win.

Their flat is charmed with the smell of citron from the scented log she put on the fire. A cuckoo clock marks each hour as Tacita moves about her kitchen, small and pale yellow. She tells me that the gastronomy of the group of artists tends toward elaborate and somewhat grotesque cuts of meat. The last meal involved a naked woodcock flambé in strong alcohol served in its own excrements, as is the custom in fine Parisian restaurants. There are lambs' brains, calf livers, eel pâté, pigs' feet, and anything with a shell. They prefer what is clear and intelligible in form, she explains. The shapelessness of vegetables is something they have no interest in. Shellfish are prized. They like the battle, jaws ripping at armour.

I think it is because they are mostly men, she says, unpacking the rest of the vegetables. Everything is a dare.

Doesn't it bother you?

What?

That kind of bravado?

She places beets on the table. The thing that bothers me, she says, is people whose imagination stops too low.

She walks out and comes back with a little wooden box. The frame is amber wood with dark black holes where the nails once were. The ground is wood, painted a thick chalky white with deep cracks running vertically. There is blue around the edges, and a thin piece of wood jagged at both ends painted the same blue. Shards of blue glass, along with a piece of white coral that seems almost the shape of a human heart. A speckled ball in one corner. White nails hang upside down from the top.

I love this, I tell her. These everyday things that together form a dream. Where did you find the coral?

Pigalle, she says. One of the streets with a woman in dirty underlinen and varnished fingers leaning out each doorway, like a play. You know, she says, placing the box on the table, people think artists live in garrets and drink cocktails. She smiles. Instead here I am in the gutters collecting dirty things and trying to arrange them to evoke some sort of wonder. Something that we know, but altered by time or circumstance. Tacita takes an opened wine bottle from the counter, pours it into two glasses, and hands one to me. Like pink glass, she says, frosted by sea change.

It's the notion of just truly being awake to everything, I say, taking a sip. Never sleepwalking and always seeing.

She says she is happy I've arrived. Before she felt that women in the group were relegated to lovers of male artists. A lot of the men looking for some form of muse, and then going home to wives who will service them anytime they want, but mostly are too tired.

I've never understood why everyone doesn't know that women are the ones who convey things in the most interesting ways, I say. We have always observed. We have been used to no audience and that has given us room to really see. I often think that's why women were put in tight corsets, so that is what their minds would focus on. Men are secretly threatened, I say, touching the back of my hand to my cheek, hot with wine. Besides, they are more compelled by action. To the sequence of events.

Maybe this is why in my work there is such a recurrence of birds in cages, Tacita laughs. I like that your interest lies in animals too.

I take another sip and put down my glass. Not the petted things. I notice that she has an astonishing ability to give herself completely to people, without distraction. A perfect and rare transparency. I learn from her that the way a friend acts toward you is a clue, it is a window into the way they would like to be treated. It is also what undoubtedly makes her an accomplished translator. She confessed to me that she'd only once taken liberties, and that naturally, it had cost her the job. It was worth it, she says. It was when she met Istvan. He was designing a theatre interior by the Canal Saint-Martin and she was hired to translate the meetings between him and the *maire* from the tenth arrondissement.

The *maire*, a big man with a long face that joined a wrinkled forehead, large sloping eyes, and an enormous nose, and who overall gave the impression of a somewhat intelligent bloodhound, said, I think we should have the building permits by April.

What Tacita said to Istvan in Hungarian was, Last night I saw that Venus was out. It sparkled above the treetops. I am in love with this bright planet.

Istvan, already alive in the presence of the translator with a scar above her lip, a silver vertical line that made her even more striking, tried desperately to comprehend how it was possible that the balding, nasal-voiced *maire* before him was speaking about the beauty of elusive planets. Once he understood it was Tacita, he began thinking of how he might ask her to dinner. A week later, the bloodhound himself married them in the atrium of the Mairie du dixième.

What sort of wedding did you have? I say, turning the thin-stemmed glass in my fingers.

I wore blue. We invited no one.

Fox

Heard nothing. Heard nothing. Rained hard.
Leaves getting green. One vixen on third night.
Barks, chilling screams, oddly birdlike.

SKEET'S BODY SHIFTS IN HIS CHAIR. Just when I thought I had figured something out there is something new to organize.

Have you slept yet? he finally asks.

My eyes meet his eyes. He knows I am a lifelong insomniac. How profound working into the night has been. It always strikes me how odd it is that we live with such divisions, that we spend half our lives lying down, in a blackout.

I must have slept last night, before I drove into town, because I woke up in the kitchen, fieldbook on my knees, with the fizz of static, the scratchy piano playing on the radio, Chopin's Waltz in D Flat, which has always sounded to me like a dog running in circles.

He twirls his finger at his ear.

I've not heard it for a long time, I say, ignoring him. It was based on an incident in the garden of Chopin's lover, the writer George Sand. As I had understood it, she sat in her garden with Chopin watching her crazed dog chase after its tail, turned to him and said, If I had your talent, I'd compose a pianoforte piece for this dog. Which is exactly what he did.

Skeet goes to the kitchen and brings back the coffee. He pours both mugs full.

I ate one of my special macaroons, I tell him, which sometimes helps.

He laughs. And then you drove?

It helps with the pain. It goes marvellously, quietly into the bloodstream. I buy the herb from a handsome young Algerian man who wears trousers of such rough fabric I am convinced they are prison-issue. And I'm not talking about one of those escaped cons who impersonated a dentist. The Algerian, as I've taken to calling him, sells on market days by the scrubby river in Chinon where the youth also go to have relations after dark. I drive there, passing the white French cows, mythic against the bright blue sky. Though I prefer the closer town, Fontevraud. There is an illuminator there with gold under his fingernails. His studio is full of brushes and stencils and fourteenth-century vellum. It is the last atelier of its kind in all of France. Mme. Tissaud would have loved it.

My initial exchange with the Algerian was somewhat embarrassing. He thought I was an escapee from a nearby home for senile females, and I was convinced he was trying to rent me an expensive boat, the kind they use to fleece tourists. I think my nervousness sprang in part from no longer knowing how to act around an impressive-looking man, it being entirely historical. Though he behaves with a brusque yet serviceable politeness toward me, everything is awkward in our communications, which is compounded by the fact that I am always confused about the calibration of grams to ounces with narcotics. Are they metric grams? Is it an American ounce? Finally a teenager standing next to him blurts, Just ask for a bag, *mémère*.

God Frame, you've got to be fucking careful.

Skeet. Mostly I smoke and think and work. I speak to almost no one.

Old shy people are ridiculous you know.

Well I want to talk with someone Skeet, I say, sipping my coffee. Just not anyone human.

There is a long silence. Which series is this one? he finally asks, holding up an image of dense spoke-like lines of geometric shapes that from a distance appear to be a sequence of veined circles, each one different, like snowflakes.

We are adept at avoiding discussing what next. Skeet seems more absent. Normally he is focused and frank. There is a thin blue static in the room. And how really can we talk about this? What I have always left unsaid. There are so many things, I'm not sure what to feel. I have no language for it. For the time when there was the possibility of a child. When that possibility was taken away, I never mentioned it again. Not to anyone. There was no one left to tell. But it is an impossible topic to escape as a woman. Reproductive activities are, for whatever reason, eternally open to public opinion. I never spoke of it. There was nowhere for it to go. Realizing that I too was falling into the line of the wordless women that I come from but having no power over it. I feel pain in my lungs, worsening in my stomach, my heartbeat pounding in my body. It occurs to me that the pain is the letter.

Morpho eugenia, I finally answer. The delicate vibration of wings. It is the vibrations of vibrations, given that butterflies don't hear, don't make sound.

It's amazing, he says, that you— He hesitates.

That I?

I don't know. Aren't you thinking about the letter at all?

The lower frequencies create less complex patterns, I say, my voice not right. But, I continue, the higher frequencies are dense and arguably more beautiful.

This one looks like something you would see on a rug, Skeet says, pointing to the Osiris blue butterfly. What's this one?

Red fox.

Looks like a prehistoric insect. He turns it sideways and pauses. Or stoner art. He flips through the stacks of images and immediately sits down. He looks worn.

What is it?

Sometimes I can't believe the scale of this project. I find it amazing that it doesn't overwhelm you.

Well, thank god the feeling of defeat has always motivated me, I say. I've always disliked the feeling at the end of an experiment. I sometimes wonder if that is why I've taken on such a vast project. Though all my energy goes to this. It takes it all now. I still have not even seen the forest at the back of this property and I have been here for over two years. The house is let from a middle-aged American woman. Its provenance, a former chicken coop, went unmentioned in her brochure on the computer.

Skeet says, Don't say brochure. Say website. It makes you sound old.

I am old, I tell him. Old enough that when he tried to lure me into technology by tapping my name into a computer, I found it dreadful that all this information about me appeared, available without my consent.

The house is made of pale heavy stone that has lasted for a thousand years and looks as though it will last a thousand more. The American suspected caves, then dug out centuries of dirt, down the stone steps, with her bare hands while on her stomach.

Swimming through the earth. It would be impressive if you happen to think that digging is harder than drawing. Or mathematics for that matter. The countryside here is strewn with caves, attracting academics and tourists, though most have yet to be unearthed. The first white cave on the property, tall with three separate entries that lead to three separate caves, has a high curved ceiling, sonically perfect, holding each note I have recorded, crisp and controlled. It picks up any vibration and renders it crystalline.

The American says there are bats and rare butterflies and larks even. I can manage only to navigate this room and to drag my bones down the stairs to the caves. Out the front door is a narrow garden to the east of the house that glitters with dew in the early hours of morning. Its terraces twin the wide flat white stone steps, thick lavender spilling over, brushing my legs when I descend to the caves, the camphor scent drifting into the air. It is so much harder to move around now. Skeet does not understand. You cannot understand stillness when you have the full range of motion. We are all just bodies when it comes down to it. Though when you grow old, you are edged out of even that. How little you are able to inhabit it. You notice that pleasures always involve verbs.

Through the window the breeze brings the sounds of songbirds, throats open, chests beating, an unremarkable greybrown. After observing southern-hemisphere birds glinting in their garish electric-coloured athletic kit, their European counterparts seem exceedingly drab. It occurs to me as I listen to them now, confined as I am, that I'm the caged one. I look down at my book full of notes. There are no signs of rests in birdsong. I flick my wrists to shake out the numbness and the fieldbook slaps onto the stone floor. I feel a jab of hunger, though I am unable to eat, my stomach knotted. Normally I take the same lunch every day, a whole-wheat cheese sandwich washed down with scotch, sometimes sherry.

After I came home from the post office, I searched the closet for the grey archival box that holds the few old notebooks that have survived, now yellowed, ink faded to grey. *Vibration of bones. Sounds not made louder by adding but by taking away. Small kingdoms of concrete music but with geometry, interstitial, ringing, humming, speaking fragments, unforeseen.* My spirits rise so high that I laugh out loud. Jejune. Thrumming with purpose. Full of ideas, unfocused but alive. It is how life is. You think it will be so different after the accumulation of time, but when I look at this I am reminded that it is still me on that page. You don't go anywhere. The past contains the future. What will become clean, unfettered observations of sound. I remember what I thought when I wrote that. I wanted to become a great artist. I thought I would uncover a new way of seeing.

With humans there is a speaker and a listener. The speaker informs the listener. With animals, it is often just a call in the dark.

I find one of my field recordings, a labelled gold disc, and press play. Howl and howl in that white silence, a high world of grey skies, hunched and shivering in the wind. Jaws clashing and paws creaking in the snow, whimpering, barking, freezing in the forest as the stars and the moon begin to brighten the sky. I play the track again, numbered, dated, and hear that the vocalizations that rip and cut and clatter and then become graceful, full of focus. It amazes me that after all this time I can hear it as both joy and agony. Fairy tales grow teeth all around them.

It is impossible to get near wolves without distorting the data. These sounds were collected with howl boxes. Devices that record and emit digital calls, broadcast from an eighty-gigabyte computer duct-taped to a tree. Skeet and I used them to research wolves following an aerial wolf-hunting expedition with its snares and poison—part of a spectacularly ill-conceived wolf extermination project.

In the Yukon, where we first meet, we stay at one of the only hotels open in winter. The restaurant is through the lobby, past the dead-eyed fish doing what appear to be choreographed movements in the aquarium. We eat eggs and unnaturally square potatoes that taste like freezer, spooned from a metal bin. They are tough and dry. The waitress seems generally annoyed at people who install themselves like this, but I think she is keen on Skeet so she allows us to spread out our fieldbooks and recording equipment on the Formica table and sit thawing in the large banquettes for hours. Skeet rests his arm along the back of the burgundy leatherette and says, Why is it that when something's fake, they add -ette to the end of it?

The oldtimers who drink their coffee here believe that some of the ravens have seen the gold rush. The ravens know where the gold is hidden, they say. Ravens can only live about thirty years in the wild, but we don't correct them.

We ride in a pickup truck with chains on the tires. It gets so cold you can see rings around the moon. Nothing moves in forty below. But in March there is a low dazzle of sun out until eight o'clock at night. The snow is so dry I finally understand why mukluks. I sip coffee from a steel thermos, its steam making receding patterns on the windshield. We wait. Then we see a large black bird, hungry, mangled feathers. It is alerting a wolf to a small rabbit below. The wolf runs across the snow, a flash of silver. The raven waits for the kill and then swoops in with its long black wings. They feed together, and then, astonishingly, they play. I am overcome. For what occurs to them, with their torn feathers and bloodied scuffs of fur in this great bleak horizon. Their daring is in seeing that even in death, there is life. I watch stunned, toes numb, knuckles swollen, taking off my gloves to work the equipment. Eyes pricked with slanted snow, eyelashes freezing together. How alert you become with this sharp startling cold. In this eternal present. The sudden hush followed by the creak of snow, the barks and shrieks, this sense of something about to happen. The inscrutable eyes, the murderous claws, the glinting fur. Today it is just braided footprints. Glyphs in the snow giving warmth and shape to the blinding white, telling me why I live for this alone.

On the ride back the grey racks of branches are corrugated with ice, a line of snow on top of every one like a seam. We pass tracts of black pines and blue ice. We don't speak for a long time. I appreciate this about Skeet. A high-pitched intermittent squeaking jangles the silence. Skeet punches the dash with his fist. I jump in my seat, looking at him, surprised by the sudden violence. I wonder if it is something he learned from his teenage mother, or one of the boyfriends he has mentioned. How could he possibly have escaped his origins so cleanly. How can anyone?

Dash rattle, he says. Once you've got one that's it. There's no way of finding the source. I've been on a whole road trip with one. Sucked dogs.

Skeet unzips his jacket and takes out the recorder wrapped in his sweatshirt. He breathes on it to warm it up. He says that this snow is reminding him of the one other time he saw his mother. It was in a ski town out West, near where he was conducting research on reintroduced wolves. She was there with a boyfriend. She didn't talk much, but when she first saw him she smiled and ruffled his hair. Skeet waited with her at the bottom of the hill. Neither of them could ski. It's for assholes with money, she told him. The boyfriend came down and turned to an abrupt stop, spraying her with snow. She threw her cigarette ember like a dart, just missing his ski. It sizzled unpleasantly in the snow. He laughed and she said, You'll pay for this, fuckface.

We pass dwellings long abandoned by prospectors. Rusted skillets and saws nailed to the silver wood. Woollen blankets chewed to lace by moths on feather beds. Raccoons the size of hatchbacks scratching in the attics. Sometimes these houses were left with coffee cups still sitting on the tabletop. Records husked from their sleeves, as though someone had meant to come right back.

A great black hawk drifts above.

Ah could my hand unlock its chain / How gladly would I watch it soar / And never regret and never complain / To see its shining eyes no more.

Emily Brontë?

It's the only poem of hers I can ever remember.

I know the one. I like how she begins by identifying herself with her hawk, saying that they are both *wholly alone*. We are quiet for a while, only the shrill bleating dash between us.

She kept a lot of pets, I finally say, watching the blurring white out the window. Of which I know the animal liberationists would not approve, but I never quite knew what to do with the information I read about her catching her dog sleeping in her bed. She punched him in the eye until he was half blind. I mean, who *punches* a dog? And then you read those poems, and marvel at how people can be two things at once.

Only two? Skeet says, turning to look at me.

We are silent for a long time. After a while I begin to hear a fragile and beautiful sound that seems to come from him. It is underwater and dusky, full of faded chords. He tells me it is from a recording he once heard. A man with a harmonica and music box who believed he could hear and play the sound of the sun humming.

In the evenings, we have started going out for a pint of beer at the Snake Pit. I leave well before the alcohol insinuates itself as it does each night—chairs broken, teeth knocked out, the floor sloshing with beer. Skeet tells me that after everyone leaves, they bring out plastic bags full of sawdust and throw it on the floor to soak up the urine and vomit. Some of the people who come out to drink here literally have dirt on their faces. The kind of characters who sound invented to anyone who lives in a city down in the south. There is a misanthropic old sea captain with tattoos of naked women up each sinewy arm who has told us he wants to be taxidermied and positioned in this bar when he dies.

Taxidermy is a revolting act, I tell him. I've never understood why exactly anyone would choose to be in a room with decapitated animals. He grumbles something and moves to the next table. I see *Flo* tattooed on one finger. Flo must have been quite something to put up with that old brute. I find it extremely loud in here, shattering crackling swells of sound, the ambient crescendoing murmurs. It batters my ears. So attuned now to singular sounds made in near silence. I find noise being drowned out with noise torturous. It makes me feel claustrophobic. ·

Dear enemy effect, Skeet says after taking a long sip. Read it, never seen it. He looks around the room. Recognize and respect your enemy neighbour's territories. Expend energy on enemy strangers only, he says, referring to the raven and the wolf from the field. I've seen it in that study we did with territorial songbirds. Skylarks can remember their neighbours' songs from one year to the next and accept neighbours as dear enemies as a conditional strategy established over time.

I have witnessed the stranger-neighbour tolerances in owls and larks too, I say. They've used the sound files to conduct audio playback studies to test it.

But that wasn't just tolerance, he says. They played.

I think that's why we still have Paris. Dear enemy. The same thing applies in war.

How do you mean?

I don't know. When Hitler supposedly screamed into a telephone, Is Paris burning?, it was not. Damaged, certainly. There were barricades, trenches dug into the streets, trees felled on the boulevards, buildings shot through with holes. But it stood, recognizable. People who weren't there began to wonder. Had life in Paris under the Germans been a bit too easy? Who had collaborated? These questions were made even more uncomfortable by the unavoidable comparisons between the still-beautiful Paris and all the other cites of Europe, devastated and in ruins.

Skeet takes another sip of his beer and then unclenches his fingers and slowly swirls the glass on the wooden tabletop. I read that Hitler was a vegetarian.

And so what? I snap. He also preferred murdering people who'd committed no crime.

He remains silent.

I cannot help my emotions, Skeet. We had no idea that the Nazis were not going to win. Everyone now has the benefit of knowing.

Just then an intoxicated young man slides over. His friend has gone to the washroom. Skeet and I have noticed this friend, a

Klondike boy one table over, who most nights sits peeling the label off his beer. You can see, even from a distance, that he has a glass eye and a rough patch of skin under his chin that looks as though it has been sewn on. Wide curved shoulders with blades that stick out like wings. Blond hair straight as iron filings. The young man asks us if we've seen his friend's father. You know, the nutjob in town, he says. You might have seen him jumping in the freezing river. Balls flying out of his Speedo. He stares straight ahead. He's a mean drunk. Messed him up enough that he wanted to blow his own brains out. He took his old man's shotgun. He stops to sip his beer, making a trigger-pulling motion under his chin with his finger. He was fine, he says, swallowing. Then he laughs with an awkward force that makes his throat sound like a cracked reed. The bullet missed his brains entirely. Came out his fucking eye.

The boy eventually comes back from the washroom and his friend returns to their table. We sit without speaking for a while.

Listen, Skeet shakes out a cigarette, to that voice.

From the old speakers comes a stalled sound from the throat, rasp and alive, and there is a slow bang accompaniment that makes me think of horsetails blown horizontal in a wind.

Wanda Jackson, he finally says. Funnel of Love.

I look at Skeet leaning back in his chair. It is the first time I've heard him say the word love. He hasn't mentioned a girlfriend. I shouldn't expect him to. What he must think of me, too. But I think they are different now. Not a lot of emotion. I think they must see everyone from the past as fools. Everything has changed. Their telephones don't ring. They are not writing letters. They communicate their bodies through the wires, not even wires. They don't talk of it and divulge far too much to the world outside, both.

The next day we drive farther out, along the potholed highway near the glaciated Tombstone Mountains where sabre-toothed tigers once roamed. Once you are in the north there is always the myth of farther out. Nothing is ever north enough. At the bar they talk of Core, a man who lives upriver and comes into town each season for a new woman. We pass the granite mountains, flat and jagged like grave markers. In this tundra, there is the beep of the sound recorder and the dry creak of snow under our feet. A large white frozen lake sits silently, occasionally cracking like a gunshot, making us jump. We find a quiet place at the edge of an opening. I look at Skeet.

What?

Nothing.

Why are you looking at me like that?

I don't know. It's just. You've been doing this for so long, but then I see the way you flick the switch and get quiet, waiting for something to be revealed. As though you've always been living one way and the plane is about to shift each time.

Because it does.

When I ask him what brought him here, he says, Does it have to be one thing?

Well, I say, just what is it that you want to do with your one wild and rare life?

He sucks air into his lungs. I was on a vigilante ship in Japan. I got aboard an illegal fishing boat. I had stolen part of their navigation system. And as I stood there, I watched a fisherman hook a shark right in front of me. He gaffed it and then slammed it against the deck. It slid right to my boots. The shark was bleeding and gasping and flapping all around, frantic to survive, while the fishermen sat there trying to figure out how to get them out of their waters. They talked and looked on while this shark almost broke its own back trying not to die. They eventually cut the line and threw him back into the water like a piece of garbage. Like he was nothing. That's when I knew.

And ever since you've never once stopped to ask, Am I doing the right thing?

No, he says.

Do you know why? Because you know you are doing the right thing.

Wolf

The wolf is the night that has swallowed the sun.
The shards glint in its borderless eyes.

THERE IS A PAINTING ON THE COVER of a catalogue Tacita
presents me from an exhibition that took place in Paris before I
arrived. It has a circle of silvery-white shapes so thick I want to
touch them. They are lit by another constellation entirely. It is
calm, luminous, almost mystical. The bottom right corner reads
in tight script, Lev Aleksandr Volkov. It is utterly unrelated to
the rest of the works. They are compelling in a more lawless way,
but this one painting stands alone. I trace my finger over the
image and two words move across my brain like celluloid. They
say, like the suck of a high edge that draws you closer, Choose
me. I rip off the cover, fold it, and begin to carry it with me, like
a magical egg, a prayer, a jewel.

The dinner party invitation arouses a feeling of apprehension.
I have shed my childhood shyness, which was where a
separateness had grown, silently, suddenly, like flowers that
bloom in the night. My grandmother Queenie always said that it
wasn't that I was shy, it was that I needed to be found. With this

group, I am aware that being a woman is harder. Tacita says some women can be treated as though they are disposable, merely promised by their looks. I wonder what it is that they wear to their parties, but in the end I wear the same white dress. I smooth my hair, conceal my accent, concentrate on overcoming my bookish French. But I am full of a wildness I haven't known for so long. A wildness when out with my brothers in the forest, peeing against trees the way they did, without shame.

I walk into the dark pink air. Through the cemetery, past Baudelaire and de Maupassant, along the dusty gravel path that slips through the bright green centre of the Jardin du Luxembourg. I walk through the remote, quiet streets of Île Saint-Louis, and eventually to the tenth. I am excited about this new pleasure of company. I thought it would take away from my inner life, but instead it has begun to outline it sharply. Oddly when there is the possibility of its being exposed, it forces me to understand what it is. It makes me aware that I have never relied on other people to know who I am. But these people, all so unknowable, are what make entering into this more extraordinary. I want to take my time arriving because I want to hold this moment, really hold it, and turn it over. I feel the cool night on my skin, and the burn of my feet rubbing in my shoes. I pass by the stare of dark windows that will fill again with bread and flowers and charcuterie by morning. The velvet gleam that recedes as the lights come on along the banks of the river in the moored barges, the quiet lapping of water against their sides.

I first met some of the artists in the group at Brasserie Lipp with Tacita, where we wrote single words that formed odd conjunctions on folded paper and passed them to the next person. One of the artists poured whisky from a flask into my champagne glass. Cheaper, he said. Something gets read aloud that sounds like, The guillotine is a lovely bitch, lazy and carnal with winding blond hair, it sleeps with its heavily ordained tongue. Tacita and I collapse from drink and laughter. And I feel not that I am becoming one of the artists of the group, but that I am one already. I have such an odd feeling that it takes me a moment to notice what it is. For the first time I can remember, it is as though I belong. I am relieved of the knee-jerk reaction to rebel. Though oddly what they rebel against, the bourgeoisie—my entitled background, with its opulent house and tutors and nannies—is the very thing that allows me to have the confidence to participate. For the first time, the action of the mind is the only thing that counts.

When I finally arrive, Tacita grabs my hand and leads me in. I see many of the artists I know. There is a thick warmth of bodies, and music, perfume, and cigarette smoke. My eyes move toward the doorframe, where Istvan is speaking to someone I haven't seen before. A man. Beautiful and filthy, like a fallen angel. I feel a flint of heat. Our eyes meet for a moment, nothing happens, but something passes through. I am handed a glass of very cold champagne, and eventually placed at the table between an anarchist and a revolutionary, their faces lit by candles. Across from me is Leni, an artist on a government grant to study rainbows. Initially there is an outlay of the sort of proper, rational food that human beings eat. A pot of *soupe aux cèpes*, *haricots verts* with *marrons chaudes au beurre*. *Galettes* rolled and stuffed with kirsch cream. Cockles in their shiny, gleaming little shells. Then Tacita winks at me as a hare stuffed with oysters is brought to the table. My plate is whisked away. Tacita by way of explanation declares, Ivory does not eat meat. She believes it is wrong to deprive animals of their life. Particularly when they are so difficult to chew. We then dine on what I believe to be tapioca

Tacita has dyed black by cooking it in squid ink, which she serves on cracked ice with lemon as though we are eating dinner plates of caviar, like makeshift Tsars and Tsarinas. Scandal threatens to erupt at any moment.

There is Satie playing, and a theatrically articulated dessert table comprising a pyramid of green figs that have been baked by the sun, crystallized apricots, translucent preserves, and macaroons in the improbable colours Istvan has described of Moscow architecture, mint, salmon, lemon yellow. And there are crates of Madiran wine that Istvan's friend Hugo has brought up from the dusty, cowboy corner of France that smells like desert. The kind of coarse unfashionable wine that Tacita likes because it strikes you alive.

Ivory, says Tacita, introducing me to the man who was speaking to Istvan. This is Lev.

In my pocket, his drawing crackles.

He is dark, vivid, tall. Eyes so blue they are almost white. He runs his fingers through his black hair like rays, tangled and rough and cut short. This surprises me. I had always thought of Russians having eyes and hair and skin all of the same pale shade. His black wool suit is tight and his buttoned jacket abbreviated in the sleeves, as though it might be the suit of another man. He has a ripped piece of fabric knotted around his neck. I've never seen a man who looks like he does. He might be twice my age, though in truth, I cannot tell.

Ivory is a painter at the academy with me, Tacita tells Lev.

And?

And what?

What do you paint, Ivory? He says my name slowly, with

difficulty, in French. It is not his first, or even second language.

What is in my mind.

What is in your mind?

The way he says this could also mean, What are you thinking about?

The forest.

Why forest? he says.

I am reminded that forest is the feminine gender in French. I like how he pronounces it, *la forêt*, as though a leaf just fluttered down. He doesn't know what his voice is like.

I think it is a place in which everything desired and feared lives. I spent my childhood escaping to the woods that surrounded my house. I always felt safe there.

He laughs.

Later Tacita tells me about when Lev was a child in Ukraine. His father came from Siberia, his mother from the small Ukrainian village where they met. He saw her, from a distance, washing her family's laundry. A line of white squares cutting across the blue sky. He saw her only twice, never up close. And then asked for her hand in marriage. Her father offered him a small dowry. Two thinning cows. Not much money. Lev's father refused to bargain for more because he loved her.

Lev attended school for exactly two years. On one occasion, his teacher told him the class was getting some books and everyone was to bring thirty kreuzens. Lev's father gave him the money, but because the books had not yet arrived, he held on to it. On the way home from school it was very cold, and he and his friends stopped at the neighbour's, Mrs. Ruza's, house to get warm. She had baked some buns, which they all ate hastily, so

Lev gave her his thirty kreuzens. When Lev's father found out that the money had been spent on buns, he was furious. He said, You have made your choice. You have eaten your books.

He was eight years old, Tacita continues, when his father took him out of school. He was conscripted to tend oxen in the forest with the other village boys. The forest was infested with wolves. There were eight boys, or *holavari*, head shepherds. At night he said they slept in the forest under the trees. They would light a big fire that they kept going all night to keep warm and to frighten away the wolves. One boy would return to the village to bring back supper for the group each night. This continued to be his regular routine for five years. Darkness, fire, yellow-eyed wolves. Istvan says this is what populated Lev's dreams for years.

Tacita, do you know about those tsunami mushrooms that grow in Japanese caves? The ones that predict seismic activity?

I understand, Tacita nods, taking my hand and pulling us down to sit on the cold street curb, marking the gravity of this. *Un choc amoureux*, she says. The body is sacred, I. It rarely lies.

Holavari, I repeat to Tacita. It sounds like a knuckle brushing across an earbone. I wonder if he is resentful. If he hates animals because of this.

No, I, Tacita says. He thinks they are beautiful.

How can he say that?

He thinks they are beautiful because unlike us, they are naked on the inside too.

It is no surprise then, Lev's reply.

Forests exist for their own reasons, he says to me, not ours. Beware of security, he warns. It is a false belief. It does not exist in nature.

There is more wine. The conversation reaches the vaulted ceilings of Istvan and Tacita's apartment. The anarchist says we must explode social order to transform life itself. The revolutionary wipes the corners of his mouth and smiles. His teeth are purple. Revolutionary-speak turns into theatre. We go around the table. Tacita blindly takes a book off the shelf. She disappears into the kitchen for three-quarters of an hour and re-emerges with Rimbaud's *Les Illuminations* baked in honey, encrusted with poppy seeds and small blue cornflowers suspended in circles of chèvre dipped in flowering rosemary. I procure an omelette with hair, cut from the beard of a dinner guest who had taken too much eau de vie and snores on the couch. When he wakes, we serve it to him on a white china plate. Ursula, a patroness in a gentleman's dinner jacket who speaks in perfectly pitched images, finds a typewriter, places it on the table, and types what she says later is the sixth Brandenburg Concerto. The harpsichord solo, we are shown, is in red. Lev then orders us to be silent. We are. Everything stops for a moment. The clattering of forks and knives and crystal glasses, chairs creaking, coughing, the striking of matches, even the paper leaves outside. It is almost funny for a moment, but then it begins to feel profound. His eyes are mirthful but in a deadly serious, funereal tone he says, Listen.

Listen to the sound of night falling.

Tacita tells me what I missed when I left. That the dainty pranks were upstaged by a giant, depressive but prolific artist named Félix, who, full of wine and out of ideas, unzipped his trousers and took out his immense occupant, laying it on his dinner plate.

Everyone laughed. The ladies did not faint, she says. They merely wondered at its pink, heavy idleness.

I am filled with unexpected joy and too much wine, and everything is starting to feel like a torpid, slow-motion game, like the pastis-dazed old men who play boules under the plane trees with knotted roots in the breadwarm sun of Provence. The decibels melting as I weave through the tangles of guests to get my coat. Lev and I knock arms in the front hall, when I'm reaching for my gloves. I kiss Tacita and Istvan, four times, and Lev offers to walk me back to Mme. Tissaud's. I don't remember my feet on the cobbled stones, or the edges of curbs.

He tells me, his voice in sharp pieces lost in an automobile engine that skids by, that he is leaving early in the morning. Obligations.

What?

It is something he cannot discuss.

We walk beside each other. My chest is burning. The city is lidded and a shiny-wet silver, rain-washed pavements that smell of petrol and chestnuts. I feel protected, emboldened, by the wine.

I remain distanced, polite. He tells me of his work, but I find it impossible to reconcile this tractable low voice with the violence of ideas that comes from him. He talks about his paintings. His cheekbones sharp, like a flicker of fire, possibly from hunger, and I am caught off guard. I say something about the beauty of the city. How it asks you to fall in love with it. He says the light is an invitation to devotion. But he says he is bored by beauty alone. He takes nothing from the outside. It's all coming from inside, he says. I am just the amusement of the forces that are born and die in me. He has an exuberance undercut with a kind of detachment. Something in his physicality, in his line of questioning that induces panic. The panic makes me suddenly feel so alive I could jump out of my own skin. It's as though he asks me to follow him, and then leaves me there to find my own way out. I love his words, the durability of them. My mind concocting desires around them. He says he likes the way I held Tacita's scissors. With grace and violence. He takes in my quietness. I see how stillness holds him.

I concentrate on the stones underfoot, and then the black wool trousers, the tight-fitting suit. I notice the outline of his body. His fingers as he buttons his jacket and turns up its collar. His gaze is startling when he turns toward me, his eyes like electricity. He asks things of me, not allowing me the shelter of my own mind. He inquires about my art, what interests me. I don't have the language to explain myself. No one has ever really asked me anything. I have always hidden. Listened to others. And why is this what I prefer? The silence began as something I practised, meant to be protective, but now it is something impossible to stop. It distresses me to think there are things, regular things I might be incapable of.

What about you? he asks. In the following silence, I hear the *tink* of the streetlamp filaments turn on, like delicate splinters of glass.

I am attracted to people who need help, I think. Not sure if I've actually said it aloud.

He turns to me. His face the map of a lost country, like the ones Tacita finds hidden and beautiful in an invisible city that overlays the one we are in.

Maybe it is you, he says, who needs help.

Deer

Small, pale messages etched in grass.

HE LEAVES ME WITH A fistful of white roses brushed with the faintest green, picked from someone's front garden. He hands them to me and then walks away, everything disappearing with him. For the next few days I watch them unwhorl with slow deliberation. I had always thought that flowers between a man and a woman were banal, but these aren't that.

An unopened heart does not bleed, Mme. Tissaud says, avoiding my eyes, when she snips the stems and fishes out a vase the next morning.

A few days pass. I cannot sleep, I eat nothing. Food is pushed around my plate. I am half-starved and liminal. Though I have no appetite, I despise my response. Hunger is not original.

I wash my brushes in Mme. Tissaud's back sink. The *chaud* and *froid* are labelled in reverse, but it makes no difference because no flat in Paris that I know of has hot water. I have an assignment to draw the same fruitbowl on five separate days. Painting food when you are not eating is useful. You see it as more of an object, more theoretically, which allows for the kind of distance required to adequately render the so-called truth. It's different when a painting comes to me. When I roll out of bed, blink my eyes, and go straight to the canvas, without washing or eating or exchanging pleasantries with Mme. Tissaud. I duck from the world, its diversions, so that I can get it down before I lose it. I squeeze out the tubes and mix the colours I will have seen in my head, and dip in my brush and begin on the canvas and stand back and feel full of electricity. Nothing can touch it.

I am trying to remain open to the tedious assignments that I am told will make me a better painter. I like how they want you to understand the chemistry of everything you use, even pencil and paper. But this assignment and the essay I just turned in on the sculptural qualities of Cézanne's fruit begin to make me unsure.

What's next? I groan to Tacita. Am I going to become one of those fossilized critics, describing the colours of a Van Gogh moon?

That's impossible, Tacita says, buttoning up her coat. The moon is not a colour.

Le loup, as Istvan calls him. Which could be a reference to his name, or his time in the woods, but I imagine it is directed more at something in his wicked, indifferent eyes. The remoteness. His separateness from his own power. Though from Istvan, this comes off as a term of endearment rather than derision.

La rentrée is dying, I think. The leaves are golden and starting to fall, foretelling the brittle cold, the one I will soon know. It is different here than in the north. The savage cold. There it is simple. It is a matter of surviving. There are provisions. Here it is complicated. It is damp, and there are cracks in the tall, thick, clouded windows. The clothing too fashionable and thin. Nothing is designed for creating or keeping heat. I can see my breath in my flat when I wake up now, but the cold is good for painting. You keep your focus.

I have been working on an animal painting, red tones in the landscape as though lit by fire, an odd white moon, birds, and a deer. A strange mist. Thick bright paint, an off-kilter feeling. When you look closer you can see that one of the creatures is a woman with an animal's face. She is like a ghost, familiar somehow, but unusual-looking. She has rain-soaked skin, like a person barely saved from drowning. But her expression is one of revolt, as though she would tear someone's hair out if they came too close. It has been slow, trying to find the right white. I've mixed red, blue, and yellow together, which becomes a dark grey. In the painting, it comes across as white. This is something I learned at the academy. We have studied Millet, Daubigny, and Corot, who are able to paint snow without using any white at all. I've fallen in love with red, not too blue, not orange, but the beautiful perfect reds you see in a child's cap in Renaissance portraits.

Tacita and I walk to a bistro where she insists we must consume frites, and wine. We pass a faded poster for the bullfights in Spain. You know the word matador in Spanish means killer, she says. Our shoes make little clicks on the cobblestones as we walk, the sound I have read whales make when meeting other whales, though usually they are silent.

The warmth of the bistro is the difference between walking from shadow to sun. Its dim chandeliers lit like a low flame against the mirrored walls. There are potted palms, banquettes of wine-coloured velvet, and women throwing their heads back in laughter. Round tables with rattan chairs on black and white tile, tasselled lamps, and ceilings a whole extra metre above normal, cigarette smoke swirling in the beams of light. All of Paris lives in cafés, I realize, in part because their apartments are too cold.

In the bistro I say, Tacita, you must tell me something.

Anything, dove. What is it?

What do you know of Lev?

She exhales smoke and runs her fingers through her short dark hair, the cigarette an inch from her scalp.

There is a long pause.

Shit, she finally says.

What?

He has a wife.

My cheeks burn red. It is as though she has struck me in the face.

In this time, Tacita, who has the frame of a sparrow, eats both our plates of frites. She washes down some wine. All right, she says, banging down her glass, feigning dead seriousness. There are two ways to become enlightened. One is androgyny.

This makes me laugh. As in a fairy tale, how every character is just an aspect of ourselves, male and female?

Sort of. Smoke spirals out of her cigarette.

Androgyny suggests completeness, the beatific condition of desirelessness. She holds the cigarette to her mouth. The coming together of male and female forces in a single individual. For most of us, she says, her head tilted, smiling, this is not possible. The other is the attainment of this ideal through the meeting of a man and woman in love. It is an ontological leap, one of great daring.

And marriage?

It is everything. She exhales. And nothing too. Though nothing isn't necessarily the opposite of everything. She pauses. Pronounced man and wife. I think it is ridiculous how in marriage a man gets *pronounced* as a man. It is always the woman who must change identities. She taps the ash. Marriage can be the highest plane, or merely a binding contract. And really, how can anyone vow they will love longer than the love might last? She shifts in her chair. I mean, I was a child, really, when I married. That day, I washed my hair in the morning. As I sat drinking coffee, an iridescent blue butterfly that looked like it came from another hemisphere alighted on my robe and stayed there. I sat, and then walked around the room, dazzled by its presence in a time when I was not sure what I deserved.

Her words fade in and out of my ears. They are just words. Her experience. What she has identified as essential to her. I can't even articulate what I feel, in part because I don't know what I feel. Ardent. Vulnerable. Dangerously inhabited. Words everyone else uses. I know it is supposed to join people, this common language, but now I think it only separates us, reducing our experiences to the same words. And really, what has happened? Nothing. Nothing that can be explained other than this sense of feeling altered. Of nerves exposed. He obliterates thoughts of my work, of myself. It changes everything. I possess nothing.

Ivory, she says, grabbing my hand, which is cold, fingernails flecked with gesso, from across the table.

Don't be a mourner. Please. Try not to think of it. It will ruin you.

I know this. I squeeze her hand, yet I am unable to perform with forced high spirits.

An obdurate romantic. *Merveilleux*, she says, placing her hand on my shoulder.

I finally reach for the wine and tip it straight from the bottle down my throat, in one long, theatrical gulp. My brother Edgar once taught me how to open my throat. We practised on lemonade, which made us choke and burn and sputter to the ground laughing.

How marvellous. Tacita smiles. How almost persuasive, she says in a way that tells me she's impressed.

I have such a vision of Lev that it is as though I've willed him here. He is standing in the courtyard of the art academy several days later. He leans against the stone wall. And even though my back is to him, I know he is there. I can tell by the expression on the faces of other women. When I turn to see him, the tangled black hair and flashing whiteblue eyes make him seem almost half-mad. Their portentous purpose startles me. In this moment I can see that something he carries removes him from the world, and from me. He is outside of time and place. Something about this, about him blinds me. He looks at me and I avert my eyes. When you are being looked at, really looked at, it is hard to look back. Standing near him is like being under a low rush of birds.

We walk through all the arrondissements sequentially until my heels blister and a small hole, the size of a centime, appears on the bottom of my left shoe. I have only one pair of shoes now, and the polish I apply each night to fill in the cracks has washed off on the wet stones, staining the foot portion of my stockings into a shoe trompe l'oeil. I barely remember what we speak of. I am cloaked in a shy opacity and become joltingly self-conscious about my slightly lilted gait, about speaking French without mistakes, about which expression I should wear on my face, how my arms should hang, what I should do with my hands, now turning red in the cold air. I am too busy noticing everything in the presence of him, how he speaks, how he moves, to remember what we discuss. There are long stretches of silence, which he interprets differently. These silences always make me think of my mortality. That there is always so much more to be said.

I like how he arrows, straight as a sunshaft, through the crooked streets. We sit at the top of Belleville, the buildings silver under the violet sky. He rips at a baguette and offers it to me. His hands are large, rough, long fingered. I shake my head and I watch the swell of his jaw as he eats, thinking that where he comes from they have black rivers, they eat black bread. I suddenly have a memory of Father telling me how the Russians loved Ivan the Terrible. He explained that for them, the word terrible means formidable. He said that Napoleon could not defeat the Russians because when his men arrived the Russians had already set fire to Moscow. They destroyed their own city. Owning a ruined city was better than giving it over.

His hands rip another shank of bread. I also think, All men are hungry.

We hear bottles rolling and clinking in the back of an open truck making its delivery to the *cave aux vins*.

What do you think of, Ivory? he turns to me and asks. He says my name, Eve-or-aya.

I wonder if he means in general, or now, and either way there are so many thoughts in this blindingly silent moment between us that I can scarcely pick a single thing. I look at the potted violets on the sill across the street that delineate the space between the shutters and think of how I love old white paint, but this seems silly after such a long silence. I think of songs that take wing. Of how when I wake up, I touch my cheek and part of my forehead to the windowpane in my studio because I like to feel the burn of morning. But I don't have the nerve to articulate such seemingly constructed responses. I'm not sure if I'm liked enough to say what I think.

We walk back to Lev's studio. It is a high white room. We climb up creaking wooden stairs. While my studio is just one painting on an easel, his has the exalted chaos of an archaeological dig. It is shockingly filthy. Something I've never witnessed in my childhood, where opulence insisted on staring back at you through crystal, marble, silver. Here there are paint-splattered walls, tins of brushes clotted with paint, photographs, magazines, books, and newspapers all torn in piles. The floor littered with coal, charcoal, matches. It is the opposite of his paintings, clear and simple, stripped to the most essential thing. In his studio, it feels as though his subconscious is leaking out. It touches even my feet. Everything in varying degrees of creation and destruction. It reveals his mind in action without ever relinquishing its mystery. Everything smells of smoke and turpentine. A fire left its black imprint on the shared wall of his studio just a couple of days ago, the room burning, banging into flames, twisting upward. He told me that you should never involve the *pompiers*. They ruin everything. Instead, he got the fire down with buckets of water. The wall, his chair, and table were blackened, but miraculously, everything else, including his paintings, was untouched.

There is no pretense. We are barely up the stairs. His rough hands on my shoulders. The dark cloud jacket in my nostrils. Wool and outside cold and smoke. When I taste him, I am tasting outside. The unshaven skin leaving a constellation of small welts on my cheek and neck. Back-seamed stockings, the ones with the pinhole of white thigh, twisting off. My shoulders fibrillating against the windowless wall, marked with black, carbon wings. New fingers, new mouths. He grabs my hair, the pins scatter on my shoulders and down my back and onto the floor, a barely traceable rain. When my hair comes down it falls over and encloses him in a dark wave. He lifts up the white folds of my dress. I am cool against him. The warmth back into the body. Delicate networks of blood. Flashing silver eyes. Sweat shining on bone. My hand on the tendons in his throat. The truth anointed. The kind of truth that can arise only from such a profound wordless moment. The far, unlanguaged precincts where there is only feeling.

I fall asleep on his bare chest, the bang of his heart against the side of my face. The only thing I think in the folding darkness, Nothing else matters.

Later he moves across the room and brings back a large canvas, its wooden stretcher striking the floor in front of me. On a thick white ground that could be Siberia, or Lapland, is a pale blue square. Blue is the hottest colour, he says flatly. When all the colours melt away, you get blue. From the date on the back, it was made weeks ago but the tiny word in the right-hand corner is unmistakable. The faint glint of those three small letters in graphite, a shining prophecy. It says, *feu*.

Nightingale

Luscinia megarhynchos: narcotic effect;
voice that signals spring.

WHAT IS THIS? Skeet asks, reading through the handwriting of voices written out on a faded blue grid.

Vocalization: 3:45 p.m. west of Albion Hills. A liquid bubbling in descending scale. Sounds like water running out of a bottle.

Juvenilia. I found it yesterday. An old notebook. Back when I only knew how to anthropomorphize. Before I used equipment. I pause and then say, Before anything had become anything.

Frame?

Yes?

I need to talk to you.

I'm trying to remember when I last saw you.

Paris, he says, slightly impatiently.

Hotel du Nord, was it? Yes. I had missed the presentation of your paper on chorus howls. I remember you walked into the restaurant telling me that you always know you are in Paris because of the tang of dogshit.

Frame, I—

God Skeet, what am I going to do? I close my eyes, still hearing the harmonic high-frequency wolf sounds, the ones associated with agnostic inner states. I understand there are probably no practical suggestions.

I've been trying to work that out the whole way here, Skeet says.

Skeet? I look around at all the fieldbooks and papers filling the room.

Yup.

Sometimes I wonder if it might be too late.

Horseshit, he says.

Science began under a sliver of a new moon in Toronto, my chest pounding like the mice hunted by owls from the sound of their sped-up heartbeat alone. I had come from Paris having trouble doing the simplest things, sleeping, eating, talking. I'd walled grief into one of the remote, inaccessible corners. But something pierced a bright hole in my mind, allowing a moment of transparency where I was able to see everything. Like sincere huge-headed woodland creatures in fables that instruct you what to do. Everything seemed clear and possible. I wanted a place that had no history. Here there were once forests of trees so thick the sky was black when you looked up. The settlers cut the trees from the water's edge and moved north, building the city out of the lumber until most of it burned down and they had to start again. On a short, cold black night in winter, whole city blocks were swallowed up, the glow of the fire seen from distant towns. Mother had once dismissed the entire country as dirty, a place full of lumberjacks, men who lived in grubby cabins and tore at meat with their fingers. When I stepped off the boat, it was late fall. Grey. I looked around at the trees and thought, They haven't any leaves. The winter light was quick and sharp, though in the summers it stretched long into night, and everything grew and grew.

I took up the hem on my wool dress so that I could walk freely. Movement was essential to fieldwork. I quickly discovered a route, past the piano factory and the brick quarry to the ravine thick with sumacs and thistles as high as my collarbone. A route that became much easier when I later had a bicycle. There was skeletal milkweed, the heart-shaped leaves of lilacs, and new bitter little smells. According to the man who sold me vegetables, not long ago black bears scooped salmon straight from the river. Crouched on the steep grade that rolls down to the water, the wet cool plants brushed my neck, flecked with dirt. Hair in gusts. I waited and heard the creak of trees in the wind, and then the haunted low tones of a pair of barred owls. Later, when I read over my transcriptions, it looked like *You you you*.

Crossing the bright green circle of grass toward the biology building at the university felt like a piece of luck. Recording animal sounds at the art academy was like trying to figure out an answer without knowing the question. In Toronto, all the lectures—evolutionary biology, ecology, organic chemistry—pointed to atoms and cells, charged with electricity. I found the biology courses exhilarating. Practical theories that would lead to magical work. It seemed a sturdier place for the mind. But it didn't come easily. I struggled with calculations. I sank into despair after accidents and failures due to my inexperience. Nothing was clear to me, just the need to immerse myself in something real. I developed a taste for experimental research right away, though learned to keep most of my ideas to myself. Or when speaking of them, to use dull adjectives and the dry technical language they favoured. I loved the laboratory, its order, its precision. Clean, with rows of glass-covered cabinets containing equipment and stacks of yellowed papers with observations, including eclipses, earthquakes, and meteorological bulletins from the past century. There was a faint, burning wax scent. Afterward, I bent silently over books at the library or at the wooden table in my rented attic room, too fond of quiet to share lodgings. I studied and worked, nothing else counting. I spent any spare time outdoors, wandering through the muddy ravine, scrambling above the river, full of curiosity and daring, with dozens of ideas in my head, while the other students were inside back at the lab, conducting delicate experiments. A return to the wilds. The green leaves and branches and vines that twined with the fallen oaks. That aliveness. The screeches and twitterings and low-rumble calls. I slowly felt a thaw, an edging toward the possibility of happiness. Not the kind that rolls in like a storm, but the ordinary kind, the kind that lasts.

An Edison phonograph and a box of wax cylinders from the music department in an old cardboard box had been left in the corridor. It was the same model that Koch used to record the owl sounds. The First World War marked his shift from music to wildlife. As a boy, he had met the great Franz Liszt and played in Clara Schumann's music room, where Brahms was a frequent visitor. The phonograph was an early model that had the ability to both record and play back sound. I carried it home and up to the attic and cleaned all the parts carefully with a cloth. There were cardboard tubes containing dark blue cylinders, coloured, I later found out, because the dye layer reduces the surface noise. I opened the window to the sterling high pitches of two mockingbirds in conversation, the whistling of a train, and played it back, the sounds magically preserved in tinfoil. I marched madly around the flat as if this could not be heard sitting down. Eventually I undressed and lay down in the narrow bed, though unable to sleep. The dark was silent, punctuated by the squeal of a distant engine, low voices in the hall below, eyes open to the ceiling.

The most important thing, Professor Tapping said, is to keep your eyes open. He first had me observing crows, which I thought perfectly suitable. It seemed folkloric, as when the hero on an adventure is advised to pick the lesser creature out of a stable of nobler ones. The simple, even ugly language asks for nothing. It loses everything except meaning, what the creature wants to say. Fairy tales and nursery lore are crammed with creatures. Coded reminders that we once knew animals to be on the same footing as us.

I read that in Greek, vulture, *cathartes*, means cleanser. Something clicked into place.

A crow will snatch a sandwich from a picnic table, Professor Tapping said. They prosper in cities, in close proximity to us. He doesn't know I've seen crows sold for fifteen francs a piece to mothers who put them in soup and feed it to their angular children.

We walk to the Necropolis Cemetery in Cabbagetown. Cemeteries are, he says, the best place to observe birds in urban ecologies.

In the afternoon light a large bird does eventually loop down from the sky, its broad black wings spread like something after a fire. Scrawny feet. Scorched-looking face. Its neurotic pinprick eyes glancing at us as it makes an unnerving sound suspiciously like laughter. Of course, I think, he chooses these birds to observe. Black with torn wings, charred voices, the carriers of death. I remember something about them as takers of the soul, to the other side. But then its head lobs down in garbage and guzzles a dropped breadslice. It is both a cindered heart and just another grubby creature. I notice the dirty feathers. How can it fly with those feathers? I find myself paralyzed by simple questions, the questions of a child.

This is good, Professor Tapping nods enthusiastically, bits of bread flinging out of his mouth. He has brought cheese sandwiches wrapped in waxed brown paper. Question everything. Learn something. Answer nothing.

Aristotle?

Euripides, he says, waving the other sandwich in my direction, suddenly making me aware of how hungry I am. We eat in silence as he pulls out a lined notebook and begins to draw what looks almost like an architectural diagram.

Was he the one torn apart by dogs? I finally say.

Who?

Euripides.

I haven't a clue, he says. They often congregate in cemeteries, the crows. They protect themselves in mobs. Unlike pigeons that require buildings to shield them from predators. The crows sit on top of the cold bones as well as the still-warm, the just-dead.

Corvus, Skeet reads out loud from one of the fieldbooks. Both crows and ravens make loud raspy signature calls, *caw* and *kraa* respectively. Why, he asks, all the birds, now?

It's what I began with. They work best with the cymatic imagery. Visual symbols and patterning give us clues that sound alone cannot, I say to Skeet, who is studying the nightingale images. You know, you might be the only person who understands my logic. I hope you can continue the work when I am—gone.

Frame—

Skeet. Please. Don't let them use the dictionary to make ring tones for European mobile phone networks, or for relaxation, like that station, bird radio. Or sit, I plead, like Mme. Curie's papers, sealed away in boxes lined with lead. It makes me think how fearless she was. But in my experience, I say, searching for my cigarettes, it is the young who are afraid of life. Only the old are afraid of death.

Except you, Skeet says.

Well when it's no longer an abstraction, when it's actually bearing down on you, it is a significant deadline. It helps you concentrate magnificently.

He shakes his head. You really are like those aristocratic women who plant goddamn rosebushes in the face of ruin, he says, handing me the small glass filter I'm supposed to use when I smoke this much. He has on a blue jacket like the French workers wear, faded to grey and missing most of the buttons. His skin is brown and the tips of his hair glint gold. The sun has both darkened and bleached him out.

I've come full circle, I say, exhaling. Reduced to my senses alone.

Hare

Millions of unaccounted notes, its blood mixed
with house paint, drawn on a tarot card.

TACITA AND I SIT in the second storey at Café de Flore
drinking café crèmes and see M. Marant, an instructor who
teaches at the art academy, walk by with his wife and their baby.
We've witnessed them as a family on a number of occasions. She
picks him up pushing the black shiny *poussette* and he routinely
invites students to his apartment for seminars. He seems a bit
stunned by his own life, I say to Tacita. He and his wife look like
siblings, as sometimes married people do. We secretly call the
baby the Larva because she is so coddled that her feet never
touch the ground, her personality never allowed to emerge. It is
as though she is boneless. Tacita, whose perceptions of people
are disarming, can divine nothing from the baby. Not even a
nascent grain of temperament.

I think I enjoy freedom too much to ever have a child, Tacita
says, jutting back on her chair. There is a part of me that makes
me wary of anything I'd have to give my whole self to, other
than my work. Besides. She bangs forward on her chair

dramatically. The violence of childbirth. The loss of autonomy. The love. That's the thing that terrifies me the most.

How exacting the knife that skinned off that desire. I say this out loud, though I don't mean to. I share her view but for different reasons. I have no growing tendency toward domesticity. I can't even remotely imagine the desire to have a child, having only just barely escaped my own childhood.

I've spent my whole life trying to avoid the notion of children, she snaps back with such celerity that it's sort of funny.

I had to look after all my siblings. My mother used to cry all the time. But her tears were different, pregnancy changed them.

She flips through the pages of her sketchbook and then shows me a drawing. It depicts an isolated woman sitting in a lonely tower, a blank expression on her exhausted face. Mechanically, she is grinding up stars that she then feeds to an insatiable moon. This would go on endlessly, Tacita says. Unless, like my mother, the celestial feeding ends because your own life does.

Tacita's composition decentres the gaze. It is oddly shoved to the left, making the woman look tiny and pale and engulfed in black. Alone.

She winces and then says plainly, Her name is Aglaya. That is the only thing I know.

What? I say, slightly nettled.

Lev's wife's name is Aglaya. She pauses. Sorry love. But all I know is that you will survive this because you are meant to survive it. You must believe this on a cellular level.

Tacita's words jam me stiff. I dangle my limbs, my heart, before a man who is married. Who somewhere has a wife. One that he loves, or has loved. One that he is betraying. His body is still on my body. This emotional tension, I say to Tacita, is like an anxiety dream from which you try to awaken but cannot.

Tacita and I try meditation. I reach for the back of my head, unfastening my hair and shaking it out. We sit on the cold hard wooden floor of my studio and chant bits of old Latin prayers I remember from convent school. *Convertere, Domine, et eripe animam meam: salvum me fac propter misericordiam tuam.* We say it over and over until Tacita turns to me. You know, hell is repetition somebody once said. Both of us try to remain silent but then start shaking with laughter. As my flanks grow numb on the unforgiving floor I wonder if my affliction is simply an interior conflict with my own art. I know, somewhere, there is a rival. A voice tells me to run away, to be free of it. To not enter into this struggle. But then he does something, turns to me with one of his illuminations, and sets me alight. I rest my attention on my paintings, pulled directly from my dreams, from my imagined world. At the academy they keep telling us that to become an artist you must be able to draw from life. I try to do as they say, but I am not fully convinced. Inside there is a growing sense of apartness. Of moving toward something else.

I have on my easel a painting I have begun with a woman in the foreground. She wears a large overcoat that could be a man's, though how the woman looks is of less interest to me than how she reacts with the landscape that surrounds her. The slope of her shoulders is not quite accurate, but the angle of her head is good. When I tilt it toward the light, it is still not right. The forest is dark and blurred, there are feathers on the ground. But there are things I haven't been able to work out. The palette seems too dusky. I dislike green right now. All I can see is blue. I have been to Sennelier, where I found the perfect blue. Cobalt glass powder. They roast ore and then remove the arsenic, sieve it, and mix it with pulverized stones. It is a stunning hue in a tiny precious package they wrap in brown paper. In my studio I smooth this perfect electric blue in silky oil with a glass pestle that I use sparingly. It is expensive and beautiful and I want it to last. The expression on the woman's face shows determination, but what is her intention? Some days I like it, others I don't. When my mood slips, the painting feels flat and obvious. Other days I am pleased with its overall effect. Does Lev fall in and out of love with his own paintings as I do? I don't ask. I let thoughts of Lev lead me away from it. He knows how to give parts of himself without losing anything. For me, his presence alters everything. I question the confines of the academy. The direction of my interests. My own artistic motives. My emotions inconstant as weather. Yes. Maybe it is that, I say, convincing myself that what rips through me is not because of a man I hardly know. A man who leaves each time, having promised nothing. He unmoors me. I forget myself with him. In these past few months, it is the memory of him that lingers the most. Enraptured. Debased. All night, all night. And sometimes I wake to the early sounds of delivery carts dragged over the stones, drivers shouting, the predawn flurry of buyers and sellers heading toward Boulevard Raspail. And in my empty room, it's as though he was never here.

He will appear when he appears. This apartness, this deep-diving absence, is essential to his survival. Because there is always a part of him that is not here, even when he is here. When he is no longer in my periphery, each time, I realize he may never enter back in. He is unnaturally adept at negative space. He is remote and then disappears. No one seems to know where he goes. Even when he himself tells his history, he seems not to want to remember anything.

But it is all outside of reason, and at moments the urgency for Lev is so strong it makes me feel sick. At other times it fades. I work on my sound notebook or paint in my room above Mme. Tissaud's atelier with its one small window in the northwest corner, and lose the feeling in my legs. I can seal it off. This is almost more disturbing than being consumed. As though I must cut off the part of the world he inhabits to survive.

I feel as though I'm only breathing through that thin slice of air between pond and ice, I say to Tacita.

I guess it is possible, she says neutrally.

But really, Tacita, what is this meant to do? How can this kind of living be sustainable? What do we learn?

What do we learn. There is a long pause. We learn to notice everything.

I walk home through a light rain, stepping carefully as though everything might spill. I am relieved to see Mme. Tissaud sewing a text block, needle between her teeth as she lines up the spines of each signature against the table edge. She motions me in.

Ivory. I have something for you.

She hands me a thick leatherbound edition, *A Booke of Secrets*, a centuries-old translation of a Dutch edition, though the book was originally published in Italian. She has rescued it from one of the bins she combs for first-edition esoterica. She has restored and rebound it. My fingers touch the whorls on the leather. You can identify which kind of animal skin, Mme. Tissaud tells me, by the marks. Ostrich has noticeable concentric circles because of the large follicles from which the feathers grow. Pigskin has hair follicle patterns on top and bottom with a uniformity that is distinct. Goat, she says, has an attractive grain, the telling factor being the size of the piece. The book contains medieval recipes set in blackletter for inks that sound more like rituals. They require such things as collecting rainwater droplets to mix in with boiled cornflowers and elderberries, clarified with the egg of a songbird, fixatives made from the skin of a hare. Iron gall, she explains, is created when wasps lay eggs under a tree's bark. The tree's own defences create a lump that becomes the gall. Those disfigured nodes are then sliced open and milked for the darkest night of pigment.

Mme. Tissaud knows of my cooking experiments with Tacita, and my desire to work elements of nature into my art. I mix my own egg tempera from a failproof recipe in her back sink where I also wash my dishes. The yolk of one hen's egg, powdered pigments, mixed and applied in thin layers to wooden panels, sometimes burnished, everything transparent. It allows underlayers to vibrate below the surface colour in three dimensions. I unscrew the metal cap of the small brown bottle and add a drop of clove oil, which keeps the colours and makes them sweetsharp. I am excited about these colours made from nature. Denatured nature, on the page. The egg tempera produces jewel-like tones, the faintly metallic gleam of minerals. I wait a day, then gesso, and sand, and only then do I begin to draw on it. The shopkeeper at Sennelier says, Mademoiselle, you do not need linen, when I ask for it. No one uses linen anymore. Here, this canvas is less expensive, he says. He directs me to a man at the hardware who cuts a Masonite sheet into panels instead of the more expensive ready-made ones at the shop.

While I wait for prepared canvases I draw in my notebook, experimenting. Bright pigments, like the Indian yellow that used to come from the urine of cows fed on mango leaves alone. Our instructors tell us its fluorescence attracted Dutch painters who wanted to paint the sun. I draw watery configurations and close the book while the pages are still wet. When I open it, there are abstract shapes that imply natural forms. It looks almost like a mystical landscape or a mapping of another moon. Accidental naturalism. I like how it removes my hand, removes me from the act of creating altogether. I am just letting it become what it will become.

Mme. Tissaud also has an interest in this. Materials becoming the spiritual part of the work. She explains that the high acidity of some inks means the paper gets eaten by the ink. I look at her in disbelief.

She shrugs. The thing that illuminates it kills it.

Lev rarely discusses his art. He hates the recent past. He is uninterested in incorporating natural materials. His time in the woods, all the living in the open, has made him devour cities, move toward the unnatural. He despises imitations of nature. In his studio is the pervasive smell, the flaking smear of glue and solvent. He reveres the tidy gardens and mathematically sculpted hedgerows of France.

It is useless and tedious to represent what exists, because nothing that exists satisfies me, he says. Only later do I realize he is quoting Baudelaire.

I once painted the village I was born in. I sat and drew it over and over again. Then I realized that what I loved was not the village but what the village pulled out of me. But you have no feeling for what you are left with. That kind of representation has no resonance. It is like a beautiful ancient religious temple. To the secular world, it retains its beauty even though its original purpose no longer exists. What it becomes is a decoration for tourists.

I think I know why he won't paint nature. His childhood. The woods to him are ugly not because they are aesthetically unsatisfying, but because they mean fear. They also mean death.

I embrace Mme. Tissaud, hard, lifting her feet off the ground and holding on for seconds longer than anyone would, the way she has shown me. She is so thick and soft to my dark and narrow, we illustrate opposites.

I kiss her. What would I do without you?

Upstairs, I lie on the bed in the corner and look up at the window. The rain is falling in straight lines though what I still see is Mme. Tissaud's hands stitching spines below. It is the kind of rain that makes you believe in weather. But then from my eye corner I see grey. It is a mouse dead and lying flat on its left cheek. Velvet fur, its thin tail behind it like a bootlace. The room takes on a slight scent of fish. I find some scrap paper to gather it up but cannot. It seems it could be just sleeping and my prodding will disturb it. It will suddenly flee in the lightning quick way mice do and I will have a coronary. The thing that we often fear in animals, like strangers, is their movement, their unfamiliar velocities. Instead I cover the mouse with paper, sit at my table, and begin to record in my sound notebook, but I cannot work. I am suspicious of other bodies, other deaths that may have occurred in my absence.

I lie down and try to sleep. The uncertainty comes at night, when everything grows bigger. We miss what we know, even if what we know isn't good for us. I lived in equal parts of fear and awe of Mother. A brusque contrarian. Her obsession with cleanliness, both inside and out, was delineated by purges, the necessary ritual for those seeking perfection. It's why she didn't like sunny days, though she would never say it. Because they show all the dust. It is also why she had to be the thinnest woman in the room. It is not only that it makes her the most envied, but that, I suspect, she is actually disturbed by her own corporeality.

Though she was not entirely a devastating presence. When I was allowed to visit her in her sitting room, she would hold me rapt with her descriptions of the paintings I loved, the Bruegels, Vermeers, and Boschs she'd seen when she travelled through Europe. But when at the conclusion of these visits I was given a chocolate, I saw what I was. A guest. Her voice was so beautiful and quiet. Her sentences were thrilling, and contained arcane knowledge. She spoke in paragraphs. She seemed to essentially be living in another century, though she could be modern when it suited her. Queenie once left the dinner table in tears when Mother came down in a dress with a neckline two inches lower than normal. It was unusual behaviour for Queenie, soft-hearted and steady. Perhaps it seemed to her that civilization was falling. When she came to visit, Queenie read Gothic tales and Irish folklore, and said we were the descendants of shapeshifters. Her stories of magic and alchemy fixed in my mind. I would sketch them on paper after she'd gone. *Do you know why they always leave a lone tree in a field? So there is a place for spirits to gather.* She would often contradict Mother, especially when it came to me. Once, after they'd argued, I heard Mother say to Father, I wonder if they forgot to screw in a heart under those toothpick ribs of hers. And I thought, Takes one to know one.

My time was marked by two distinct lives. During the day I took lessons, studied, played the piano dutifully. I sat with a straight back, occupying the strict space reserved for children, especially girls. Sunday meant wearing a starched dress and sitting on the couch with my hands folded in my lap. Not moving or speaking while they received guests. In the evenings before dark or early in the morning I was allowed to ride. Every day I walked out to the tall wooden barn, its roofline like a church. In the early morning my leather boots were hard and cold when I pulled them on. I took the bridle from the hook in front of Admiral the gelding's stall and pulled it over his ears, my other hand slipping the bit between his teeth, the sound like a metal file scraping something hollow. It was almost impossible to see the outline of his outerspace eyes against his jetblack fur and mane. A tightly braided whip sat in the corner, but I never used it. The saddle creaked like a ship as I rode into the forest, climbing the sharp angle of the hill, ducking under low branches, sometimes slapping and stinging my face. I noticed how the birches held thrushes and that kestrels would circle in slow motion far above. I was always moving toward danger—a thunderstorm, slick trails, the low sun barely casting light, tight unknown corners, cantering down steep rocky ground while the mist blurred the land from the sky, thrashing through water, losing my sense of time and coming home far too late to be acceptable.

The house was seated in front of fields and woods, on the edge of a slope, at the bottom of which wound a river. In the distance was a singular conical hill, and when the trees were bare you could see the dark blue waters of the small lake nearby. It would take me fifteen minutes, ten at full canter, to get through the forest and cross the stream into the back field. I could no longer see the maples, reduced to squares of light in the cold black. All that distance shook off constraint. My days consisted of what I could not do, all I couldn't say. I stopped in the field, leaned over Admiral's neck, and patted it. Steam came off his shoulders. He blew out a long ruffled breath that shook his whole body, and then jerked his head down, ripping at the grass with his teeth. Out of nowhere came an explosive whir of a partridge taking off from the ground as they do. My heart jumped, he jumped, but I managed to stay on. Steady old boy, I said, leaning back, my hand on his flanks, watching the orange sun dim then drop below the tips of trees. I pressed my heels below his ribs and cantered back in the dark.

I never tell Mother where I go, I say to my oldest brother, Albert. And she never says anything.

Then she knows, he says.

If she knows, it means it is only a matter of time before I am stopped. Her concern seems to come from appearances, not true worry, like most mothers. I hear her murmur that there is a wildness in me that makes her uneasy. Why does she require so much air? Things she doesn't like, she tells Father, she describes as suffocating.

I started to keep secrets. I decided everything out-of-doors was my own. I don't tell her the day I punched a boy for setting a fox trap. Or that my broken front tooth was from when he punched me back. It is a milk tooth, she said standing back to get a better look, thank god. Her own profile is exquisite; a portrait of it hangs in muslin above the fireplace.

I don't tell her of my collections I have begun to catalogue in notebooks: leaves, nests, insects, the hollow bones of birds. Or the day I stood in a field of Queen Anne's lace and in a few short moments was covered with tiny flapping wings. I was with my brother Garnet. At first we laughed. I said, Listen to the sound of their wings. Garnet looked at me. You hear what other people don't, he said seriously. Don't try to do anything, I whispered. Feel it. And then we both stood perfectly still, feeling the little brushes of the wings on our necks and arms, in our hair. Their bright wings fluttered and fluttered and we didn't move. Open arms aching. Sunshine blinding us. The clear gleaming sky. My body flooded with rapture. I felt my face was wet and realized that tears were running down my cheeks. We stood there, long after they went, saying nothing.

The day I come home, clothes soaked, wrinkled against my skin, Mother's voice spikes with anger, though she appears calm, neck tall. She wears elegantly sewn dresses from a woman who comes to the house and measures her with a tape, not the kind other women order from the catalogue and have delivered the same day by horseback. Why, she says slowly, must you choose to go out in violent weather? It is unnatural. Her tempo making it hard for me to know what will be next. I have disappointed her. I am not sure what to do, so I stand there, dripping onto the glossy hardwood floor. I know that she has attended finishing schools in France and in Italy. That she had a coming-out ball where she wore a silver dress with long white gloves. She has a way of making something trivial seem as if the entire world hinges on it. She seems to have constant issue with my brothers and me, agitated by what she sees as our inattentive and erratic nature.

You will hate yourself, I overheard Father cautioning Mother, if her behaviour allows her to win. Though I wonder, when a mother disowns a daughter, who it is exactly that wins.

Hyena

Hyena; points of stars, cackle.

BRASSERIE LIPP IS BOISTEROUS. There is a gathering, a corralling of performances. This group has such a hunger for radical expression that almost any ludic gesture could gin up a constituency. Hugo with his hallucinogenic speaking style conducts spontaneous writing, passing a blank book for collective contribution. He writes, *Broken*. Tacita wonders when that word could ever be positive. When you're talking about a horse, I say. Or an engagement to a lecherous man, she says. A large roll of thick cream paper is unfurled, the ends taped to the long row of tables. Everyone is a prisoner and must draw a map of their own escape. A scene is performed for a play in which a black swan lays an orphic egg. Tacita gathers the contents of each person's pockets and recreates their dreams out of paperclips, matches, a Jew's harp, centimes encrusted with grime. Yuri, who once slept on Lev's floor, juggles lit candles that surprisingly do not extinguish on the downdraft. He was once a clown in the Russian circus but was kicked out because of his drinking. They told him he was murdering himself with liquor. When he came back sober, he wasn't able to catch anything. His body had compensated for the offtime of alcohol. When I hug him there is the familiar slightly musty animal scent, but the smell of brandy is staggering.

Tonight, I am invincible. I kick off my shoes and dance on the tables, my ankles brushing the heat of the candles, while Lev deadpans poetry made from Victorian department-store catalogue clippings. When he snaps the book shut, I walk off the table and into his arms. He kisses me slowly, deeply. He stands so close I can feel the heat of his body. We look at each other. We barely speak for the rest of the night, but our bodies glint awareness. He is amused by the group's antics and has a genuine affection for them, but his artistic affiliation is elsewhere. He is tolerant to a point. When one of the artists does something like dye a toy bear pink and build shelves in its stomach, he just shakes his head. Though mostly he is alone, he seems to like something he gets from the group. Istvan says it is like interbreeding, given the polarities between his art and that of the group's. Like a donkey and a horse.

And who exactly is the ass in this scenario? Lev says.

This morning we dyed our hair blue. Only both being dark, it is a halo of cerulean, faintly suggested.

Grind the blew cornflowers gathered in the morning before the sun riseth, with faire water very well upon a stone. Then put them in a horne or shell, and pour water theron, stir them well together, then let them stand half a day, then pour out the water, and take the gaule of a great fish, and grind it with gum and the white of eggs, and use it when you thinke good.

It is night. We fall into the cold sheets, our hair leaving watery blue bled into Lev's pillowcase. Blue is benign. Despite what they say, it is a happy colour. A whole universe from red.

There is one star over Jardin du Luxembourg that can be seen through the window from the bed. I appear to be asleep but am not. In truth, I find it impossible to sleep when I am near Lev. I am also kept awake by a little dry grinding sound that is him, in typical lucubration. His paintings happen at any time, but he draws only at night, when the shapes from dreams emerge. I see that he does not want to be interrupted. This is clear.

Punishing silence, the stretch of days between. I paint when I first wake up and then late into the evenings, adjusting to the light. Through my small window, a view of the tree branches. I am conscious of the smells of oils and turpentine that fill the slanted space. Occasionally there is a voice on the street, birdsong, a reminder of another reality. With the apartness, I cannot help the feeling of abandonment. There is a violence in absence. These rhythms of closeness with Lev that upend once he leaves. A stiff formality returns when we first see each other after days apart. We act like wildlife, tentative, despite our bodies bristling with intent.

I have a board on my easel, gessoed and ready, staring at me, but I keep working in my sketchbook instead. The closing facing pages experiments as well as animal voices. This is what I am drawn to, but at the academy they continually dismiss my interests, reminding me to remain on course. They impose the ideals of classical art: order, proportion, symmetry, equilibrium, harmony. I see the other students adopt these intellectual concepts and determinedly incorporate them in their work, but feel as though something vital is being repressed. Instinct. And though I want to hold on to something solid, I am starting to have the sinking feeling that the academy is the wrong thing. What they want is for us to meet requirements. What I want is to ignore them.

I have no way of contacting him. When I say goodbye, I don't know if I will see him an hour later or a week later. I have no rights, no hold on him. There is no plain dignity in the waiting. Waiting has become a habit. He barely exists in this world where we overlap. I know with absolute certainty that any dialogue around it would make him recede for good. And though I have become used to being silent with him, I am still struck by how many things I can't say.

Over a week later, when he arrives at Tacita and Istvan's he takes the small flower from his buttonhole and puts it behind my ear. An electric shock. This happens every time.

I say, Only you.

His lips on my ear. You have been in my mind, between my fingers.

My face and neck flash red. Truth makes heat.

I watch how he puts his hands on Istvan's shoulders and looks into his deep eyes and greets him with such assurance. Though within the possible conduct of every human being, he alone is magnetic. I feign a great calm.

Tacita and I drink tea out of chipped blue-and-white china cups.

The problem, she says, is that I am in love with everything. All of these things. These broken, dirty, miscast things are imbued with such significance I can barely walk down a street. Istvan is wondering if the boxes of things that pile high will take over and we will become diminished souls. I spend so much time collecting, but haven't been able to work on anything.

But this is the work, I say, lining up the cup directly in the saucer's circle. The art is in the choosing. Assemblage is restoration.

Extraordinary.

What?

Your ability to see so clearly.

Everything is easier to see when it is about someone else.

I think, though he deeply understands, Istvan feels weighted by objects.

So. The worst version of collecting would be that you are held ransom by the objects. That they hold you, that they block your mind. You need an uncluttered mind.

She fishes in the tin for a cube of sugar.

And I guess the question you would have to ask is what it is exactly that you're holding on to.

Life, she says as she drops in the sugar. Her spoon clicks against the side of the teacup. I, sometimes I don't know what I'm doing.

Does anybody fully? I like what the objects are to you, each with its energy from where they have been before. Each with its own democracy.

It's similar to your paintings, I. You show an alternative world, where humans, animals, plants, and inanimate objects are on an equal footing. Where do they come from?

Dreams.

Tacita slaps me on the back as though we are sportsmen and I have just scored a point. She walks across the room and uncorks eau de vie and pours it into our teacups.

I think of this place. Full of its imagery. The poetics. The corners of antiquity. The disquiet. As though the city was invented for Tacita. And here I am looking for things elsewhere, like the crows that fly over it. It's ridiculous. Like saying yellow is the colour of that red painting. Tacita says we need relatively. How else can we measure? It is not new, the idea of the thing farthest away being the most desired. With longing there is velocity.

I think of Lev. How I trick myself into believing that I don't need to know the things he is unable to tell me. We have never discussed his wife. I don't think I'll ever know him, but there exists a part of him that is mine. My understanding of him is more physical than intellectual, but it is that too. Though it is also what he senses from me that, in part, attracts.

The prophet with Siberian eyes. Tacita and I secretly name him Rasputin. We laugh, though it doesn't have the effect I want. To render him harmless.

I measure the time differently, with all of my body. But I refuse to simply wait for a man. If nothing else, it destroys all notions of the present. And still I can't help imagining him. Getting up. Moving toward his easel. Mixing paint. Layering paint. And going out to the cafés where women smile and come to his table and he talks and moves as though I do not exist. I think, How ridiculous. Somewhere he sits in a café and I find this an assault. Although sometimes I feel I'm the luckier one. To have this obsession. To be so alive from it. Yet when I conjure up his face, the tendons in his wrists, the way he walks, I am aware that there is little difference between this and a hallucination.

I continue to make regular visits to the zoo at the Jardin des Plantes, with and without Tacita. As a result, all the pages in the notebook of animal sounds have completely filled and I've begun a new one. I have no idea what I will do with it, but I feel excited by simply seeing the tilted violet script sitting on pale blue lines. *Vibration of bones. Sounds not made louder by adding but by taking away. Small kingdoms of concrete music but with geometry, interstitial, ringing, humming, speaking fragments, unforeseen.* I have befriended the mid-sized mammals guard with the lopsided grin who at the beginning would make me produce my acceptance letter from the academy each time to qualify for the less expensive ticket. There is a spotted hyena there that I have been thinking about. The larger animals often seem sad and filthy, and I find it hard to connect to the fish, but when I saw the hyena, something was set in motion.

At the Sainte-Geneviève Library I consult various texts, learning that spotted hyenas live in large matriarchal clans and have a startling social intelligence. Though they are capable hunters that kill most of their food, it is also true that they will eat garbage, which I find a virtue, not a character flaw. I notice that when she is fed she makes an almost giggling grunting sound of laughter that exposes her jagged, yellow-brown teeth, so dirty and crooked they feel like something private. And then I discover her small golden eyes, ringed with black halos, and her sharp pointed face. Every few minutes she pricks up stiffly and looks around.

Medieval bestiary says that hyenas are immortal. That they are highly sexualized and can change their gender. She looks at me with those yellow truthful eyes and I feel helpless merely being a witness, while her nobility remains intact. I am slightly afraid of her. There is a stone in the hyena's eye, the old scholars say, that can, when placed under a person's tongue, predict the future. I like to think I am not projecting any of my uneasiness— about her capture, her environs, her general station—onto her consciousness. The gold eyes continue to stare back. And in truth, she appears a bit despondent, spending altogether too much time lying on the floor of her cage.

What do you want, Ivory? Tacita asks.

What do you mean? I say, leaning in. You mean from Lev? From life?

Yes.

Yes what?

From life.

I don't know, Tas. I feel like one of those people of old who are told to enter the sacred groves or the remote areas within an Egyptian pyramid. You know, the ones who must pass the harrowing tests of fire, air, water, and earth in order to learn the universal secrets.

Which are?

If I knew I wouldn't be undergoing the tests, I say. But even with Tacita I hold back. My mind always reaching forward, thinking of how little security there is from the past. And now even less from the present. I was sent to convent school when I was little, no more than ten. I never dreamed that small acts of rebellion would lead to exile. Once Mother had her mind made up, there was nothing to say. She was appalled at my behaviour. I was to be hidden, locked in the attic like Rochester's lunatic wife in *Jane Eyre*. When I left, Arthur handed me his copy of *Greek Myths*, which I knew was his favourite book, and my eyes filled with tears. We had read countless myths and fairy tales and stories rich with escape and adventure, but in this one, there was only me. When I read on the train about Persephone being dragged to the underworld by Hades, over and over again my stomach churned as I looked out at the colourless sky, the trees blurring farther away.

Days pass. Tacita has an idea. Do you promise to say yes even though you don't know what it is?

What choice do you give me?

A few days later we walk down a stone lane, arms entwined.

It is dark. I don't know why but I am afraid. I can feel it in the stiffness of my spine. My quick steps.

Tacita tells me that the woman is the eldest of seven sisters. She bought this apartment from a famous theatre actress, only when they signed the papers, she met the actress and was disappointed with her appearance. She had an uneven gait. Her husband was distant. There was a big white baby with navy blue eyes on her lap. There was an issue with the door, and its not closing shut. She had the feeling of history repeating itself. She moved into the apartment anyway. She found out that the owner had five wives. All of them, except the last, the actress, had died in childbirth. There was something strange about the children. This woman has always known her predisposition. She does readings with big candles. Her first reading, Tacita says, was of her own death. She stops to look at me. You know, we don't see death the way people in other centuries saw it.

Which is how?

All the time.

I haven't heard what Tacita says. I realize I am shaking. I don't tell Tacita. Instead I ask if she is one of those women dressed in black. Lips and fingernails painted blood-red. Fantastical name.

Her name is Dot.

Dot?

I think she's English.

That is a name devoid of all magic.

That might be the point.

Tacita has told me about the time her mother took her to a village reader when she was young. The woman had an almost priestly energy. Flowers mysteriously fell from the ceiling. Tacita was told she would die young, in her childbearing years.

From blood. I've asked her if this is why she has vowed to never have children, but she says no. It was her mother's death that made that choice. Still, she is attracted to ritual, the idea of constructing a religious system of her own. The mystical life.

Aren't you afraid that what she said might be true?

I think what is meant to happen works itself out many times, in many guises.

There is some mystery there that I honour. I think some people really do have a gift of seeing. And if they truly do, then most likely whatever they do will be transformative. But Tacita, you know that you already do what they do. The contemplation of the surfaces of things that stimulate visions.

Dot's apartment is through a hidden courtyard off a dead-end street. An interesting choice for a channeller, Tacita says. We climb the spiral stairs and slip past a thick door to a wide and dark apartment on the third storey. The apartment is depressing. Dark and ugly and very cold. The front windows have been blacked out by swaths of black velvet. There are sheets piled in a glass cabinet so white against the dimness they hurt the eyes. There is a silver tea service, of the kind Mother had, displayed on a burnished wood credenza. Candles burn on a large oval table covered with a red-embroidered cloth from another country. Astral bells. It seems a cliché and completely singular at once.

Please. Sit down, Mme. Szalasi. Mlle. Frame. Her voice is flat and lifeless, like an artificial lake. The apartment has a strong, nauseating perfume, one that is clearly concealing something else.

She speaks, unnaturally, with her back to us.

I look for something barefaced and fraudulent. But there is nothing overtly damning. A thin uncertain noise hums in the room. There is an obvious construction of dramatic elements I refuse to be unnerved by. But still I feel as though I'm being dragged through deep reeds toward a river. I remind myself that it is of my own invention. Captive to a mood, a state of mind that she has worked at manufacturing.

I have taken part in the group's séances. But they separate themselves from this experience. The air prickles and is electric, but everything feels slightly funny. The holding of hands, flickering night-moth eyes, the droning speak. I am always on the verge of laughing. I stop myself because I understand what they're trying to do. To gain direct access to the unconscious. There is always a presence of animals. I like how they emerge, marvellous and sacred, conveying messages through their appearance in dreams and trance.

It is in this moment that I realize that I don't believe our future is meant to be known.

The air is sliced in two by an unfamiliar voice.

Dot changes her accent, her entire voice, altering its pitch completely. It is thick and lilting and full of heavy consonants. Russian. The hair pricks up on the back of my neck. I stand still. She recites in the low hushed tones reserved for children after dark.

> *Baby baby rock a bye*
> *On the edge you mustn't lie*
> *Or the little grey wolf will come*
> *And will nip you on the tum*
> *And will nip you on the tum*
> *Tug you off into the wood*
> *Underneath the willow root*

I feel a wet, cool line drip down my stomach. When we go around the table, I see her face. She stares at me in a way that is terrifying, as though I am being dragged by my hair. She has one walleye and one piercer. No categorical questions, inquiries into age, or preferred colour or animal. I suddenly see that her skirts are hitched up and she sits with her knees apart, feet on the seat of her chair, like a bird. Her hand, resting on the table, is upward. The thumb and index finger touching, forming an O. *They will take it*, she says, in a thin whisper voice. *They will steal*. A sickening feeling. A sharp pain and waves of flushing heat and nausea. I turn and run, Tacita behind me. We pass by the blind in the window, cracked in a half smile. I hear, Pretty thing, the way she runs.

Our shoes scattering across the floor with a graceful urgency. I run so fast that I fall on the uneven stones down the lane outside and skin my palms. Tacita stops and takes my hands in hers.

What is it, I? What did you see?

My breath is hard to find. You didn't see it?

I ran because you did.

An amethyst.

There was an amethyst?

Yes.

What do they symbolize again? I think amethysts—

No, Tacita.

Ivory, what?

That woman had an amethyst the size of a human heart between her legs.

Tacita takes out cigarettes, but her hands shake too much to light one. She fumbles the pack, avoiding my eyes.

I am filled with an unnameable fear. *Take what? Steal what?* Whatever she was trying to say, Tas, something bad is going to happen. I know it. Did you hear how she changed her voice? And that stone. With her one terrifying eye she looked me goddamn straight in the face.

We take a tacit vow of silence around the channeller. I recognize the fear in Tacita's eyes. It is the same as my own. It is the first time I realize that Tacita and I have the same eyes.

Reindeer

Rangifer tarandus. Reindeer husbandry;
day by day, lichen. Sense of coherence of
reindeer herders and other Samis in comparison
to other Swedish citizens. International Journal
of Circumpolar Health, Vol. 72.

THE SKY IS EDGING TO BLUE. Skeet stands at the kitchen sink, high-pitched clinking and the low rumble of submerged objects. He relieves me from the mundane routine, these ritualistic gestures that over time take on small ceremony. He finishes the dishes and wipes his hands on his pants. In the Yukon he had said that he was amazed at how I always knew which direction to walk in without frightening the animals. He wanted to know where I learned it. Lapland, I tell him. Reindeer there have been hunted for forty thousand years. They know a few things about avoiding humans, sensitive to the very smell of us. You get to know wind, and approach, and how to hide your humanness.

It was a disaster that trip, I told him, at a time when I could scarcely afford disaster. I didn't know the protocol, and had failed to apply for a permit to research in the field there. When I returned, the conservatory was furious. It's the kind of misstep that can end funding. I had flown over Moscow, over St. Petersburg, its dark rivers, and over thick leafless forests, tangled black. It is where I met Ondine. At the only tavern in a small town in Lapland.

She is with radical cartographers. After a few weeks fog makes aviation difficult, and, grounded, they install themselves at the tavern, run by a Sami ex–reindeer herder, a few short hours from the Arctic Circle. The bar accepts gold dust as payment for liquor and has thickly lacquered knotty pine everywhere, the kind with black routed edges. Cups go cold, ashtrays overflow, liquor is consumed. We don't talk about the weather.

Do you know that the Finns have their own unit of measure? Ondine says. *Poronkusema.* It literally translates as reindeer's piss. She looks up from the map. It measures about seven and a half kilometres. Apparently how long it takes a reindeer to travel before it has to relieve itself.

It's true, I say, unlacing my boots and rubbing my toes to get warmth back. They have small bladders. Comparatively.

Are you a reindeer expert? she says, a smile breaking across her face.

God no. I began with birds and then started researching based on the communication, not the animal. I had an echolocation phase for a while in the seventies, marine animals, which then led to bats. I focus mainly on birds now.

There's not a lot of birds around here, she says.

I've been recording reindeer near the easternmost part of the park. At the sound lab, we've created baseline data so that changes to sites can be compared. Forests can look unchanged, but recordings of soundscapes, over time, can reveal things that aren't obvious to the eye. I'll take the recordings back to the lab when I'm done.

Where is the lab?

Oslo, I say. I had to do a lot to convince the university of my animal language project. I published papers, passed stringent peer review, made the rounds of scholarly conferences. Eventually I built a lab out of a white square they gave me, with two small windows that face Kuba, a greenspace with tall maples. I had to acquire all the instrumentation, rewire the voltage to accommodate the sound equipment. Half the time I forgot to eat, and ended up resorting to those revolting nutritional shakes, the kind they give convalescents. All the reels of analogue tapes and books of discs are being catalogued digitally. The sound data and the cymatics images are being translated into computer-generated spectrograms. The music of insects, vibrations of bones, everything from hummingbirds to whales, I tell her. Every single object in the lab has a purpose. There is not a lot of space, but it doesn't really matter. It is a self-contained world, possibly the closest thing to a home I've ever known. Ondine nods. It still amazes me how surprising sound is. You know if you slow down a hummingbird chirp, it sounds like you're listening to a dinosaur.

So, what will you do with the recordings, this dictionary, when you are done with it?

There is a movement in Japan, I tell her, where people nominate the most beautiful soundscapes. Thousands and thousands of people responded. The way the waves hit a particular shell from a sea creature on a particular beach, they said. The queenly creak from roots to sky that a particular forest of pinewood makes swaying in the wind, they said. And so the association went to listen to each sound, and if they agreed, it would become one of the most beautiful soundscapes in Japan. These places are now protected. They are like heritage sites. If you wanted to build a factory next to one, you would probably have a hard time. They are protecting the environment by using sound democratically. It's exactly what I want the dictionary to do for animals.

She nods, her eyes strikingly bright.

What about you? Where did you last fly?

Chernobyl. When people moved out the animals moved in, she says. She was there to chart the zone that has become an accidental wilderness. The levels of radiation meant that first there were no humans. Fifty thousand people had fifteen minutes to leave. But birds, and wild boar, elk, deer, bison, lynx, and wolves all came back. They thrive in a deadly forest where the reactor still smoulders. Now there is a ring of silent fire that encircles the pine woods, the abandoned apartment buildings. Some people still live there. They choose the post-nuclear world, the winding forests and dark bogs. They say they are not afraid of dying early.

What *are* they afraid of?

Modern life, she says.

Ondine is like no other pilot I have flown with. They are always men. Either too quiet or not quiet enough. She calls everyone she flies with *pal*. She picked it up when she flew in Texas. She says that around the pilots, the less female the better. Mostly, she says, they are pretty macho. Not one of them would look me in the eye like I belonged there. She takes a sip. My co-pilot wore a cowboy shirt. A leather belt with a big silver buckle that had an oversized star in the middle like a bull's eye. Stiff, dark jeans with a perfect white seam down the centre of each leg, where no doubt his wife had ironed them into existence.

The seams were distracting. I remember thinking, How do you get laid in those jeans?

People get laid in jeans? I think but don't say.

Anyway, she goes on, it turned out his wife was cheating on him. When she left him, she demanded half of everything he owned. He was so pissed I was scared to fly with him. And then one day he flew *under* a bridge in a fully populated town. He lost everything. His job, his licence, every single penny. And he couldn't have been happier. That was his plan. To give her half of nothing.

Ondine is tall and lanky, with wide-apart eyes and hair now flecked with white that she wears up, keeping it back with a clip near her temple. She has one grown son, Lucien. When she is flying, even when he was small, she says she is so engrossed in what she is doing she forgets she is a mother.

Flying was always at the centre of my dreams, she says. It didn't come to me naturally, but once I dreamed it, I knew it. I went to the hangar the next day and could suddenly fly. My instructor just looked at me stunned.

Did anyone try talking you out of pursuing such a dangerous profession?

Like who?

I don't know—parents?

I never knew my parents, she says. I was left at a convent in Paris, raised by nuns.

I know about the nuns, I tell her.

When I turned eighteen, they pushed open the doors and directed me to the street. Your time here is up, they said. *Bon courage*. Whatever you do, do not become a prostitute. I worked a bunch of destroyingly boring jobs until one day I went up in a plane. I loved the sense of freedom. I find it impossible to tolerate anything slow. To be passive. So I spent every single franc I'd ever earned, liberating them from my pocket, large as folded flags, into the air. She drains her glass.

We drink several more glasses of whisky. Ondine finally says, All my hours logged, all your animal languages. Are we just like everyone else, she asks, obsessed with collecting things?

What does everyone collect? I ask, genuinely interested.

I don't know, she shrugs. Friends, money, objects. I think it comes from a fear of dying. As though things will somehow hold you here.

Well what does have permanence?

Good question, she says, fishing in her bag and pulling out reading glasses. Apparently not my eyesight. God, I despise getting old.

Which part?

All of it. Feeling like I'm running out of time and there is something I have yet to do.

What would you want to do?

I don't know. That's the problem, she says. And then you lose your looks. All these seams on my face. She takes another sip. Your powers flag.

It's true, I think. When you are old you are transparent. Is it possible to hide and yet be annoyed when no one notices you? I was almost hit by a car crossing the road to this tavern and I thought, I don't want to die here, run over like a dog. Beauty is wasted on the young. Like leaves in autumn at their most brilliant, when the tree doesn't need them. But it's just some inches of skin, I say, realizing how truly indifferent I am to minor vanities. All women eventually become invisible in the same way. For someone like her, there is more to lose. Where does the thing that is left over after the attractiveness has served its purpose go? But what I say to her is, Aren't you bothered more by not being called upon to give your opinion? Or, by eventually not being here at all? Besides, I tell her truthfully, you are still beautiful.

She laughs. When something is still something, it's not.

Ondine produces a small glass jar of lip balm. She unscrews the lid and holds it in front of me. I shake my head just as the lid falls from her fingers and rolls on its edge along the wooden planked floor. It wobbles loudly and trundles into a large pair of brown leather boots.

I feel dazed by the alcohol. I realize that when I was describing the dictionary to Ondine, for a moment, I felt a twist of regret that it began as something else, and that I had to alter it to see it through. That I let go of art because it meant Tacita. It meant Lev. With painting, I felt a sense of completion, laying down brushes, standing back to look at a canvas. I couldn't really explain it to her, but the project doesn't just involve collecting data. It involves releasing messages stored in the voices of animals that represent the memories of all we have lost. *Edison believed that after we die, memories disperse or swarm like bees and enter other human skulls.*

Ondine looks at me intently. You know what I think? she says, her expression suddenly becoming serious. I think that we are all fallen creatures who once knew how to fly.

I excuse myself and in the lavatory splash cold water on my face though the tiny room itself is sealed off and startlingly arctic. The loo paper has a ghastly scent and is dyed pink with perforated rose patterns, discarded in a pileup of squares like deleaved cabbage in the white plastic pail beside the toilet. It smells of floor cleaner and cold. I have spent so much time alone. Though it strikes me how hard it is to really be alone. It is one thing humanity has never really valued. I remain still in front of the mirror. *Temps morts*, as the French critics say of the Italian filmmakers when they keep the camera running after the acting has finished to record the moments of error. The back of a head, an empty room that waits for an actor to drift back in. They see what the error is. The error is life. My own eyes meet my own eyes. I've been looking at Ondine's bright eyes for so long I am almost surprised by mine. They are shining black. They tell the deep time of things. I am suddenly reminded of Tacita. How much living she has missed. Being in Ondine's company makes me think of her. Her courage, her heart, her brain. I feel the sharp agony of her absence. Why did you have to go? I think. You have been gone so long. Come back. I can't remember the last time I've spoken with anyone, really spoken to them. And suddenly I think I might be crying a little.

When I return to the shiny wood banquette, the suffocating heat in the bar hits like a change of season, making the time lapse feel pronounced. There is a sticky smell of liquor and stale cigarettes. While sitting in one spot you can become deeply intoxicated without knowing it. There is nothing to measure your sobriety against. How long was I in the bathroom? Ondine has gone. She leaves a note written on the white scallop-edged paper placemat, weighted by a triangular glass ashtray. The leather boots say the weather is clearing tomorrow. She has gone to sober up and suggests I do the same. I wonder for a moment if this is a euphemism for a sexual encounter. I know there used to be talk at the university. Has she slept with a researcher in the field? Is she a sapphist? I speak of it to no one, of course, how lovers leave me empty. Why talk and eat and make up other arrangements with other people? Why look at each other from across a table to see that you know nothing of each other? We all just tell each other stories about our lives, decorating them with the most compelling things. For me, everything is too difficult to explain. I don't want to tell my story, I want to listen. When I am alone, I work with astonishing energy. As soon as I am at a social gathering with others, I become sluggish, I fall into lethargy. I am lucky. Happy to find that the work is the best expression of who I am. My eyes slide to the left where the bartender is quarrelling good-naturedly with three men on barstools, wolfing down plates of god knows what. The men are small and pale and presumably half my age. They are a bearded, cheerful people, though addicted to spirits.

We will meet at dawn, her note says.

But we don't. A blast rips through my dream. I find myself thrown from the bed. Snow dusts up the night sky. There has been an explosion. The nickel plant glows orange, hotter than lava. The conservationists and cartographers are rounded up and questioned by the authorities and made to show their papers. Everything that was once in order, now is not. This curious system of exchange that occurs when authority is threatened is far too familiar to me. It has the internal logic of a nightmare.

I am held in a small, brutally lit, thin-walled room, the low buzz of the fluorescent tubes above my head. One man asks me to detail my "activities," which would be frightening if the other man hadn't seemed so utterly bored as to be cleaning the dirt under his fingernail with his thumbnail. My head pounds, eyes burning. It is hot and dry in this dingy little room. My activities. They largely consist of lying silently on my stomach, cold on the dry snow in a husked silence. Time tripwired. They tell me I am here illegally. They have no record of a permit; I cannot take this data out of their country. I close my eyes. I forgot about the permit. I've been given money to look for signs of the effects of industrial activity on the reindeer and their habitat.

Land use changes are the greatest threat to wild reindeer. There is so little funding for this study that I considered sleeping in the truck, which I have done before. Avoiding losing daylight hours setting up a tent. But here it is far too cold.

They empty out my bag, full of cassettes. Their fingers pull at the reels of shiny brown magnetic ribbon that form tangled heaps on the table. Later Ondine will laugh and say, Well that was a bust. The university will not find it funny. But right now I think of staying up all night, analyzing all the sounds because I need to know what they mean by morning. Weeks of research. I feel like crying. But I don't. It is exactly what they might expect a woman biologist to do.

In the field there is so much white my eyes see things that are not here. The same way someone shipwrecked who stares at the sea long enough will start to see a sail rise above the horizon. The cold is bitter but preferable, they tell me, to the swarms of mosquitoes so thick in the summer that they duct-tape the cracks of the windows. So thick that you swallow insects when you talk.

The scrub fir forests are misshapen from weather, flecked with lichen. I have started to anticipate where the reindeer will be. They are quiet animals but the herds become vocal when there are new calves. The females grunt softly while the males sometimes roar loudly or emit a rasping, guttural noise. I am deposited here each day via a wooden sledge hitched to a herder's snowmobile. The reindeer herder wears fur boots that stick out like paws from underneath his Gore-Tex pants. Reindeer hair is a good insulator, he says, it being hollow.

I am vague about what I'm doing and he doesn't ask. His utter lack of curiosity verges on eccentric.

Reindeer have two extra bones in their feet that click so that they can hear one another in the dark.

The only reason the reindeer herder takes me is that he needs money. He has had some animal rights people campaign against deer hunting. He sizes me up, alone with my recording equipment and fieldbooks, and determines that I am not here to distribute virtue. That I will leave the landscape, the creatures, inviolate. This is when the objectives of those who save and those who kill overlap.

On the long ride in he tells me about how when he slaughters deer he uses every part. He sells the meat. He uses the skin for clothing and blankets. The heads become dog food. The hooves, boots. The antlers, handicrafts. The antlers are also ground into a powder and sold to the Japanese—a cure for sexual weakness.

It makes me think of Duchamp. He once walked into Café de Flore, and Tacita leaned in. Two words, she whispered.

Porcelain urinal? I ventured.

No, she laughed. Notorious impotence.

That is not what I expected you to say, I whispered back.

She told me that he had married a lascivious peasant girl from Normandy, who, as it turned out, had little interest in his cleverness. When he started to launch into one of his ideas, she would say, Look, we're here to fuck. Stop telling stories and get on with it. This did not go over well with Marcel. It made him incapable of sleeping with her, so she left him. He was crushed. People said he was a destroyed man after that, in a sense.

The truth is, the reindeer herder yells over the sound of the engine, it does nothing, but they give me a good price.

The herder unhitches the sledge. The trees are being cut, he says. It is so far north it takes three hundred years for them to grow again. He pulls a piece of lichen off a tree and holds it out to me as if to accentuate his point. If they cut down the trees, the reindeer can't eat. It means more hay, which costs too much money.

The hay?

The gas for the snowmobile.

I feel alive in the cold. Sharp. Starved for sound. All my training funnels into this skill, remaining calm and quiet. I wait. It is so still, I can't tell which way the wind is. I watch my breath, visible in the cold. Not sure if they might be picking up my scent. Then I see them. After all this time, random flashes of pale fur across the white, like a hallucination. They come toward me, loping and arcing. Dancing. Hooves barely touching snow. They come close to where I am lying. Close enough for me to see the soft underfur, to feel their shudders, ear twitches, everything in them that is wild. I am cold. My heart hammering. I can see their eyes, two shiny black pearls, moist noses. I can hear their nostrils take in air. I feel the electric intensity that trembles from them, what they know. That there is no order in the world, nothing at all except for this very moment, sure as death. We are the only creature who has the knowledge of our own mortality outside of imminent danger, and yet they know more. They don't have reason. They don't do anything. They just are. What is my snowblindness is their articulated forests of ultraviolet light. And then something extraordinary happens. They stop. The whole herd, over fifty animals, have been doing myriad different things, long legs loping and pawing, bodies at every direction. In a flicker they all stand completely still. Every single one of them freezes. It looks like a photograph. I hear the trees creak and the snow skimmed off by a faint, low wind. It lasts at least a minute, which in close proximity to a herd of wild animals feels like a very long time. When they are still, I see only their ears lift. They are listening. They are concerned with what is happening over the horizon. After a long while come the clicks. They are clean and sharp, like a glass slide placed on a microscope. In the dark blue light, it startles. Eyes closed, it is the guttural voice of a farm animal, but here, it sounds like comfort to sorrow.

They twitch and paw and push their noses in the snow. And then they turn quietly and run, legs angled like lightning bolts, vanishing as swiftly as they came. I look around. There are vast plains of nothingness. Being in a northern place so cold and white, so absent of detail, can cancel you out. You have to keep your focus. There is no distinction between earth and sky, this repetition, this feeling of waiting for the inspiration, as in painting. It makes you see everything, hear everything in all this white. You notice that there is still black in your heart.

Swan

Long neck with dead space. Can hiss like a snake,
speaking fragments, unforeseen.

WALKING OUT INTO THE FILTHY daylight knocks me awake. Day is harder than night. My eye sockets burning. They sharpen when out in the cool air. I should feel brazen with matted hair in the morning and the same clothes from the black moonless night. I see shoals of knee-socked shins of schoolgirls in the cold streets, kilts with knife-sharp pleats. Lev has been drawing all night and my head pounds, my shoulders ache from sleeplessness. My body still in disbelief, replaying itself like the way you are tricked to feel waves after you've reached solid ground. A bruise near my collarbone contains the violence of nights before. Blackvioletblueyellow. Each day I carry it, the only thing that links him and these acts to the days between. I lose track of street names, how long I have been walking, which way the light is coming from. Has winter yet passed? I think suddenly in a panic. A striped awning clicks forward. The *boulanger* can tell. I do not see the scorn on the faces of the women gathered in front of shops. Women who are eager to pass judgment on the authenticity of a woman's honour. Though they misinterpret where exactly this is located. Still, in France, however far from admirable infidelity is, if conducted properly it is as acceptable as a standard piece of furniture.

I try to send my mind somewhere else. The things to hold on to. I have been meaning to visit the Muséum National d'Histoire Naturelle. I have been wondering about the hyena. I haven't gone to her in a few days and worry that I've mythologized her too quickly. Tacita is set to paint her portrait. There has been some shuffling of animals at the menagerie and I am convinced that the monkeys are no longer there. I even inquired directly of the mid-sized mammals guard, but if he knows anything he's not saying.

My pace quickens and I am soon in the familiar courtyard. I've come straight to the academy, without washing or changing my clothes. Without eating. I find the capped cardboard tube stowed in my desk in the studio. Inside my drawings are furled leaves that I will remove and flatten to show M. Marant, though this does not happen. There is no doubt about the intelligence he possesses but there is something that feels anti-democratic about it. He has a reverence for callow religious painters and for coldly impassioned painters with immense technical skill. He is not convinced by my paintings nor by those of the artists in the group, but he accepts my meticulousness as a kind of mutual consent. I can tell that he has found my deportment at odds with the increasing horror and bestial fictions of my work.

The last painting I submitted was not received well. I had the usual animals, birds, horses, but the main subject was a ritualistic meal. A banquet of cannibals that Tacita thought to be a blasphemous take on the Eucharist. There is a group of gluttonous grotesque women, with heads that she described as phallic though I had thought of them as equine. They sit at a table, abundant with extravagant dishes. It is all writhing and moving and somewhat alive. There is a woman alone, with a neutral expression on her face. She is off in the corner of the painting, and appears to be unaware that her fork has dug into a plump, live baby. It was part of a series of banquets I had begun sketches for. The last being one that depicts forest animals who turn against the humans they encounter hunting boar—the prey eat the predators.

The instructor was silent. All he said was, The assignment was for a still-life rendering.

But doesn't a banquet constitute a still life?

I'm not certain one could call something this—he pauses— *perverse* a still life.

I look at M. Marant and tell him that I am withdrawing from the academy.

When he registers my determination, we walk through the high halls to a small office, his heavy oak desk under a pile of papers with tidy paragraphs and aligned paperclips. After some rustling, he produces a document that I sign with the slim pen he holds out for me.

Thank you, I say.

I am swaying back and forth from lack of food.

Remember the rigour with which you have learned to draw, Mlle. Frame, and keep it with you. An artist must have dedication, ideas, and technical ability. But ultimately, they must be better than the sum of these parts.

The absoluteness with which the instructors speak about painting feels like learning without belief. It seems they explain everything without explaining anything. Being preoccupied with the sound notebook, and contemplating how to make this into something, I showed it to one of my instructors tentatively, after my life drawing class. The students filed out. The air was dense with cigarette smoke. But what is this? he said. His broad hands leafing through my writing dismissively. I felt my neck grow hot. He shut the notebook. Spend your time working on paintings, he said with the long dramatic pause of a man who is used to being listened to, or you'll not improve.

M. Marant finds a key threaded with a white ribbon and fits it into the lock on a wooden filing cabinet. His soft small hands flit through the files and for a moment I think of the Larva and that she may stand to inherit these soft hands. But then I realize that for a girl, this is desirable. He touches his necktie as it swings forward while he bends over the files. He produces my tuition deposit, which oddly bears my father's signature, and looking over his eyeglasses, hands it to me. I will be able to live on this money for months.

Bon courage, Mlle. Frame, he says, with no trace of irony. He extends his hand and I shake it. It is limp and warm. It is the first time I have chosen to leave a school without the involvement of my parents. I am sure of my decision.

Je vous remercie. He has allowed me the dignity of uncontested escape. How lightened. How free. With every step away from the academy.

Tacita and I sip kir royale. She is supportive of my decision. The unlikelier of the two of us, she will remain at the academy.

I like the rows of seats, the wooden lecterns, the professors who have studied every corner of an Ingres, Tacita says. I prefer practising my art within a structure. I've had so little of it. It seems something to push off from. But you, I, you come from that controlled world. You are right to rebel. Besides, no one can teach you to be an artist.

The same applies to you.

But I didn't come to the academy out of escape. It was pure practical desire. I never really learned how to draw. What I want is technique, not ideas. We all have those.

Our tangents have crossed and are headed in opposing directions. I have begun to consider alternative semi-abstractions that may not involve putting pen to paper at all. Tacita is increasingly interested in the mystical immanence in portraits, in landscapes, that she was once dismissive of.

But, I, in the end it doesn't matter. It isn't the ways in which these things meet the eye, but the ways they take form in the mind that count.

The door opens like a blade.

A tall, fine-boned woman who formerly danced with the Ballet Russes brushes past us. A woman whom I have been told Lev has been with. A welter of jealousy. A slow flush crawls up my neck, my face. She has an exacting part down the centre of her head. A swan neck. She sees herself in the mirror above the bar. Glued to her own reflection, as swans are. She wears her long pale hair drawn into a low bun that means her ears are covered. Sharp Slavic cheekbones, glacial eyes. A sensual mouth, long dancer thighs. A calm but unmistakably predatory way of turning her head.

Despite my own will, I am decentred and seeing how Lev would see her. Does she know who I am? Does she call me l'Anglaise and make jokes with the other dancers? Do they speak Russian and laugh at our alphabet with all its childish roundness? The consonants of tin? Does she offer her body to Lev the way she does with her art? I envy their shared native language, which I imagine to be far more nuanced than English, where everything has to be pinned down. Because to feel connected with someone is to have the kind of dialogue where you don't have to think, however imperfect. And in this they conspire together.

Ivory, don't, Tacita says, in characteristic telepathy. She's a fish. Remember that jealousy is more a matter of self-love than love.

What's wrong with self-love? I say. Besides, who is speaking about love?

Oh I forgot. Your northernness comes out when you're mad.

I'm not mad. I'm, for the first time, scared. I've given up the academy, the one steady thing, and my life now hangs like a question mark. And with Lev, I have rendered myself helpless by succumbing to something that is outside of me. Though I say nothing.

We will finish this champagne and then drown ourselves in red, Tacita says. We will join everyone at Le Dôme later.

The only thing I can think of is the dancer. Her small high head and drawn-out neck make her seem ethereal, longer-limbed, taller than she really is. Do our eyes meet? They are beautiful, vacant eyes, though she is not unintelligent. She walks straight up to me and says my name the way Lev does, her r's deep and palatialized.

She looks at Tacita and then to me. The silent language of the eyes. I think she is not speaking because she is preparing what to say, but she is merely taking time to see who I am. I can see from her eyes that for her, everything is absolute. She has the look of someone who is bad at life, though somehow without losing her advantage. She wears a long scarf wound tightly around her neck and has filigreed earrings that swing and flash when they catch the light. The immense bag on her shoulder is cream leather like the underbelly of a snake. Its size makes her seem even narrower, as though she might have one less rib. What does she carry? I imagine it to be filled with all her portable possessions that she brings with her, never trusting them to anyone. When she speaks I cannot believe this is what she intended to say, but there is no mistaking it.

You should not open your legs for him, he is not for a little girl like you. In his head, there is always something more beautiful. Go home, English, if you know what's good for you.

My hand burns. I am shocked by her vulgar words, her brazenness. I grew up with emotions kept in line by the notion of proper appearances, even in the absence of witnesses.

I rage inwardly for my lack of control. But I am raw, a vulnerable version of myself. I feel bonier and stiffer in her presence. She has a tensile strength enough to break me in two, but I can see that she is frailer than I am, in a different way. I observe that jealousy spoils her face.

She touches her hand to her cheek and then laughs and says what someone says later means virgin bride in Russian. It is a ridiculous laugh, but one with warning. She turns away.

It is then that it occurs to me that this woman could actually be Lev's wife.

Well, she knows that Lev has chosen you, Tacita attempts to say jokingly, so naturally she wants to kill you.

Neither of us laughs.

She is not a happy person, Tacita says, lowering her voice. People who are happy are harmless.

Dolphin

Ceta cea. 21" length of symphysis . . .
5'3" of ramus . . . 16'6" end of muzzle to
palatal notch . . . 13'10" to preorbital notch . . .
85 teeth incurved, fang compressed . . .
Habitat, unknown. Creates rings out of blow hole
or creates water vortex ring and blows air in.

AFTER SWITCHING OFF CHOPIN, I take my woollen shawl and wrap it around my shoulders. Two jumpers layered over pyjamas. I slide my feet into my sandals, my ungainly limbs labouring up the courtyard gravel to the car parked on higher ground by the wild blackberries shot through the tall grasses. My bones feel too large, too heavy for my body, though when I catch a reflection of myself I am so slight I am barely here. After Paris, I refused to look at myself in a mirror. For years, only catching flickers in windows, the glint of a knife, fingermarked lenses. Afraid to look and find that grief had altered my face.

There is the absence of sound and visible objects in these tracts of land. All the evenings, across these violet-lapped fields from setting suns, I watch from the front door. Cool to the heat of them, emotions dulled by the simple act of time passing. The darkness unrolls, the white-tufted moths fluttering in confined circles around the light. So much of making something out of life comes from the physical world, from really looking at everything. The smell after rain, trees illuminated in a storm, the sound of a screen door, the first star, all the things that compose your existence moment to moment. It forces you to live in the present, which is the only thing I've ever known to stop the sinking fear of death.

The American found me this car. I'm not sure the era. From some friend of hers who summered here from California. This is his dead wife's car. I wedge the cuttingboard behind the driver's seat and feel it jutting into the small of my back. Did his wife do this? I wonder. She was a young woman. It makes me feel ashamed at once, to still be here.

When I reach the village I realize that I don't remember the drive. I've unintentionally driven to Chinon, twenty minutes to the seven of Fontevraud. My mind elsewhere, and time moving still. The shops and flats are quiet, shuttered in. No sign of the tourists with their canvas hats, hauling around their ridiculous packs, and maps, and cameras, and plastic water bottles, as though they were going on safari and not to a French town with perfectly potable water.

I park along the river at the foot of a plane tree and slowly walk to the river's edge to the payphone, with its clouded plastic scratched with graffiti, and begin pressing the small grubby metal squares. My hand judders. A calling card, strings of passwords. I let it ring. Six, seven, eight. I am rehearsing what to say. Then nothing. No one answers. There is an answering machine detailing various extensions, gallery hours.

I find a park bench illuminated and slowly walk there. My legs ache. I conduct what I might say on the telephone, the stillness creeping. Though the village is quiet, there is the odd low rumble of a truck, a distant voice. I sit in silence for long enough that I drift off. I wake to a young woman in a white nightgown and complicated sandals, with straps around the ankle like a slave girl's. Mostly they seem to wear cheap, ill-fitting garments with exposed midsections. For all its practical improvements, feminism has not yet freed women from a sense that their value resides in how they are seen by men. The woman has a tattoo above her ankle that I can't make out, most likely something banal. It used to be just sailors and criminals. Not much interests me about fashion. During the war it froze for six years. Now there is clothing manufactured to look like what was once worn by the bone-poor, and somewhere somebody profits from this. I picture how many times I mended my one pair of stockings in Paris. How unshined shoes were tantamount to the end of civilization. The modern expression of rebellion seems sadly commodified. When out with the artists, I always felt a nervous sort of energy. As though anything could happen. Because the revolt came from within, and how can anyone ever predict what might come from the mind? Change life, Rimbaud said. There were naked bodies, objects on fire, magnetic fields, clouds eaten by the moon.

The young woman and I are like churchgoers, an extended polite silence between us. But soon her sobs punctuate the night air with a violence that almost gives me a coronary.

Mademoiselle? Qu'est-ce qu'il y a?

She turns her pale oval face and looks at me suspiciously with blue-socketed eyes, as though she has just now been alerted to the fact that she is not alone. She must think me mad, this old woman in striped pyjamas piled with sweaters on the other end of the bench in the middle of the night.

She tells me that she can't sleep. That she's so exhausted she cannot even sleep. A small baby. No husband. The baby sleeps twenty metres away but inside it is a dark and shrunken world, one she feels she'll never get out of. She needs air. She needs to feel part of something bigger than her apartment, with its hushed tones and sour-milk smell. She says no one ever told her about the loneliness. I am the first adult she has spoken with all day. The days are without end. Nights are the worst. They are as deep as black water. It is only me, up with the drug addicts, the mentally ill, and the old people— She stops, embarrassed.

Ça va, I say. It is the first time I've heard my own voice in days. Old people actually aren't usually up at this hour.

She lets out a small laugh. She wipes back the wetness with her hand. She says that when she pushed out the baby, a whole new magical life came with it. People stared, saying a baby this new still has angels around it. She felt enchanted, altered. Her own sister didn't even recognize her voice on the telephone. But then you don't sleep for months and you are stuck in this gruelling toil and everything slides to a brink. It makes this bunched, plain life it came crashing down into all the more desolate. If the baby is screaming and I am half-starved, do I still make a sandwich for myself while he cries? While he sleeps inside, is it illegal for me to be sitting here, on this bench? I feel unhinged, she says. Like I am capable of doing something crazy.

I think all women carry something of a rebellion inside them that often goes unexpressed. Because we think we are not in the race—or game, or whatever the sporting analogy is—we have a sense of anarchy that I think is an advantage. In times like these it threatens to erupt. It is not such a bad thing.

I can't shake the darkness that rips through me, she says. It's so strong I could harm myself, or the baby. She pauses. I've been thinking about death a lot lately, she says, blowing her nose.

Well all the thinking you do, I doubt you'll figure out much.

I'm so tired, she says. Sleep like a baby, she mimics. Why does no one talk about the fact that babies are insomniacs? I'm so exhausted but I'm just sitting around doing nothing. I sit inside all day. Laundry piles up, the refrigerator empties. Nothing is ever finished. I never realized how hard it is to do nothing. To do nothing and be okay with it. To not become impatient doing nothing. I can't rely on anything. Each day I think I learn something about him, about my situation, but then it changes. She slumps against the back of the bench and mutters what sounds like, He seems somewhere between human and animal, though more animal than human. And what does that make me? Someone told me to keep a journal because you forget everything. And you know that in ten weeks, I've only written one thing. One word. She laughs. Milk. I feel like a farm animal. Like the goats on my aunt's farm that I helped milk when I was little. We would get them on the milking stand with the lure of grain, then we would keep them in by their necks with a long piece of wood that had a hook and eye at the top. I always liked the sound that streams of milk made hitting the pail. It sounded so rustic, so comforting. Now I don't feel that way at all.

Mammals are so dependent on milk, I think but don't say. It's why we will never be as free as the birds. Because I have nothing subjective to contribute, I tell her about sleep. Dolphins don't sleep for a month after giving birth, I say. It's how their offspring avoid being prey.

C'est moi. Exactement, she laughs, wiping her eyes.

Well there are better stories.

How do you know that?

There just are.

No, I mean, how do you know about dolphins?

Oh. I study animals.

What do you study about them?

I work a few kilometres from Fontevraud in the white caves near the house there. I am transcribing animal languages that have been recorded.

I didn't know there was such a thing.

It's been over a hundred years. The first recordings were birds on an Edison phonograph. But those birds were captured. Which isn't the same.

Oh.

The first wild bird recordings in North America were made in 1929 on a movie soundtrack because no one had invented a tape recorder yet.

She looks at me with the look that people get when they are determining how old you really are, patronizingly, as if I am a small child. And what I want to say to her is, Don't do that.

Maybe you can tell me, she says. I think I saw a jackal by the river late at night.

Egyptians used to read the *Book of the Dead* on how to navigate the underworld. The god of the dead had a jackal's head. He determined who could enter by weighing the heart. If it was lighter than an ostrich feather, the soul would be allowed to ascend into heaven.

She shifts on the bench.

Jackals are opportunists. They often steal what others kill. I think what you might have seen was a wolf.

You know a lot about animals.

I've observed them my whole life. We are quiet for a while, both staring ahead.

Is the work lonely? she finally asks. I think of sitting for hours silently on the ground.

It's like being in love, I say, feeling oddly candid at this hour with this stranger. Your interest in everything else is lost.

I wouldn't know, she says, the baby's father left. We aren't—close.

I am relieved she doesn't use one of those tinselled words like soulmate. People should leave each other's souls alone. Untapped parts of a person used to be called charisma. Now they are cause for therapy. What's inside you is a precious, essential thing that must be left inviolate otherwise you risk ruining it. The radiance at the centre of your very own life. The thing that makes it worth living. Without it, no one is truly independent.

To be understood is the worst disaster, I finally say out loud.

What?

Valéry.

Who?

I tell her that I am writing a dictionary of animal languages, of species on the brink of extinction. By listening to wildlife, we gain understanding of animal communication, and the health of wildlife populations. I am looking at the patterns that have emerged from the sounds. They allow us to see what we normally could not. There are innumerable little extinctions occurring all the time. We are living in an age of slaughter. But modern society seems to operate with no sense of the past and even less regard for the future. I have no idea why extinction isn't more a source of horror, I say. I once ended a lecture this way, and surprisingly a student's hand shot up. And do you know what he said? He said, Stalin said one death is a tragedy, a million deaths is a statistic. I was so angered by a rhetorical question being answered with a fascist's justification of mass murder that I was actually shaking. After I calmed down, I thought about it a lot, and realized that I had to admit he had a point.

And what brings you here, she inquires politely, at this hour?

I've come to speak to the person from the gallery. The one who sent the letter in my pocket, knife-sharp. I thought I was coming here to confront Valentina about the complete silence around my work. *S'affronter.* Already it sounds like a dustup. But it is the letter that occupies me.

Work, I finally tell her, and quickly feel ridiculous.

You know, I say, switching the subject. You will open up into motherhood, you just must remember to do it without losing yourself. Let the laundry accumulate. There is more danger in getting too good at being practical. Women who do this are never fulfilled. My tone is of a calm parent, though this is not my intention.

You must have children.

A grandchild, I say. The word hangs in the air like a bird testing its voice.

She looks at me oddly. Both of us are calculating how this is possible, or maybe only I am. She is distracted, looking at her hands.

I am trying to not think of the letter. As though it has not precipitated a new and exquisite pain. Why is there no mention of a child? What kind of terrific odds could produce such a preposterous outcome? My entire life I have been persecuted for living, in essence, like a man. And now this absurd claim like a thousand forces doing their best to pluck things from me, designating my own inadequacy, my own insignificance. Only for a moment did I let thoughts of motherhood take shape, but even then, especially then, it was set to fail. The choice was made. And once a choice is made, it cannot be unmade. I tried to not think of it. Looking too closely at things changes what you feel. And now it doesn't matter how much or little I thought of it. Why repeat sad things?

Ask for help, I tell her. Sleep. You will find that you will get through it. The night is difficult, but the night can also bring solutions. She looks up. You need to sleep long enough to dream.

She slides over and collapses in my lap holding on to my waist, and then starts shaking with tears.

I've not been held like this for years. It is uncomfortable, verging on painful, but I do not move.

I wish I could help.

You already did, she says, wiping her eyes with the tips of her fingers. Though everything she says sounds open-ended.

She gets up, holding her small body with grace, and then glints white through the cool grass and across the park. A pale shape moving, through the navy blue light. I think because of my age and opinion, she mistakes me for wise and maternal. The truth is I'm neither of these things.

Snake

Sun jerks in its eyes as it slicks through
grassblades, blood heating.

HAVING SEEN THE DANCER means I can't go to him tonight.
I make these interior arrangements. I need to see friends, laugh it
off. Stunned that I am capable of violence. I know that hurt, I am
dangerous to meet.

Tas, all I can think, that woman is so overtly sensual.

Tacita lights a cigarette and hands me one.

Okay, I, but that woman is not Lev's wife. She's a dancer. Her
name is Ulyana.

Great. So now there are at least two.

I asked Istvan about the dancer. I think she's from Leningrad.
Istvan says that Lev found her beauty gratifying.

Is this supposed to make me feel better?

Her self-involvement is legendary. Istvan says before parties
she makes herself cry because it makes her eyes bluer. He said
her birthday is on Christmas Day.

God Tas, what does that matter?

She is used to ruining festivities. That relentless need for an audience. You know, if she were religious, she'd want to be Jesus.

I laugh and Tacita says, Finally.

Istvan also says she's the sort of woman who can change the mood in a room with a single remark. He calls her a cage in search of a bird. She kills everything, including conversations by saying things like, I dance like no one.

What else do you know of her?

She once told Lev that when she has a blister on her foot before a performance, she shaves off a thin slice of raw meat, usually veal, and places it on top of the wound. After she dances, at the end of the night, the meat is cooked. It's the only thing that works. She says all the dancers do it. Tacita winces. I think this image has possibly ruined ballet for me. She pauses and then says, She might be half crazed with hunger. Her only food is vodka and cigarettes.

Vodka and cigarettes are not food, they are an addiction.

I, let's not talk about her.

After a moment, I force myself to ask, Do you know anything of Aglaya?

No. Istvan says that Lev never discusses her. Istvan doesn't even know where she lives. She sucks in her breath. He wonders when Lev has long absences if he has gone to her.

An inward shudder.

I wonder if they have children.

There is only silence around everything with Lev. He does not want to talk about it. I, let's not talk of it either. All of this. I wonder if it even seems like you.

Tacita—

She squeezes my hand. It was the dancer who went outside of courtesy, she says.

I reach for Tacita's coat and my own, a cream wool coat,

stitched by Mme. Tissaud, who prefers creating clothes of her own style rather than the fashionable thing. She has drawers of ribbons and fabrics and underclothes from bygone eras though everything she makes is unfussy. A wise man, she says, wears simple clothing and carries a jewel in his heart.

We walk to Le Dôme hand in hand. The cold air is sobering. For a moment I can see these unsettling things. The three-inch newspaper type. The sparse grocery stores. Museum collections slowly trickling from the city to the provinces. As I feared, each week another rare animal vanishes from the zoo. Monkeys. The python. The hyena is still there but the guard informs me, after much pleading, that she is soon to go. There is a danger of not taking danger seriously enough. And yet still my world exists only within my desires, and two arrondissements. We walk to a group who seeks mappable routes to the unconscious. The underworld preferable to the sliver of land we precariously stand on.

Istvan comes toward us and kisses us both warmly. My eyes flicker across the room. Lev is not here, though many of the women who look for him are. Unlike everyone else, he does not recount amorous episodes from the past. I hear about them from other people. I think of what Tacita said. That maybe he and Aglaya are together. I have offered myself up to my beloved. I am acutely aware of the geometry of desire. Of the fact that somewhere he too could be doing the same.

I excuse myself. In the *toilettes* women jut out their lower lips applying red lipstick, their mouths o's while their eyelashes coat with black. Hair in waves. They wear complicated constructed dresses and garter belts and silk-seamed stockings. They are ravishing. They smell of perfume and cigarettes. I am overcome with love for them, for bothering. Of course beauty also destroys beauty. Like the iridescent peacocks now gone from the zoo. Tacita and I observe that they prefer to eat chrysanthemums and roses rather than the granules and grit consumed by the dust-coloured birds that nobody notices. I see myself glint across the mirror. Dark-circled eyes, angular lines, messy hair braided and pinned up around my head. A white dress with pleats that fall to the ground. I look wrong. Out of time. I have a certain ignorance in complex barters of social currency. With women, appearance is most definitely one. I know that solitaries look odd. It is mostly when I am in a room with people who have a common goal that I feel remote. I have grown used to being separate, but wonder what it would be like, just for a moment, to be them. Women who wash their hair in dead champagne to make it gold. Women who sleep with pins and strips of rags tied around their hair to wake up to curls. Women who wear the newest thing. Would I know which dress was the right one? Where to find a small mother-of-pearl mirror that clicks shut? Queenie had one, Mother, an army. I wonder if because I had only brothers I have never really understood why people choose to determine women by their outsides, and not by their brains or hearts. I don't want to be admired like Ulyana. I want to be given space so that I can paint and record and unfold into what I'm making. Without that, I see that there are parts of my life that run thin. I see how the best things are made in solitude. These women who seem to live in front of the mirror, this flash of beauty, fleeting, like glitter at a party. But, I remind myself, I am not a solitary anymore. I have Tacita. I have Lev. And with him, I am alarmed that my words are stunted and rusted from being so deep inside of me I have no idea if they are even really there.

I emerge back into the noisy room, gather my coat and gloves, and kiss Tacita.

Oh Ivory, don't go. We're just beginning.

You must tell me what transpires.

We will re-evaluate in the light of day.

The walk back to Mme. Tissaud's is rainsoaked and the lights get mooned in the dark rivers of streets.

I take my key and unlock my door, the damp cold is startling. In the dark, I see a thin film of water from the rain. I left the window open. But also sharp frilled edges of roses.

How? A locked room and only I have the key.

I can't stop thinking about Ulyana. I can't shake her image. Acting as though nothing has happened is like having to speak to a stranger in the morning, when there still exists the remoteness of an intense dream. I wish I could live without this interior drama. I think of Tacita and Istvan and the way they move together, without question, or conflict. Though I know living by comparison is living in shadows. I wonder if she experiences this. The feeling that if I hear from Lev, if he is in my room, or we meet in the street, it is a marvel. That he is even there. I cannot imagine a world that he inhabits sturdily, enduringly, without fail. I cannot imagine living together. A shared key, food, space. Instead we move like animals, cautious of coming in close. What is it that is feared? Capture?

There is a distant thrum of an airplane above. Lev once told me that he was interested in aviators, until he actually met one and then was disappointed to find that this person was just normal. A sportsman. No inward struggle, just a tightly focused mind with little self-consciousness.

What did you think they would be like?

Adventurers.

Well isn't travelling adventure?

People who travel for recreation are limited by the part of

themselves that's only interested in elsewhere. Travelling is a substitute for real activity.

What would you consider real activity?

Anything you do with your mind.

Later Lev explains that he stood below waiting for me, and when I didn't come out, he began to toss the roses through the open window. Without staying any longer, he left.

But that's impossible, I say. They were placed there so perfectly. As though they had been arranged.

Bee

Solenius vagus (female) skilful borer,
behaves differently from the Osmia,
(condition of the) sense of smell.

ONE, THEN TWO. And then Valentina's voice on the telephone saying hello like a question mark.

It's Ivory, I say, annoyed at my thin voice that resembles none of the fury inside.

What time is it? Valentina says, her voice full of sleep. Clearly I've woken her up.

I don't know.

Suddenly she's pricked alert. Have you seen Skeet? Is he there?

What? Why would he be here? Isn't he in Oslo?

A pause. Relief trickles through.

Can I telephone you back in the morning? It's the middle of the night, Ivory.

Valentina, there is no telephone reception where I live, as you well know. I am in my nightclothes, standing at a payphone that I travelled to by car. You could ring this number in the morning, but I assure you it will not be me who answers.

What is it that can't wait until morning?

You cannot tell me you did not expect that I must be upset, after all the time I have worked with the conservatory. Valentina. I need to know what's going on. There has been no communication. I sent all the skylark files over six months ago. Some of the most beautifully complex recordings.

I think of how the slow methodical work put me in a reflective mood. All the power the sounds contain, like precise little jewels read inside the cave walls.

To think that skylarks die because we eat cereal. They can't find food through the densely packed winter fields. St. Francis once petitioned the holy Roman emperor to scatter grain across fields on Christmas Day to give the crested larks a feast. The fields in England used to be clustered with them. We can see exactly the effects that moving the spring sowing of the wheat and barley crops to winter has had on the populations, I tell her. All so we can eat more cereal. I've—

I can hear a sigh, the telephone receiver unmuffled, as though she's reconciled herself to the conversation.

I don't know what I'm expecting. Valentina has only ever had a touristic understanding of what I am after with my work. She is the person now who has known me the longest. A biologist-turned-bureaucrat, she clicks down the halls to her small bright office at the university where she tracks projects, allocates funding for the conservatory. Something shifted years ago between us. We now use a brusque more informative style of communicating with each other. She has always been unwilling to accept that my life, for the most part, is not what anyone might call domestic. She hates the clutter of bags of nuts and fruit and vegetables I leave on her counters, one of those modern kitchens that look like a morgue. I don't believe in refrigeration, I say. She glares. It kills the taste in things.

I wouldn't think someone who is used to gritty sandwiches in the field, who drinks nutritional supplements in the lab, would care about taste, she counters.

She admonishes my utter lack of style, but I've also never understood the thrill of feeling enhanced by a garment. She says I have it wrong. Clothes can be profound. They are signposts of the interior. When I would stay at her apartment in Oslo she would offer up her enormous toiletry case. You could do something with your hair, she ventures. Horrified that I would enter a public building barely combed, in an unironed shirt. What about some makeup? You know women use lipstick to tranquilize, I say. She ignores me. Her hair is swept up in an old-fashioned businesslike style. She wears what seems to be the same structured dress in different colours that she used to make from brown paper patterns. It hides all my sins, she says by way of explanation. Her elegance is out of place, against the modern triumph of comfort. She cannot stand all these people now, no difference in droopy attire between the child and the adult. Perhaps our generation, so consciously assembled, wanted to avoid the complacency of comfort. As though we secretly found it necessary, the need for small pain.

I did apologize for the way the last batch of notes reached you, didn't I?

Ivory, it's got nothing to do with that, though if you'd not smoked so much perhaps your writings would be more legible. Besides, you know data is required to be in digital form now.

I've never wanted to rely solely on technology, Valentina. The resistance is active, not passive. My method has forced me to recognize each voice individually.

That's precisely it. You hold too much information in your head. You are probably the only person in the world with these decades of fieldwork, this intimate knowledge of behaviour.

I think of Mme. Tissaud's voice saying the death of an elder is like the burning of a library. They are like palimpsests, she once told me. Those very old documents in which the original text has been erased and replaced with new writing. Within them is a record of layers of natural and human events.

Ivory, she interjects. I don't want you to take it personally. We've all had to undergo a fair bit of restructuring since so much funding has been cut.

Restructuring, Valentina, I say, wanting to sit down. That's damned rot. You know I detest these modern euphemisms.

Well, it's what's actually happening. We've amassed a sizable library of your recordings, which will remain in the bioacoustics archives. But the linguistics and your cymatic imagery are not where the conservatory is interested in putting resources at this point. It's a direction things have been going in for some time now. We've lost a considerable amount of our funding, Ivory. It's—

But, Valentina, you just said I am some sort of singular repository. A pause. Some time? How long, Valentina?

There is no answer. Oh Ivory, she sighs. Mea bloody culpa. What do you want me to say? Her tone faintly hostile, as if to say, Do you have no idea that you are so old?

All that beeping and whirring of the extraordinarily expensive technology that's been brought in. Remember when it was just pencils and recorders? People look things up on a computer now and think they've found something out. That they know something. But you need to really observe something, really be with it, to know it. That is learning— Valentina. So?

So?

So, it is a quaint project by an old woman who should have retired long ago.

You wouldn't have received funding for so long if that is what it was, Ivory. You know that. But it isn't daft to consider that maybe it's time to stop work. Relax a little. You could travel, get a pet—

Become one of those old women with a dozen cats wrapped around their ankles? I stare into the receiver, and attempting composure, say in a lowered tone, Of course, Valentina, you and I well know that for anyone who even remotely considers the idea of animal liberation, eliminating the word pet would probably be the first step.

Valentina laughs tentatively. See, that sounds like you, she says, loosening up.

I revere the work.

She remains quiet. Well?

Well the French have a saying. If you piss in the violin it doesn't make much music.

How—vulgar, Valentina says with a laugh.

I'm like a bee, Valentina, I must keep moving to stay still.

I am reminded of recording sounds of wild bees nested in lightning-struck trees. Knowing which chemicals were hitting them through the sounds they made. When Valentina proposed that I focus my research solely on bees, all I said to her is that people notice the bees and the monarchs because they are iconic insects. But what do you think is happening to everything else?

I am now desperate to sit. There is a faint scent of urine in the phone booth. It authenticates my theory that the world is covered in pee. I say to Valentina, Of all the hours I've spent on my stomach in the dirt, really listening to the world. In ditches with clouds moving across the sky. The astonishing intensity of it. I wish I could use words that we use when we talk about love, not these drab ones we reserve for work. It has given me a wonderful release from the consciousness of self. I need not speak, just listen, and remain marvellously alert. And then I look down and see my hands. Or the small flashing red light of the recorder. Tears fill my throat. And I'm amazed that I'm alive. Struck by the notion that I myself am here at all, that I am simply here.

I understand this, Ivory, you know, she says quietly.

Everyone wants something nice that relates to them. Like we are preserving this rainforest so it will be around for our grandchildren. You know that I think that is the worst reason. We should be preserving it because the plants and animals deserve their rightful habitat. I do it for them, Valentina. They should be allowed to exist.

Well they are lucky you have saved them.

They have saved me, don't you see? It is something of great importance in my life, I say, trying to gain some composure. I am lucky. Not everyone can say that.

You have fulfillment, is that not enough?

Fulfillment. That is a dead word, Valentina. In the eighteenth century they would have called it inspiration, which I prefer.

A car rattles off past the river.

Anger is already turning into something else. Despite its being the appropriate response for what is being meted out.

I look down and see that at the bottom of the telephone booth there is a collection of dead flies, like raisins.

I hear the deep tiredness in Valentina's voice. There is also a certain nervousness I've never felt before. Because I know her so well, amid the warmth there exists a sliver of condescension. My age. The restructuring. Of cutting off any drain. It occurs to me that I am a drain.

———

The conferences I used to travel to, often with Valentina, weighed on me. The urbanity, the people, the requisite small talk. Dry scholarly symposia on subjects such as Linnaean taxonomy. We would walk past the dull corridors that smell of desk, past the students huddled in the courtyards in conversation, stubbing out cigarettes underfoot. Valentina always dressed strategically. Tight dress, sharp heels, lipstick. There was a feeling of confinement heading back to our hotels. I can never seem to help that feeling of absence in what others consider a gratifying present. That need for male identification, which I have always associated with young women who have little choice, which she plays in to. Always we are being reflected in the eyes of others. They ask so few questions of us.

It's not possible, Valentina. My work has never been about surrender, I say into the phone.

Please. Let's talk about it in the morning, Ivory, okay?

I hear a metallic hum. The card has run out of time. She has told me nothing.

Damn it, I say into the dial tone, jerking my hand back as I slam it into the receiver.

I hear the wind ticking over the plane trees with their pale calico trunks like the flutter of the white queenly moths flickering across the caves at night when I work. My body vibrates. From emotion, or cold, I'm not sure which. I gather my shawl about my shoulders. This isn't dignified.

Buck

Colourblind mystical eyes; freezes at the unknown.
Brays, small kingdoms of concrete music with geometry.

A PAIR OF YELLOWHEADED BLACKBIRDS pick at their feathers and rasp through reeds and fronds as though they are a couple that has grown old together, comfortable in each other's personal hygiene and itinerant bodily noises. At least, this is what I imagine when the thin paper takes up the walnut ink. There is the lyrebird with the tail feathers of a dandy and a voice that can mimic everything from the circular rhythm of a tin-bladed fan to a barking dog. I have been saved from abject poverty. I am drawing biological illustrations for M. Barbary, a professor at the Sorbonne and an antiquarian book collector Mme. Tissaud knows, who deals in lithographs from early nineteenth-century publications. Butterflies, grassland animals, plants, birds, fish, crustaceans. These tender-faced creatures labelled, ordered, once drawn alive in their native habitats. I am replicating them, in my cold Parisian studio. Overcoat on, fingerless gloves, enough francs to pay for my flat, food, for coal and art supplies, though everything is getting harder to find. My own art waits on the easel. A group of horses in different colours with human eyes, in a dark stormed landscape. Tacita says she likes the way the wild eyes hint at a disturbing unnameable confrontation. Flowers grow from underneath. There are smaller scenes in the underpaint, in the corners.

The gallerists have taken an arm's-length interest in Lev, but still treat him as the parvenu. I have been with him when a well-regarded gallery owner approached. She had a foxfur collar, tall shoes, and hair the colour of whisky. She found his poverty attractive. I could feel her appetite for him. She spoke with him in a low provocative tone, her hand on his arm, as though I wasn't standing right there beside him. She wanted him to come to her gallery, to meet with her there. He remained cold, unreadable. Though she didn't seem to mind. We weren't introduced.

Some of his work is sold for good money. Though I really don't know how he lives; he never discusses practical matters with me. I know from Tacita that he can spend whole weeks in his studio with no heating, with only tins of herring and alcohol to drink. He works so prolifically that he hangs his art by clothespegs like laundry.

He tells me nothing, I say to Tacita.

Well people who are too direct are uninteresting.

She is silent for a moment. Lev said what most fascinates him about you is your ability to read other people's thoughts, to see other people's dreams.

Other people's dreams can be tedious, as it turns out, I say to Tacita, who ignores me.

He told Istvan that you are like one of those animal deities that lead people to the afterlife.

Really? I say, surprised. I am reminded of how his sensitivity

135

stops me. This is not straightforward. I think of you and Istvan. So simple and quick.

God, I, you make it sound like a murder.

Oh, why not the kind artist from the academy who sends me notes and draws tiny still-lifes on sheets of letter-sized paper?

Yes, everything would be so much better, she says with fake excitement.

All right, Tas.

You would never be happy in such a slack union, I. Everything would be well arranged but lifeless. You would be adored but numb, without feeling. Besides, you'd feel guilty about eventually turning against someone who would have done nothing but continue to be himself.

But I wouldn't be so troubled. I feel like I never get my fill. And then I worry that I am letting him absorb too much of me, so that he can use it to do what he needs to do. But this I don't say to Tacita. Once things are said out loud, they can become true.

My last letter before Paris: *Dear Mother, All is well. Am settling in nicely. Thank you for the notecards. Love to all.* Though in truth, I am dying inside. And when they receive word of my expulsion, the only thing they are surprised by is how easily duplicity comes to me.

At convent school, I am an unenthusiastic student. My thoughts readily stray from the classroom to the outdoors. I have filled notebooks with drawings. I barely pass an exam. Every day I stare at Jesus, pretty as a girl, on the giant crucifix in the chapel where we say our morning prayer. All the girls' eyes on the first naked man they've seen. They say he is handsome. They hold up fingers, blotting out the hipbones and blood. I count one hundred and twenty-seven references to animals in the bible. Forty-one of which are dogs. There are no cats. At one point, when they have us memorize passages of the bible, I refuse. Why? Sister Agatha asks, eyes narrowed. Because it is a book of fairy tales, I say standing against the wall, and not even good ones. Are you not concerned about the side effects of your godlessness? she asks. By side effects do you mean sound mental state? That was the first expulsion. Another came after I decided I wanted to be a saint. Mainly to see if I could levitate, something my brother Edgar and I had read and marvelled at. I was also caught listening to the nuns' crystal radio. I didn't have enough time to find a station, but felt life rushing in at the whistles and pops between stations as I turned the silver dial. Later I argue with the doleful Sister who taught science. She had a mouth twisted in a permanent scowl and smelled like an old book. She had us filling out qualitative analyses of the elements in writing, like a police report. The Sister performs experiments in the chemistry lab mechanically, with a sober rigour that borders on humorous. I feel an almost violent enthusiasm and am unable to wait for her droning instructions, managing to create a small explosion with potassium dropped in water. It sounds like a door slamming. I don't hear the nun-shoes squeaking on tile as they all come running in because, for a moment, I've lost my hearing. I am stunned. I feel an excruciating sharp pain, and then liquid leaks out of my left ear. When I look at my fingers, I see that it is blood.

Mother is horrified when she hears. Though astonishingly, she acquiesces to my pleas to attend the art academy. This is the last one. After this, she says quietly, you are on your own. She agrees to it only because of Queenie. A week before I woke with fierce pain in my chest. All day, I was unable to breathe. Mother called that night. She didn't have to say it, I already knew.

Queenie had died. A heart attack. There was no space in my body for such great agony. I felt vague, rudderless. I wanted her to say something more, but there was just a low buzzing sound on the telephone during a long awkward pause. Well that's it then, I said. No one said anything back.

A bright knock in the cold. He is in my room. Always north of him I see a light. He smells like the sun. From his coat he produces a lark's nest woven with dark hair that could be mine. He holds it out to me with both hands cupped, like an offering. He also produces a pair of worn leather riding boots. They are for me. I immediately question where he got the money. I know he is hungry. He says he traded a painting. They are completely impractical, reflecting back my childhood with its opulence that makes me almost ashamed. But at the same time I realize how remote it is too. How there is very little of my childhood left that feels real anymore. He says, No. They are verging on a beauty that is in no way material.

I show him my illustration. He studies it for what feels like a long time and then he asks me what I'm doing it for.

So that I can live.

You should paint, if you want to live.

It seems so odd to be talking at all. I have been aching to see him. It has been days. The last time I saw him he held an olive in his teeth, passing it to my mouth, warm and salty and filling me full of desire. My cool fingers on his warm neck. Ravish me. We are surrounded by people in the dark and riotous café. He rips the shoulder of my dress with his teeth. I drink wine with my coat resting on my shoulders for the rest of the night, and listen to a café luminary recite long passages of Dante and Verlaine.

After the cafés close, the artists will go to one another's studios, taking bottles. Behind its shutters, Paris is a late town.

It almost doesn't seem real that he is here, in this small blue room with little ornamentation. I hate myself for not asking all the things that have been occupying me. Ulyana. His wife. His absences. But instead he returns to silently alter my existence.

How difficult it is to say what you actually feel. Rough hands, blue refracting eyes. I find his presence blinding. I see how rare communication actually is. Real, true communication. So much remains unsayable between people. All the secrets we keep.

His mouth on mine. Brushes drop. Abandon. Pleasure bursting into a thousand pieces.

Tell me a story, Ivory.

Imagined or real?

All stories are real.

A long silence.

I look at the familiar corners of the room. My voice has a different sound.

Once there was a raven-haired woman with skin as white as marble who had a daughter, a feral, woodland child. It was difficult for the girl to live as a regular child, as she had been given the extraordinary gift of hearing the voices of living creatures. This did not please the mother. The child would only become herself alone, deep in the woods, which pleased the mother even less. One afternoon, the woman threw a garden party where she had servants put out triangular sandwiches, trays of teacups, cakes piled high on glass plates, everything creamy and opulent. The woodland child was forced into formal attire, a shiny red dress, with a sash that wound tighter as she breathed. She tried to creep across the gleaming wood floors, attempting to slip out unnoticed. The raven-haired mother caught sight of the red swirl out of the corner of her eye, and in a few strides her hands were on the woodland child's shoulders. You remember Mr. Winter don't you? the woman asked the girl. A dark eyebrow arched in disapproval as she conducted the girl toward the man with kind, wet, bovine eyes. The girl nodded hello. The man was tall and awkward, with a shyness almost worse than hers. She could see that he was fighting down his embarrassment. Clumps of his hair fell forward and bobbed up and down when he spoke. He did a sort of clipped head bow every time he acknowledged the girl, which she found endearing, though he often knocked heads with maidens who made excuses and scurried off. If he were an animal, the woodland child thought sadly, he would be prey.

I am told you are an accomplished rider, he said to the girl, his eyes like someone carefully not looking at a rat they've just seen run out of the host's kitchen.

I am fond of horses, the girl said, looking at her shoes. The mother hooked a finger under the girl's chin and directed it up.

Just horses then?

All animals, she said, unused to the interest of an adult human. It's unfortunate we've not figured out how to communicate with them better, she added.

The woodland child's mother remained tensely polite and was about to speak when she was abruptly led away by a birdlike woman. This was the girl's cue. She slipped two hard-boiled eggs from their delicate arrangement into the pocket of her dress, and moved with arrowing purpose.

The grass was damp and glossy. The woodland child's shoes were painted with mud as soon as they left the flagstones. She ran, the sun-striped oaks blurring. It was so quiet she could hear the sound of her own heart beating. She could see the house, a dot in the distance. The windows were like flashes of mirror, giving shape, small fragments of civilization in the brush. The woodland child stopped when she reached the trees. The woods that surrounded the house—unlike the ones she would later know that form tidy colonnades—were clumped, thick, and deep.

The girl was slightly afraid of being caught, though she knew the raven-haired mother would never leave her party to look for her. And so she let herself relax a little. She knelt down on the forest floor, carpeted in bluebells, and loosened her sash. She snapped a twig. And in an empty space on the shiny mud, she wrote. She didn't use ordinary letters. It was a message for the forest animals, so she wrote the way they do. But as she dragged the stick, the hairs on the woodland child's neck bristled. She knew she was being watched.

The woodland child jerked her head up. It was a buck. A huge rack of antlers and wide dark eyes. Its body stock-still. Even though it was a calm and gentle creature, she was terrified at being so startled and alone, this deep in the woods. Her heart beat wildly. She could hear its breathing. Its fear. Air released from its nostrils. She looked into his eyes like dead angels. Neither the girl nor the deer moved for a very long time. Their breathing was synchronous.

A faint gasp escaped through the woodland child's lips. And then the strangest thing happened. The buck made the same sound. She stood paralyzed in this moment. Their eyes locked. The girl understood that if you gazed into someone's eyes long enough, there was no need to ask any questions. What passes between galvanizes. Children can look into eyes forever. But when you look into a creature's eyes long enough, everything they've ever known passes through you too. The shelterless life. Running until their heart is about to explode. The life that occurs in the open, and in part-darkness.

It was at that moment the woodland child understood that a mystic and a solitary creature were the same thing. Hours deep into the thicket, a darkness grew. The girl became aware of canopies of sound. Her attention was on the deer, but at the same time, on everything around her. A collusion occurred. The woodland child would protect the deer from the bows and bullets, and the deer would teach the woodland child its language.

The raven-haired mother had rays of anger radiating out of her when the woodland child finally returned home. The trays and glasses had all been cleared away. There were only small signs of the party that afternoon. Flowers throughout the house, the smell of lily-of-the-valley perfume mingled with tobacco in an unholy union. The girl knew to remain quiet. There was no use in attempting to defend herself to her mother, it was like burning green wood. But the raven-haired mother was oddly good-humoured, calm even.

That night she sat on the edge of woodland child's bed and informed her that she would be sent far away. The forests and the animals were turning her into something unrecognizable. The mother knew, even then, that part of the girl already belonged to them.

Swallow

Pair; nested in a fissure halfway up a 400-foot
precipitous rocky wall. Vocalizations muffled.
To reach them would require 300 feet of rope. Or wings.

WE'VE REHEARSED THIS BEFORE. Skeet asks, Why a
dictionary?

Each time I answer him it is at least ten degrees different.

It started with a professor in Toronto, I tell him. When I
discussed my applied linguistics class, and my interest in what
happens when a language dies, he said that we cannot measure
what we've lost. The effects are culturally devastating. Each
language is a key that unlocks the knowledge of entire
civilizations. It's everything, he said. It's medicinal secrets,
ecological wisdom, weather patterns, spiritual attitudes,
mythological histories.

If what we say marks all that we know, then a dictionary is the
most important human document. Is it not?

But wherever there is language, there are borders that limit
our existence, he counters. Not to mention nonverbal thinking
and feeling. Wittgenstein, he continued, said that if a lion could

speak, we would not understand him. Language being the place from which compassion grows. But of course this is precisely the self-serving tautology used by people who defend things such as animal testing and slaughterhouses. And then there are the silent languages. Silence is not acoustic. It is a state of mind. Moths and pheromones, the flashing of fireflies, honeybees dancing on hive walls, the leg waving of spiders. Glasswing butterflies. They read clear to us, but to one another they are rainbow coloured. Sound packs the most information the most rapidly, but the interesting thing about nonverbal communication, he says, is that it is harder to lie.

I found a flat on a little avenue by the university, and dragged my trunk upstairs to the tiny room under its angled ceiling. There was just a small stove and a narrow bed. I found a wooden table and chair, and a jug and a washbasin, on the street, it being impossible to throw things away in a city. I noted down the dates of the exams I needed to pass in order to register as an undergraduate and taught myself biology from a book, one I might have illustrated when I lived in Paris. It felt like a return to childhood. Born by a lake, sworn to water. When I crossed the sea, my suitcase had contained white dresses from another life. The brass latches clicked open, the contents emptied overboard into the black, cold underworld. Gusts of white, like live feathers falling on the dark swells. But the little money I had was giving out, and I was so often cold or hungry or both. I had only one practical grey woollen dress. My face was bare. There were no flourishes. Everything was scrubbed away. My gait felt lumbering, not graceful and light as once it was. Clipped wings against a bitten moon. The only way I could mark the changes wrought to my inward self was by altering my appearance. Before I came here, I cut off all my hair, dark ropes on the floor.

The only way to bear the loss of Tacita was, in part, to become her. Small ways.

In a desolate moment, I wrote a letter to Mother that came back months later, unopened, the foreign stamps a ruinous luxury. I eventually received word from Arthur back in England, the one brother who survived the war. He wrote only "flat feet" by way of explanation. He wired money without my even telling him how grim my situation was. We exchanged respectful, affectionate notes at long intervals. Neither of us mentioned our other brothers, though their memories darkened over us. A shell exploded. A plane was shot down. A gun was fired. Uniforms rusted with blood. And then vanished. As though they were never here. It becomes another thing to forget. I think of them as boys, and still they were. We are not readied for such violent loss. So we vowed to make new lives. Singular, where everything is precious. I confided to him that I was gloomy but carried a secret about my future, which I promised to reveal later.

The air was different here. The light. The sidewalks even. They were flatter and wider, gutters tinnily gurgling at the edges of cement curbs. The empty shining streets. The air smelled like nothing. A faint scent of trees and brake dust. There was nothing in the sky except billows of grey smoke from the chimney stacks and the hum of factories. There was no war here. They were not used to death. They did not know my past. They did not know that for a time I ceased to be an honourable woman.

Professor Tapping could get so deep into his work that I would often see him cross the campus in his laboratory gown, having forgotten to take it off. I wanted to take a course from the music department, which I was told is strictly forbidden. But what he said with his limpid eyes was, Your studies can all intersect. In one of his lectures, I thought Mother, with her acute desire for tidiness, would have approved of the precise geometry of cells—Latin for small room, oval and orderly. Everything seemed so absorbing, with no weight of memory to it. *Even insects express anger, terror, jealousy, and love*, Darwin wrote and I underlined.

Everything sounded amplified to me. *Songbird migration happens at night. Whales are composers, their songs are clicks that rhyme like words. Animal voices are important because so many animals are difficult to see.* My behavourial biology professor pointed out that we were in an age of intellectual revolution. Biologists and evolutionary psychologists were disassembling the consensus. Everything was worthy of re-examination. Don't ever hold back in pursuing an idea that might seem mad to others. He told us that after Einstein published his theory of relativity, one hundred physicists wrote a paper condemning it. Einstein's response: if the theory is wrong, why wouldn't one author suffice?

I wonder if being truly successful at something means that you are simply bad at everything else. Years later, Einstein's letters to his wife depict certain strict, somewhat cruel domestic arrangements.

> *You will make sure—that my clothes and laundry are kept in good order; that I will receive my three meals regularly in my room. You will renounce all personal relations with me insofar as they are not completely necessary for social reasons.*

After a short time, I received an invitation to Professor Tapping's house in Forest Hill. The dark wood, the antique rugs, the thick velvet curtains, and his punctilious manner comforted me. The housekeeper let me in to the sitting room, with visible hesitation, having been used to admitting only male students. I waited while she told him I had arrived. My eyes moved toward a framed photograph in the hall; in it, Professor Tapping looks very young in his black suit. There is a woman next to him in a hat. He holds her elbow. They wear the same stern expression that everyone did then, even though it is clearly their wedding day. It reminds me how photography can be a form of lying. I never ask about the photo, or the woman in it. He carries a forlornness the way that only men can, men who have been left to go on living alone. His two sisters are clever, unmarried, and most likely would have been scientists too if they had been male. I wondered if they had stories of fiancés lost in the war, or secret lovers met through the university, or maybe, as with me, none of it would even matter now. There are not many versions on offer in this town. Everything seems to favour an inert sort of morality. Couples who don't seem to love each other very much but get along well enough. They mate for life, rearing their offspring in sturdy houses with large lawns.

Each Sunday, there was bread, cheese, baked fish, cake, and Paganini's virtuoso violin solos on the record player. I was almost embarrassed by it, making me aware of how the crudeness of my life bordered on the masochistic. It took a moment to adjust to proper food and conversation outside of school. I had become adept at concealing myself, offering up only one of my profiles.

In the laboratory I am made to slash the throat strings of animals with a knife, spending hours dissecting and sectioning, making paraffin slides. Birdcalls I'd not heard since childhood drifting through the open laboratory windows, everything a song for hard sorrow. The classrooms were crammed with men back from war, their long legs sticking out from underneath their desks making them seem like overgrown children. Though the nights were feverish, work shutting out despair, my days were calm, concealing all the determination that I possessed. I received a first degree, and then a second in quick succession. Because I excelled, and because I did not have any money, I spent my summers at the lab.

The warm months, the room broiling. My mind torpid and thick. There was not a surface or object that did not feel hot. In winter, the wind roared in the chimney, banged at the windows. One night it was so cold I wondered if it was safe. I ran my hands along the wall and found that the reproduction Constable that hung here when I moved in, and for some reason I never removed, covered a hole right to the outside, cold air streaming through in a circle where a stovepipe must once have been. I heard the gnawing of squirrels in the walls and felt half-mad in the boreal air. The kind of cold encountered by some of the soldiers I had seen. The kind where corneas freeze, teeth shatter, faces are eaten by frost. Those men marching who looked off, only to see what it was. That they had no eyelids. Their eyelids had been torn away from cold. I piled everything I owned, including my textbooks, on top of me. A thin layer of ice formed on the washbasin.

If it is cold enough, birds in flight can freeze, and then drop from the sky like stones.

I received my first cheque, a small bursary in the mail. I exchanged the cheque for a bicycle. I rode it through the city, and to the ravines. It was spring. The weakest season here, though small leaves sprouted from trees that had pretended to be dead all winter. There were sudden yellow flowers, and cherry trees with warmed branches clotted in pink bloom.

Professor Tapping and I drank bitter English tea that he sugared heavily in a matching cup ringed with gold. I remember him looking up and saying with warmth and determination, You will accomplish a lot. But you must know your own response to your work, Miss Frame. If you don't, his teacup clattered delicately, you will miss the reward.

Ivory, one of his sisters said, leaning her head in from the hall and then walking into the room. She handed me a parcel. I have a dress to give you, one that no longer fits. I think it will look smart on you. I had shown up in the same one each week, and all I think is, Please let it be practical and dark so that I can wear it to the university underneath the laboratory smock.

I became a research assistant to Professor Tapping and a Professor Ellis, a migratory bird expert who managed to wrest fascinating research from the most interminable fieldtrips that continually tested the limits of human patience. Hours spent watching an empty grey sky for wings. Though he taught me that another way to look for nests was to listen. He was also incredibly adept at Latin binomials. With biology, taxonomy is essential. It gives the chaos of nature a form. Aristotle once grouped animals in a hierarchy by whether or not they had blood, or whether they lived on land or water. Humans, he put on the top. Like Descartes—who once nailed his wife's live poodle to a board to prove that it did not have feelings—his relationship to animals was immature.

Even early on in my studies, I found myself turning away from empirical science when I saw that it wasn't able to speak to the kinds of questions I wanted to answer. They are vast, possibly ridiculous questions, too large for the fine-grained grid of specialization. What is communication? What is silence? Can animal vocalizations and their meanings be made into a dictionary? What would it accomplish for extinction? I have listed a litany of questions. How should the listening be translated? As a kind of diary entry? An emotive expression? A reaction? Or is it an act of discovery? My questions filled an entire notebook to get to a single sentence that I voiced in a meeting with Professor Tapping. He answered me in measured tones, attesting that scientific discovery does not always mean accumulation of data or measured consideration of facts. It often requires a leap of imagination. True scientists do not simply conduct prescribed experiments, they develop their own. Sometimes it's the only way to get to new knowledge.

You start with a fantasy, which you must ultimately prove in reality. An essential aspect of creativity is not being afraid to fail. You know— He pauses. Scientists do the same thing as artists, they just use the words hypothesis and experiment instead.

I found all the field recordings the university had, seven in total, including braying Antarctic emperor penguins and hornbills from the Carpenter expedition. I wore enormous headphones, sat in a small wooden carrel that smelled like varnish and dead skin, and counted the seconds between the sounds, listening to the static, the dry little scratches of feet on snow, the timbre of trees creaking in wind. They let me sign out a microphone and heavy recording equipment from the university. I lugged it out to the ravine. The silver discs spin and click to a halt after I replay the sound of thrushes. Their voices telling interior things. Night descends. Everything quiets for a moment. Moonsoaked. Treeglitter. The air held on to this distant, vanishing sound of swallows. There were large gaps of silence. It made me think of Satie's Gymnopédies, which had been playing quietly in the dining room when I first met Lev at Tacita's apartment. The music was so far from my mood, slow melancholic notes floating in space. I stared down at the recorder, moonlight on my fingers. This blue dusk, the birds' voices, invitation. A great calm washed over me. I knew what I had to do. And for the first time, it felt like the beginning of a new age, the one after the king has been killed.

Black Swan

Each breath is the dark corner of an echo
and contains the energy of wind, like two
people whose paths are about to cross
and then don't.

A DARK VERTICAL LINE divides the mist. I recognize his gait and watch his shadow move across the grass. He has such radiance, you forgive him anything.

First he cannot see me. I am white, clothes waving like a flag, hair in black gusts. My breathing is slowed, the taste of his coppery mouth on my tongue. His hands on my fingers. He says, You're so cold. And puts them inside his shirt.

We climb a monument modelled after an ancient Roman temple. Lev prefers this strange park sculpted from the ruins of one of Napoleon's gypsum quarries. Despite the careful curation of exotic plants, it cannot shake what lies below. A history of blood and industry. Battles and bodies and murder, though now beautiful flowers grow. The swans are black. Paris from up here looks small. The silver rooftops and the domes of Sacré-Coeur appear over the treetops. And unlike every other park in Paris, here you can sit on the grass.

Lev is part nocturnal animal. He leaves the studio at night and wanders for hours, walking though Place des Vosges, through the cemeteries, behind the Pantheon, exploring the old Paris. Only sometimes can I come.

There are wet-root smells soaking through fog. His eyes whiter. My eyes blacker. The grass cold under his hands, he opens his eyes to the dark sky. A farness that makes him near. His presence all over my body. Hands on my ribs, hipbones. His mouth on my throat. Stars falling on skin. Fingers in fingers. The parts of the moon that glimmer through. Warmth. Violence. Bones licked clean. The thing that happens to us. Its full pleasure beating through me, shaking me awake, head clear, mind stilled. Longing and abandonment skinned off to ripeness, a daze of rapture.

When I first made the lines, he says, hands underneath his head, I was actually thinking about the honesty of trees. I think of the Buddhist monks, being silent, sitting. Who does that better than trees? Our backs on the damp grass as we look up, the sky pierced with sharp black branches.

In Siberia, near the Tunguska River, he says, when I was a boy, I heard about what the villagers thought was the end of the world. Everything shook. There was a cracking sound like lightning, and then a column of blue light brighter than the sun. Windows broke hundreds of kilometres away. All the trees were on fire. Eighty *million* trees burned to the ground. It was so isolated there that no one came to investigate. He closes his eyes. Twenty years later someone came to look at the hole that was left. Thousands of square kilometres. He laughs. It was a comet. The largest one to ever hit the Earth. Almost no one died because of where it was. If it had exploded four hours later, it would have taken out the whole of Petersburg.

I'm trying to picture the size of that, the terror of the not-knowing. Living in a permanent stoop, waiting for some unnameable violence that might strike again and take you out for good. For twenty years, not knowing, when Lev turns to me.

You will like this, he says. The peasants said they could hear the trees hum long after the explosion.

I am about to say something, but see he is already somewhere else.

Later he will show me all the thick white and pale grey shapes spaced symmetrically. The icy lyricism of his work makes me think that it is impossible to escape our geographies. I also know what it is to feel air so cold it burns. So cold that animals cannot be born. So cold that if you die, no one can bury you. An endless rhythm of cedars. The bleak north wind.

His work is intelligent and beautiful and unsentimental. I see how directly it comes from what he left behind. A realism in what most people call abstraction. Vicious cold, exhausting heat, relentless insects, black dust, everything covered in ice. By way of compensation, they are given an unending sky. Where he comes from has a heartless logic but it is also sublime. It exalts and destroys. As a result the people carry a humility that allows them to think majestically.

The Greeks, he says, knew that there were no perfect circles, straight lines, or equal spaces in nature. They had to create them.

I know he finds it impossible to put down the first mark, and this series of gratifying experiments has altered his mood.

Where did it come from? I say. A prick of jealousy. He has seen me hunched over working and reworking. Changing the way I work makes me anxious; with him it is the opposite. He is emboldened by it.

The error, he says, is thinking that you have a part to play in the process. You need to receive everything. Cling to nothing. His voice drawing a line, There is no halfway.

Our eyes meet for a moment.

You see what's already inside you, I say.

You could tell me anything, and I would believe it. You have the eyes of a mystic, he says, putting his hands on either side of my face.

Though distant, he has the ability to establish deep communions. Why was he given over to me. Choose him. Do not choose him, I think. Blinking back the emotion.

There is something in these animals, I say, changing the subject. The ones I have been drawing. But I'm finding it hard to know what exactly is real.

We make our way down the hill, past the taverns with their overhead shutters closed, the windowledges of geraniums, pert and anxious in the cold. He stands at the door of Mme. Tissaud's. I feel his mouth on the back of my neck. The only thing real is feeling, he says. I twist the key in the lock, and when I turn around he is gone.

Bat

Mammal (not bird); uses polarity compass;
can sense the direction of the magnetic field vector.
Knows which side the arrow is located.

I FIND MY WAY BACK to the car at the foot of the plane tree. I see the bluelit town in my rearview mirror and wonder how it is I am here, by this place I don't even like. Everyone shuttered in and then tomorrow it all starts again. One might die, another might be born. There might be a boy who thinks he can fly and ends up in the *salle des urgences* for stitches. There might be a woman who as a girl sprayed her wrists with perfume and wore a flower in her hair when she thought she might see the man who would become her husband. And now they might sit silently with their dinner on their laps, light from the television blinking across their faces. The clock will chime each hour, they will do it all over again. Routine lures you, it makes you feel your own identity. Though I often think the opposite. That in repetition, you can lose sight of yourself. Like women imprisoned in housework. Isn't the very definition of insanity repeating the same thing over and over again in the same way, expecting a different result?

Out of the black there is a flash of bright. Two low fixed stars. I swerve. A pair of eyes. A dull thud, then the squeal of brakes. My heart pounds. My palms slip on the leather grip. I turn off the engine. My heart racing. I brace one hand on the wheel, the other on the car door, and slowly hoist myself up. My legs unreliable, as when I was small and broke the left one falling off a horse. The X-ray terrified me. A skeleton, no different from all the other skeletons. I had a plaster cast and had to scratch my knee with a pencil. When the cast was sawed off it exposed a strange leg, bony and brushed with blue. It looked dead. Not my own. I realized, after limping around trying to walk the way I had before, that your mind is part of what makes you walk. It also made me realize how easily things could break.

There is a thick dent and a bright star of red with a few coarse brown hairs on the far right of the bumper. *Tapetum lucidum.* I've learned about the membrane behind the deer's retina that increases their ability to see in the dark. It also makes their eyes shine in headlights. The body went down, I am sure of it, bent at an odd angle. I know that I cannot walk in the tall grasses that join the blacktop. The slivermoon casts little light. In the almost eerie silence I hear the scraping of dry sunflower fronds against one another in the wind. I see nothing but the endless flat fields and a solitary tree. There is no body.

Deer sleep in beds of deep vegetation they press down with their quick bodies, tangled thin legs, in order to hide from predators. They never lie down in the same bed twice, but the imprints can remain for several days. Years ago I followed the whorls of grass. Each time I came upon a deerbed, it felt as if the deer had just departed, leaving a warm impression in the grass. I remember taking a documentary photo of the first bed I saw, the smell of sun still on the lens cap. My hand touched the grass.

Before I knew I was doing it, I got down and lay on the imprint. My body curling into the existing form. First aware of their proximity, and then the quiet embodiment of absence. It made me think of my own mortality. I closed my eyes though the light came through my eyelids. Grass prickled my cheek, poked my back where my coat had ridden up. Lying down, I was struck by the hard band of loneliness that encircled me. Everything crystallizes over time. Like deer who begin with soft velvet antlers and then they calcify underneath, eventually turning to bone.

After the engine fan cuts out, there is a hot wind and the quiet buzzing of cicadas. I run my hand over the dent and lean against the warm metal of the car. My eyes burn with tiredness. I feel the trace of Valentina's voice telling me it's time to stop working. But I want to do it because I want to do it. I am not happy when I am not working. We let some people continue, I think. Painters don't retire—they die. Though I have read what the critics say. They say in the history of art, late works are catastrophes.

I look out at the silent fields. A bat jags into view. Its webbed wings misshapen and black, like a broken umbrella. Its movements jerky, the only mammal with the ability to fly. And I think, It's never the grand spectacles, but always the small intimate moments that hold me rapt. I look up and see part of the moon weakly illuminating the grass. Another bat. There must be a cave nearby.

When I open my eyes again, I can see Lev's shoulders. My feet finding depressions. I clamber down slowly over stone rubble, my back lit by the sun. Through a little vestibule and a densely mudded floor. Caves are not to be entered lightly, I hear his voice say.

Why?

The lower world. A doorway between our world and the otherworld.

We lie on our backs and stare up at the smooth, pale rock. I see something glint. Jewel-encrusted. A bat wrapped in itself. The condensation droplets on its wings glittering. The still-warm sun on our shoulders goes cold in the compressed dirt, the dampness of the cave seeping into skin and holding it there. I stay still, listening to the sounds for a long time until it feels as though I am inside a hallucination, not my own. I start to hear something. Who is there?

When there is a spring in a cave, Lev says, it sounds like voices.

Ever since, it is his voice I hear when I enter a cave. For a period when I am deep into recording bats, it is often. I never get used to the feeling that I should not be there. I remember in the southwest, moving through with the recording equipment. The cave begins to narrow until I am crawling on my hands and knees. Then flat on my stomach. It gets so tight my arms become pinned in front of me. I cannot move them back to my sides. I try not to panic. There is the familiar acrid ammonia scent. It reminds me of the shock when I first started life drawing at the academy. I had pictured the painters during the Renaissance who worked in palatial ateliers with velvet and sun streaming through the high windows. What I found were dark little packed studios with models, sometimes taken from the street, unwashed and looking entirely out of their element. The rooms were overheated and stifling and the models would perspire heavily under the electric lights, making the air sour with sweat sharpened by the scent of turpentine and tobacco.

If I squirm and wiggle, there has to be a way out. Despite our prejudices bats are essential to the balance of nature. To our foodchain. To whole economies. They are in peril. Hanging by their feet with their gnomic faces and leathery wings and ultrasonic cries, the little licks of echolocation. They might be one of the most reviled groups of animals on earth.

My knees are shredded and I have cuts all down my arms when I finally come to the cave mouth. I put the earphones on and play back the tape. All I hear is the sound of my shallow breathing.

Later, in Paris, I will hand Ondine the earphones. She says she wants to listen to what noise pollution destroying bat populations in southern France sounds like. Little clicks and a low hum like a vacuum cleaner running, it turns out. I look around at the city that after all this time in the field seems full of barricades. Buildings, gutters, pigeon spikes, exhaust fumes, barred windows, sirens, pavement mottled with gum and spit. We sit and drink café crèmes at the Café de Flore where the waiters with their starched white shirts seem to be frozen in time. Though I wish I could walk all the way through the Marais, over the other side of Canal Saint-Martin, we take a taxi across the river. We pass the Palais Royal, and then a street of beauty parlours with coarse hair extensions inexplicably strewn on the sidewalk like horsetails. I see a man who holds a hamburger grinding out a cigarette with his foot like a chicken scratching at the dirt under a red and white Quick Burger sign. Paris can be both ancient and garishly new, never going through the awkward jerky passage of adolescence, just existing in two different times, one running under the other.

Ondine's flat is near the oldest hospital in the city. She has sculptures and books and neoclassical French chairs, silk dresses in the closet. She believes in working for people who pay. I scan the photos on the wall, mostly of her and her son, Lucien. Ondine never takes pictures of places, only people. Always get a person in the shot or it will look like a postcard, she has told me. There is a photo of us in Lapland. We are laughing, wrapped in enormous coats, huge hats, snow everywhere. We look happy. Younger. Every photograph has a bit of death in it, Barthes said. But here they seem like life to me. A child in a garden. Ondine standing beside her plane squinting into the sun, Ondine lying in sand with Lucien as a meaty baby in her lap. It occurs to me that I've never been surrounded with artifacts. I've never had a framed photograph of anything. I've always felt that life runs dry in a house, with its traditions and accumulated objects on display. But here I see how they can bring you into existence. She turns on the radio in her kitchen and opens the refrigerator. Debussy's *L'isle joyeuse* is playing. She immediately snaps it off. I can't listen to that. He was such a dog, she says and then laughs, uncorking a bottle.

Isn't he just like any other man who thinks he can cheat death by having mistresses? I mean you of all people should understand, I say teasingly.

I suppose living hidden lives makes it seem like you've outwitted all the poor sods that get only one.

Seem like?

Well, so often the first thing people do with their freedom is to just exchange it for another version of the thing that imprisoned them. Besides, we all know how it turns out in the end. Here, she hands me a glass.

Oh, it's good.

It's Greek, she says, showing me the label, though I find it hard to read with my minimum-efficiency eyes.

It tastes like pine needles.

Let's sit on the balcony.

Slowly night comes. There are people walking hurriedly home, a couple holding hands, a white Vespa zooms by. A teenager walks a small dog. An older man who looks like a playboy from a bygone era, the pomaded kind with a thin moustache and mahogany tan, buys a lottery ticket from the tabac. A young man eating a banana jumps off the bus at his stop and I am reminded of the fierceness of youth. The physicality of it. Everything they do is beautiful, every moment full of what is to come. How utterly sick of the body you become when you grow old. And conversely, how protective of your own thinking. Uninterested in fictions, I have no tolerance for novels now. I look to things for my own imagination to work through. Romantic slush holds the least appeal. I want information, things that are real. There are voices and laughter from nearby cafés, the honking cars, the *tap tap tap* of metal clinking down, closing the boulangerie below, the butter pastry smell still in the air. I think of how rarely I set foot in this arrondissement when I lived here. Where Tacita and Istvan first met, decades ago. How Paris can be different but still so much the same. The long colonnades of wet chestnut trees. The silver rooftops. The patisseries with names and interiors that haven't changed in three hundred years. Everyone revering a different era, always from a time that came before. I have never felt of this time. Not of any time. Why here? Why now? It is just an improbable series of events.

I'm going to Iceland next week for work, Ondine says.

Have you been?

She shakes her head.

It is like a fairy tale with all those fjords and volcanoes.

I always picture it covered in ice. Like that book you lent me. Which one?

About that big flood in Italy when millions of important books and masterpieces were underwater. And while they flew in all the experts and desperately raced against time trying to decide how to save them, they realized the answer was to freeze everything until they figured out what to do. Ivory?

Yes?

She looks at me, uncertain. Tell me. She takes a big sip from her glass. Are you happy?

Oh, Ondine, I say, not you.

Well I know you don't give anything away easily.

What about you? I say flatly.

She tucks her legs under her and takes another sip. Me? I don't know. I love to fly. There is Lucien. My boyfriend. All my boyfriends, she laughs. It's just. I see you, alone in your Spartan accommodation wherever you go, stooped over your work. And yet when I am with you, I always see the heart of another woman. One who likes to laugh. Enjoy herself. A strange expression on your face sometimes when you are in Paris, a smile that contains such warmth and then suddenly it goes out, like a match.

Don't you find, she says after a moment, that even when you're not working, you are always at work?

I don't separate the two.

So often I never hear back from you. Sometimes I worry.

About what?

You.

Don't. I am not grounded to this livelihood you know. We grant men a right to solitude, why can't we do the same for women? I exist more completely in it, I say. Though I suddenly wonder how she sees me. I remember reading about Nikola Tesla. Old and alone, living in a rundown hotel with a wounded pigeon he dragged back from Central Park. He never had a relationship his entire life but was said to have feelings for the pigeon. He said he loved her, *like a man loves a woman.*

I look down at my glass. You ask about happiness and I think, I am not really interested in happiness. Happy people have nothing to tell. They have been happy and that is— perfectly unproductive.

Well, she says, reaching over for the bottle. I have seen you working in Lapland when you came in with your face red from the cold, grinning. Playing me the reindeer sounds, madly drawing your ruled parabolas all over sheets of graph paper. Or when you figured out that foxes have that system of twenty vocalizations or whatever it was. She laughs. You know you are like the veery birds you have recorded. A songbird able to harmonize with itself. It's just that— She hesitates. I wonder sometimes. You wear your work like a shield. You have no— attachments. You resist mightily any talk of the past.

We sit in uncomfortable silence.

And— She hesitates again. I think that, for instance, you've probably always known that Eudoxie, my sculptor friend whom you've met before, was friends with Volkov's wife, the French writer. The one after the short-lived American—

Ondine, please.

You know she said you are the only one who ever left him.

I stare fixedly ahead. A woman waters her plants on the balcony across the narrow street. We are both silent. Ondine doesn't know what's going on inside of me, and I don't know what's going on inside of her, and the woman watering plants has started to talk to a baby two storeys below. I know that Eudoxie knew Lev's wife. Istvan did too. His letters always in their architect writing, in perfect French learned from Tacita. Lev's exhibitions. His images, fame, his name everywhere. These bright hard little facts recede against my own beliefs. The belief in what I chose. In wanting what I chose. I don't really know how people whose lives have a clear before and after can possibly continue to live the same life and still survive. For me it was necessary to alter everything. And speak of nothing. Of all the countries I have been to, conducting research in the field, the gold-eyed creatures darting through foliage, the conferences in cities scattered across the globe, the labs, and sound rooms, the whole world dropping away while I am filled with these sonorities, this opalescence. All of this against the ridiculous fact that we could never get very far from each other. These places and moments in time on which we have been caught. Of course I am not unaware that most people observe holidays, and fill their lives with firelit rooms, children running through—with laughter and meals. Children cast your life wider, you get to live beyond your own generation. It's so obvious why we domesticate. But these things to me are both dreamlike and dull. I would never have allowed myself to want them, let alone go near them. I have always traded on the notion that I did the right thing. But how does anyone know for certain that they have done the right thing?

Ivory, I can hear Ondine say, I don't mean to upset you. I only bring it up because sometimes I think that *you* might one day want to talk about it but not know how. Or find that it's too late, after all this time, she says, resting her chin on her hand. She gets up, putting her hand on my arm, and fills my glass.

I know she feels genuine concern. But my entire life I've scarcely been the object of it, and have no idea what to do with it now. I know that Eudoxie was friends with Lev's wife. The French writer whom I could never bear to read, though I heard she was good. He had wives, children, exhibitions, all of it. With him it was always a widening beauty. Nothing could be changed by an irreversible act, because that would be admitting the darkest version of life. I am not that different except in my work. I know I have been strict with myself in an unforgiving way. But I needed something more durable than love, more subterranean.

She takes the thin clip from her teeth and repins it in her hair. You want food?

I nod. I thought I was having a heart attack but I think I'm just hungry.

Don't joke about these things.

You know people give women bad advice, I call after her. She is inside for a few moments and comes back from the kitchen with cheese and olives and small red tomatoes on the vine, and two triangles of cake from the shop below. We eat with plates resting on our laps.

How do you mean?

We are so rarely left alone to love what we want to love, I say. Happiness comes from accepting the world the way it is. I've worked against this notion my whole life.

You seem to have no need to transmit anything to anyone. You know that's odd don't you? Maybe it's from all your time alone. Unlike someone like Eudoxie. I find her madly absorbing but also overstimulating. I always have to lie down right after seeing her. She holds the cake to her lips. But are you not worried that as you get older—

I am older, Ondine.

For most people, she ventures, work is utilitarian. Or I suppose, in some cases, decoration.

I don't know, I only think about what I'm going to do tomorrow. And what I want to do tomorrow is my work. Most times I am so interested in what I'm working on that I can hardly wait to get up and get at it in the morning.

That makes you a child, she laughs. Only children can't wait to get up in the morning to get at what they want to do.

Well isn't that the goal?

I guess because you're always on your own I just want to make sure you have what you need, what you want. I don't know, she sighs. What does anyone live for?

These are questions you don't really ask if you are truly occupied.

Most people never seem to have the time to consider it, she says, brushing her fingers on the parts of the geraniums that are dried out, the stiff petals scattering over the balcony.

Most people dull their wits, Ondine. They don't stop to think about just what it is that's disappointing them about their own lives. And they spend even less time on what to do about it. Though if they do, it is always something inconsequential, like a new town or a new job. It's at the end, when it is all running out, that people finally feel the weight of their own lives. And then they die leaving their plates and books and closets full of old clothes, and hearts blank as walls.

Starling

Wings across the star field,
across the crescent moon, closing the evening.

THE LINEN THREAD FINDS the holes Mme. Tissaud has
measured and punctured with the awl. She works on an order of
two dozen volumes bound in white that will eventually dwell in
the smoking room of one of her clients while I also sew.

Why white? I ask her.

His name is Angel. He is from Latin America and grew up
with the white libraries there. They are vellum or alum-tawed
bindings, not the tanned leather that we are used to here. She
describes the tanners who sell her leather—toothless, criminal
eyes, hairless up to their elbows from their arms in the chemical
baths—as arrested characters. *Un sale métier.*

Some of the leather is tanned with brains, she tells me, not
looking up.

That is grisly.

She shrugs. It is the fattiest organ.

What will Angel use these for?

We go to the things we know from childhood, she offers up as explanation, needle between her teeth. South America, Eastern Europe, and the Middle East are mostly white. Libraries covered in frost. Northern Europe's libraries are mainly brown, she says. It is the white libraries that have far less deterioration.

It makes me think of Archangel, the medieval Russian city near the White Sea where Lev has told me his father came from. Where deterioration does not occur in real time. Lev says that, as with the rest of Russia, Stalin is destroying their churches. Archangel's was dismantled by some of the men whose own grandfathers had built it. Pride in the shining domes now beaten with sledgehammers and then burned to the ground. The priest taken out and shot. Fire is so complete. Gleaming golden domes, and the sublime bells, once treated as living things, believed to be not a note, or a chord, but the voice of God. Lev said they smashed the bells and melted them into a tractor that gleamed gold along the dusty tracts of land.

I try to explain this to Mme. Tissaud. For someone who stands in darkness, Lev's ability to bring such beauty and jubilance seems a feat of alchemy. But his complexity startles.

In other words, says Mme. Tissaud, a real Russian.

I bristle at such generalizations, but with Mme. Tissaud, it is different. She eyes my hands. I know what she thinks. She thinks, How dangerously inhabited she is. I am sewing buttons onto Lev's coat. The needle stabs at the ends of my fingers. He didn't ask for this. I know that he will meet a woman in this coat. And though I feel no neutrality in this, I am complicit.

We stitch in silence, drinking our café crèmes that Mme. Tissaud prepared on her hotplate at the back of the atelier, with its smell of matches and violet lozenges. She takes theatrically loud slurps from her mug, letting the liquid sputter through her lips. This, from her, is endearing. The front windows are still warm with sun, though the grey looms.

Mother found my contact with nature almost carnal. Now Lev is the wilderness, only this one is hard going.

Mme. Tissaud gazes at the window growing moist as the darkness begins to fall and says quietly, *Entre chien et loup.*

Pardon?

The time when night moves in, *entre chien et loup.* Haven't you heard that expression before?

Why between dog and wolf?

The uncertain light, where you cannot distinguish one from the other, she says, going back to stitching. The shift from domestic to wild.

Though she carries with her a very cultivated set of beliefs like Mother, the way they are decanted is far less aggressive. With her it is all feeling.

Cocotte?

Yes.

Please be careful.

Of what?

Of him.

These words leave a small scalded space between us.

She makes these concise delicate prophecies. Ones that, despite her not wanting them to, become true.

In the evening, Tacita and I meet at the café where Istvan and the other artists are. She shows me a song sheet, starling feathers, and three miniature spoons she found in a rubbish bin, though she is unsure how she'll use them.

Group them together in one of your boxes. Call it Game.

This is why you have been called upon to contribute to the

publication—the only woman. You are always so sure. Like a man. Or a cliché of one.

What is the word for cliché in English?

There are some words that cannot be translated.

Why is that?

I don't know. There are just some points when a translator knows when to stop. Like cliché.

I cannot think of a single one other than that.

Avant-garde. Blasé. Coup. I could go on.

Of course. I always forget that you are a translator.

Was a translator, she says, tilted smile.

Anyway, I don't know if "like a man" is quite right, Tas. That some of these men we conspire and create art with, these men interested in invention and uncharted realms, still uphold such dated conventions. Is this what you are referring to?

I think you grew up unaware that you were meant to consider yourself inferior. You have always been fully formed. It's given you the confidence that most of us have yet to completely inhabit.

I've never thought about it.

See!

Well, that isn't entirely true. Remember when I asked why we don't study any women artists?

I remember. The instructor said, Because there aren't any. The room went silent. And then you said that there have always been female artists, but since females have been considered inferior animals, we don't know too much about them. Everyone laughed. He didn't like it. It's the kind of misstep you are only allowed once. I think it was the first time that he didn't know what to say.

But he did say. He sent me out for disrupting the class.

I remember what you looked like, she laughs. You looked like you wanted to stab him with a knife.

Well, normally I am rather quiet.

Really, I? she says, raising an eyebrow. What about Félix? Istvan told me that when some of you were in his studio, he turned to you and gave you a handful of centimes and asked you to get him cigarettes.

All I did was look around the room and see that I was the only woman. I said no.

Istvan told me what you said. You said, Bloody well get them yourself.

I see a flash of dark, like a crow's wing. I know that Lev is in the room. I have lost count since the last time I heard his voice. When we met in the night at Parc des Buttes Chaumont and he told me that in my white I looked like his dream. I appeared, illuminated, licking icing off a knife. He says my white fills an empty space, it is both a cure for isolation and a mystical pronouncement.

Since that night, I have been hiding in the ordinariness of my days. Absorbed but uncertain, like the morning after a dreamless night. I spend time illustrating, stitching. These things that occupy the hands but not the mind. Like Mme. Tissaud, who when not binding books is knitting. All the knitting. All those women who incessantly click their needles on the benches in the Jardin Luxembourg. I think some women knit because doing something with their hands means they are doing something with their lives. But not Mme. Tissaud. She makes things out of zeal.

I am possessed but do not possess. I have submitted myself to this, with all its risks and cruelties. None of the single sentences and kindness of Mme. Tissaud or the inspiring sistership of

Tacita can save me. I have brought it on myself. I haven't had a choice in the matter, though if I did, it would still be the same. I cannot get far enough or near enough. Everything depends on Lev, whether I see him or whether I don't. Each day the world larger/larger then smaller/smaller.

I've taken on a few commissions from the antiquarian book collector for biological illustrations of birds despite Lev's dismissal of such work. Mme. Tissaud lent me a copy of Audubon's *Birds of America* for reference. She tells me his project began by attempting to paint a bird a day. I see that he has used coloured pastels and layer upon layer of watercolouring to add softness to feathers, which is useful for the owls and herons I am drawing. I learn that herons have three-metre wingspans but weigh only a few pounds because they are mostly feather and large hollow bones. They move slowly but can strike like lightning. They are both optimistic and awkward. Under each coloured plate Audubon writes, *Drawn from nature.* I learn this means that he shot the birds. He killed them for pleasure and then took them home to stuff them and prop them into rigid poses by filling them with armatures of wire. There are no heads drawn back at majestic angles. The larger birds are contorted because he needed to fit them to the size of the page. It explains why you can look and look but what you are seeing is not really a bird. Where is the bird? Each illustration carries the weight of Lev's disapproval. He believes in submitting to your art, regardless of hunger, rent, or other practical matters. I realize that sometimes I am a bit afraid of him.

Lev. I turn his name over silently. It sounds so close to love, though I'm possibly the only one living in a language inside which this is true. There is this feeling, a feeling of the bone-deep exhaustion of translation. Would something occur differently with Lev and me if we could communicate using the language we spoke in childhood?

I can see him speaking to people I've never met. He holds their eyes. Everyone wants to be near him, not just women. Despite this, he is encircled in a kind of untouchable loneliness that I understand, so deep it goes underground. Like rainbows, Leni, who I met at Tacita and Istvan's dinner party, has explained. They are actually round, only we don't see the full circle because the horizon gets in the way.

We pour wine. Leni tells us that she is being made to pay back her grant money, even though, living frugally, she has spent almost all of it. Most of the time she is in libraries, clicking down the metal stairs with her documents. She has also been ordered to return to Germany. She confides to us that she won't. Our glasses clink in solidarity, but I can tell from Tacita's eyes that she is thinking the same thing I am.

It is no different with Lev. Threatening letters have come from Russia.

He made an installation, a complete departure from his usual work. It was a reanimation of a Russian folk tale. A grubby doll without clothes, encased in glass, slowly drowning in wheat, which he called *Untitled (Murder by Hunger)*. He said, How do you tell about Stalin's imposed starvation, which killed millions in an attempt to extinguish the Ukrainian independence movement, though miraculously, nobody outside seems to know? The Holodomor. Extermination by hunger. Aimed at the Ukrainian peasantry. How to tell about how they were destroyed? Stalin's men say people were so hungry they ate their own children. The Soviets falsified everything and banned all discussion of it. Lev's installation went directly against the party. And though Lev values only art that generates feeling rather than art created from religion or politics, this once, he cannot resist defying his own edict. Dictators decide anything. They are reanimators, he says. Under Stalin's rule the Church of the Nativity became a holding pen for circus lions, the Cathedral of Christ the Saviour the world's largest open-air swimming pool.

He has been under a watchful eye. They demand his return. But Lev says he will never go back. To where? Where he is from in Ukraine, everyone is now forced to speak Russian. They are told what to read, what to think. Entire histories altered. He finds this pretense of believing in an age of community repellent. What kind of community lets the individual perish? He lets people call him a Russian and doesn't correct them. His mind refusing blood. Refusing slaughter. Glassed-in and rigid as winter. He ignores the strings of Cyrillic, with its ligatures and clustered consonants, and drops them into the iron stove in his studio, setting them alight. *Whump.*

They are almost beautiful to me because the shapes against the thick white paper take the form of abstract geometry, not threats. He doesn't read them anymore. I see the unopened envelopes in the cold ash, powdered silver and propped like tombstones.

The swan-necked dancer kisses him and slips something into his pocket with her long fingers, but he does not pause in his conversation, which gives an odd intimacy to her gesture. Her shoes are high, she sways on heels sharp enough to stab anything underfoot. Tacita knows I am elsewhere. Under siege, I become quiet. I think, Do not show your arrow. None of this has been rash impulse. My very way of being has, whether I want it or not, prepared me for this, this singular devotion. First in the woods, then drawing. I can grow quiet in something, isolation canting me in deeper. The ability to shut out distraction and furrow into my purest form. Tacita can get me talking, and telling her makes everything seem less severe. She can get me out of my head, diverting the feeling that everything rests on the pleasure of the one moment I am with him.

Leni has returned with a large *pichet* of beer and three glasses and pours. The liquid foams and rises, streaming down the side of my glass. As I look for something to stop it, there is the dunk of a man's finger. Lev. He grins, saying it works every time. He leans down and kisses me decorously. His tongue grazes my lips, though no one can tell.

It is not possible to be grateful without showing it. I look up, collared light, whiteblue eyes, and I know what he thinks. He thinks, Didn't I just see you? And I think, How different your time is from mine.

Owl

White mask of feathers like a sonata by Ravel,
faded chords of the underworld.

STARS THICKEN, GALVANIZING THE SKY. Night jewels in.
We climb the stairs to Lev's room.

He makes hot verveine. Often it is this or Armagnac or any
number of other quarter-hour rituals.

I want to show you something.

He bangs a wooden stool from his studio on the floor in front
of me. Sit, he says.

He has something in his hands. It is the fabric of a scarf. He
ties it around my eyes. Blueblack filament, his smell touching my
face. I like that he wants to show me something I cannot see.

I hear little clicks. A low rasping croak.

I smell turpentine as serene glimmers of sound wash over me,
intoxicated, blood pounding, palms damp. Small, bleached
messages from the world, silences interspersed. Sound that
comes from such a singular plane it cancels everything else. In
some way it is like a last word, a held note, but its resonance is
something other than an instrument. It is a voice. There is

nothing remotely intellectual about it, though it does not come from the heart either. Instead it is something profound from the outside, like rain or wind. The silences are uneven. They make you wait. And there is a moment in which the ear no longer attempts to hear. A sound is formed by something else, coming in as from a dream.

All that emotion and I can only find words to say, Where did you find this?

A man selling 78s by the river. He said that two hundred years ago, it was debated as to whether all owls hooted in the key of B flat—also the key of trumpets and French horns. There was a man who recorded animal sounds with a gramophone.

It is the sound of owls and other nocturnal truths. When the needle finds the first ring of the record, it signals night like a stone. I am stunned by the sudden feeling that I am happier than I have ever been. That I have found something I've not yet known from regular life. But it is a dangerous joy. It is similar to those dreams in which you feel so strong and jubilant that it is ruinous, because you know something horrible is about to happen. The sensation is immediately followed by one of equal but shattering gravity. I will never be this happy again.

How?

Lev's hand detains my ankle. A hand that found a record, its flapping shape that maps my interior world.

Separation creates hunger. Fingers trace up my shin, slide across my hips, between my thighs. He kisses my mouth, my neck. My eyes slowly closing. The touch of his hands, the bones of his wrists. I feel his fingers, the power they contain. The touch of his tongue on my neck, his hand spreading wide under my back, tightening my body, gathering me into him. My mouth curves around him. Breathing slowed. And then I take him, my whole body toward him, our skin, our fingers, all the remote corners. Slow lasting waves of pleasure as though we are both encircled. Over and over again until we both fold into the darkness.

We are stunned awake by a bloodcurdling sound that is bone on wood. The knuckles of uniformed men in field-green who speak German, or is it Russian. In my half-sleep I wonder if it is not a horrible dream.

They come in the night, Lev has said. It demonstrates their power.

I try to suppress the choking that fills my throat until I cannot breathe. The water is too high. We are beyond our depth. Strings of words puncture the air like gunshots. Lev is pushed against the wall, the horrible, dull sound of a head hitting a hard object, a trickle of blood from under his eyebrow, each arm clamped with a square-knuckled hand. The men are large and with thick shoulders but Lev's body is taller and tensile and somehow more unpredictable than theirs. It provokes gratuitous force where none is required. There is no time for any kind of exchange. He is barefoot. They throw his boots down the stairs with unnecessary aggression. I see rolls of fat at the backs of their shaven necks, red and fissured, like corned beef. Lev looks back at me as he is forced out, two doors at right angles to each other. A foreign look on his face. A look that changes everything. I have never seen him caught. It is a plea that binds us.

All my senses are tuned to a higher frequency. Silence hurts my ears. I have Lev's blanket around my shoulders. The wool sharp against my bare skin. His presence strays over my body. I realize that I've never been in Lev's studio without him. Studio visits are, even between us, by invitation only. Only he has the key. That I am here alone seems a breach of protocol. Its flaking plaster and weathered planks spattered with paint and glue, and torn paper in piles reflecting the gleaming chaos of his interior world. But in his absence, the space appears immense. A cold ungilded squalor.

It is only when he is gone that I understand how completely altering his presence is. He has always come and gone, the time slipping. We are sensually bound. Voluptuous hours. Our skin together. But, I tell myself, there would never be a way for this to be constant.

I light upon the paper that Ulyana gave to Lev. It has fallen on the floor. I feel shame at once for considering reading it. I wouldn't know what it said, though no doubt it is not a harmless document. I swing open the iron door of the stove and gather the remaining unopened letters, taking them with me.

Out onto the street with intense sun. I had thought it was still night. As though it should remain as dark as when the sound splintered through the door. Neither day nor night. But it is startlingly bright. The light shot onto my face makes me squint. A ripple of high-pitched pain shoots behind my eyes.

I ask a man, wearing a navy overcoat with flat metal buttons that flicker sunlight into my eyes, for the time, as though it would matter. He could say anything and I would believe him. Instead he stops and presses a coin into my palm. Blanketed, unfocused eyes. I realize he thinks I've asked for money. That I'm a beggar. This actually makes me laugh the kind of half-crazed laugh that is useful in that it stops me from crying.

I decide to walk north across the river, purposefully avoiding the plenary comfort of Mme. Tissaud, the wide smiling wrinkles around her eyes. I continue until I am up the hill, Belleville, and then to the park. I try not to look at the parts of this city, every sidewalk, every pane of every building. Instead, there is deafening squalling metal. Shuffling feet. Half-smoked cigarettes ground out with hate. Heavy overcoats weighing down skeletal shoulders. Hats stuck with feathers yanked from the backsides of extinct birds. Gun-hipped men. Thin-hearted women. Dirty-faced children never staying in school. Louse combs. Breathing, cracking sidewalks. Greasy handkerchiefs. Slanting wind. Spitboxes. Downtrodden men who open their trousers. Brown-streaked statues. Castrated newspapers behind clouded cracked glass.

I am walking so violently that drops of perspiration dampen my forehead, under my arms, and I am glad. I want purification. The sun is warm. Bad things don't happen in the sun, I reassure myself. At the foot of the park I walk directly into a charcuterie and pocket a jar from its sparse shelves. It clinks against the centime and I realize I could have used the beggar money. I am sensible, even as a lunatic. I stop only when I reach the top of the rocky belvedere. It honours Sibyl, who wrote her prophecies on leaves and let the wind scatter them. On this bench Lev and I once came to each other as in a dream. He walks toward me and I marvel at the precision of his body and how his limbs seem to be catching the entire wheel of the moon. I breathe deeply. My mind stills.

Ivory. He is telling me about a new technique with ink that takes only a few seconds, each one a *mise en acte*, he says. Ephemeral. More about the way the act of making them is occurring. Everything left to chance. But he likes it because the fleeting moment he is creating exists strictly in the eye of the maker.

Of course, they are just inkblots, he says. But they are footprints to absence. The presence of absence. Unlike most people, he believes creation is about subtraction, not addition.

I unscrew the jar and scoop out the mustard with two bare fingers and swallow. Again. A ripping burn in my stomach. And then the vomiting starts. I lean over the rail, above the manmade lake. I want to jolt out of this sudden sorrow. That someone can just suddenly be gone. Always the simplest things are the hardest to grasp.

The park was just as I'd hoped. Balding gothic hills, cliffs and streams and exotic trees from the Orient that perform out of season. At night it has a dark energy, like how even gentle creatures can scare you after dark. I take the soft paths to find Lev on the cliffs above. Feeling the blood that moves underneath. I lie down, my face against the cold hard stone bench, so tired I can only think with my eyes closed.

I can tell from the look on their faces that Tacita and Istvan are frightened by how I come to them. This much I can see. But they remain calm, because someone must remain calm. They also do not judge, which means seeing in parts. Seeing in parts being worse than seeing nothing at all. There is solace in Tacita and Istvan's apartment, its pale, bright rooms. The rows of Tacita's objects, the Poulenc nocturne on the radio, the smell of food, all the human things that can wend away sorrow. Tacita cuts a thick slice of bread and hands me hot tea. I cannot eat. They are the ones who uncover the names of those to whom I need to write to plead for Lev's release. The address of the camp where I can send provisions, art supplies, letters. Though in the end, everything will be met with nothing.

And when I return to my studio, Mme. Tissaud has left a hyacinth, its scent pressing through the room. There is a cream wool cape with white stripe embroidery. It is folded on my chair alongside two jars. One of dried cornflowers (blue) and the other of hawthorn berries (yellow). These offerings, found and homemade, come not out of a spirit of thrift, but of goodness. They are majestic and hopeful.

There is still a part of me that responds to the idea of creation. I force myself to grind and then mix pigments in the back sink late in the night, quietly so as not to wake Mme. Tissaud. I wipe the brushes, one after another, on a ripped piece of cloth. The water runs cold for whole minutes, it numbs my hands and escapes thinking. I take small glass jars and fill them. A drop of ox gall. Bright colours glimmering life back in. A slash of moon throws light onto the countertop. Everything gleaming like the new illuminated sphere of Earth ascending in the Hieronymus Bosch painting that I like, because along with destruction, it reveals new stages of existence. I gather everything in my arms and walk quietly up the wooden staircase. Each board creaking from all the people who have walked before.

In my room, I place a prepared board on the wooden lip of my easel. I dip the brush Lev gave me, tapered and sable—it pulls the paint more than all my brushes combined—and begin the silent work. Quick precise strokes. Almost like drawing at first. Then I thin the mixture, add salt and poppy oil. Something clouded and living happens between my careful composition. I let it come. Time vanishing inside the work. As in childhood. Time stalls, then speeds up, never in the right order. I take another smaller brush adding deep red. Translation is the most difficult. The space between what you carry in your mind and what you can put down. I know right away if it is working. But not by eye. When we walk by a Vermeer or Velázquez, I tell Tacita that when I get a burning feeling in my chest, I know that what I'm looking at is good.

I can't decide what colour it needs. I think of Lev always urging me to put on paint.

But you can't just end a painting by suddenly throwing something at it.

Why not?

And then it surprises me. Despite the anguish, I enter the space like a new year, pronouncedly, full of belief. I realize that with Lev my solitariness had been violated. Everything takes on new shape, and for a moment, I find my pitch. The painting is working, I am barely mixing, using the crude pure colour from the tubes, layering. Only one touch of black in the yellow makes an electric green that I need. It gives the painting weight and form. Blueblack bodies of trees have a new layer of soft grey. Colour becomes an armature buried under colour. It connects these elements that have no necessary relation in the world, a moment of beauty wrested from fear. But there is a danger in that beauty can also disguise the truth.

I've just learned that Lev's last name, Volkov, means wolf in Russian.

Of course it does, says Tacita. And we all know that no one can tame a wolf, she jokes, as we sit in Jardin des Plantes, days before.

But he lives in a city. Shouldn't he now be domesticated? I say, reaching across for her pack of cigarettes. Perhaps more like a dog?

Even dogs are recently wild, cherie. They are stoic creatures. They show only one sliver of what's really going on with them.

I take Tacita into the zoo. All this glass having replaced the bars. They have created a living tableau of animals, shielding us from their disagreeable odours. It looks more like a fine art museum.

Tas, I think we should alter it all.

How?

Well, they contrive to exploit. Placing large animals in the centre. Surrounding them with lawns of small animals to make them seem larger and more exotic than they are.

A tableau of a different scale.

An altered symphony. Turn the insignificant voices into first violins, I say. As when Millet painted *The Gleaners*. To everyone, they were just worn-down peasants, scrambling for the fallout after the harvest, the lowest rung of society. People said they looked as if they were painted with the earth they were sowing. He gave them the attention and size of a religious, mythical painting. He painted them as royalty. Those peasants contained the knowledge of weather and land and living, and also of misery, but were utterly invisible to society. And how the bourgeoisie hated that painting, most likely because it made them feel shame.

What are you suggesting?

Your animal portraits, and my sound transcriptions. We can put image and text together. Hang images beside writings. I could construct the animal sounds into languages, with symbols and whole alphabets. We could break down all the formal elements, these inherited conventions that don't speak to us. We could get to the heart through eyes and ears. Make something outside of existing order. Almost spiritual.

She closes her eyes in thought.

Tas, don't you sometimes wonder why for centuries all art, paintings, music, has been produced for the indoors? Maybe that's why I always liked the cellist-with-birds concert. I would like to go to a gallery where they make you leave. *Take the south door, walk six steps, follow the sidewalk until you see a path in the courtyard. If you haven't been in a forest for a long time, stop. Listen.* You'd pick up irate curses, the occasional drunken shout, some poor bird struggling to have its voice heard and then it could slip through the green and back to your paintings.

It could be like an undersong to the paintings and alphabets, she says. We could take something, like a Stravinsky rhythm, and use that structure to fill it with your pitches and then make part of the whole experience be an act of framing.

But there should be an element of disturbing rather than completely comforting people.

She nods. It could be a museum of sound, the art in the experience of it. How Duchamp always says, non-retinal. Maybe I abandon my paintings entirely. It could be for the ear-minded. We could write out instructions. Like a star chart. But I wonder, how would we convey the sounds? Recording equipment is scarce. I have only ever found one ruined cylinder, she says, holding her cigarette to her lips.

Maybe we could instruct the people at the gallery to make the sounds, I say.

She stubs out her cigarette and straightens, looking at me, her whole comportment almost heraldic, saying slowly and purposefully, Yes.

Magpie

Corvidae. Frantic, jumping around fields then forming great clouds in the sky. Recorded early, 5 a.m. (Compare with recordings from Bitterroot National Forest, Custer National Forest, Helena National Forest.)

I DRIVE SLOWLY, obeying every signpost. I hear the lurch of the engine fan despite having taken the key out of the ignition. The seat skates backward, bumping up against the worn leather of the backbench when I remove the cuttingboard. I pull myself out of the car gripping the cool metal at the top of the door and shiver at the dawn air. Age makes you sensitive as a Geiger counter.

When I slip the key into the lock, the door is already open, which stops me. I know I left it locked. The American insists there are thieves, though I question what exactly they would want from her overstuffed shelves full of cheap crockery. It looks like the work of a magpie. The love of small bright objects that compel it to steal, with all the associated risks and triumphs.

Magpies are one of the few animals that can recognize not only themselves in a mirror, but that what they are looking at is a mirror.

I remember once aiming my microphone at the sky and

picking up thousands of their flight calls, the black-and-white bodies across the landscape like writing. They have the ability to mimic and layer sound. One shiny black head darted through the foliage startling me, calling, *Kill her! Kill her!* Well not exactly. But I had a nervous energy. I'd left the house with my nightgown tucked into my jeans. I had just heard that my first cymatics paper would be published, and I had received more funding from the university for the sound lab and field research. It occurred to me that I might be a magpie too. But the thrall of accomplishment can fill you the way love does. Still, there were rewards and no one to tell. I put the headphones on. The recorder picked up the bumping sounds of a tractor rolling downhill in the distance. There was a slight buzzing sound that released something in my throat.

In Mexico, the journalist had the bad luck to arrive on a day I wanted to see no one. I was in the middle of the cymatic translations. I had been offered a research residency through the Library of Bird Sounds in Mexico. I had been using a metal plate with a thin layer of sand hooked up to an amp and speaker. The conservatory had dispatched a crew and we had been photographing and filming the patterns for the past ten days. The whole setup filmed from above with a copy stand. They had all left the night before, and I was looking forward to being alone.

There is a dampness to every object. All my books are beginning to smell of mould. I lay them out on the grass in the sun.

The journalist was sent to interview an illustrious biologist but instead comes upon a woman in bare feet knocking sand out of her boots outside a wooden cabin with a corrugated metal roof. Books are spread everywhere in the grass. She asks me, Do you know if Dr. Ivory Frame is staying here?

The journalist's name is Marisol. She was born in Paris to a Mexican mother. It's a story for a magazine in New York that Valentina says is read by everyone.

I instantly bristle. It's not scientific.

Relax, Ivory. They have a wide readership.

Tell them I'm a hermit, I say to Valentina. When I am interviewed, it is always Paris, the famous artists, that people are most interested in. Why? I think irritatedly. It is so utterly unrelated. Besides, it is always something ridiculous. How they heard a woman say that when you made love with Brancusi you absolutely were not allowed to touch his beard. Or that Picasso incessantly wore shorts because he thought his legs his most beautiful part.

It will be good for the project.

When Valentina says good, she means money.

Marisol is embarrassed by her mistake. You don't look like your picture, she says, shading her eyes with her hand. I'm sorry, is this a bad time? She offers to come back later.

I squint at her. She has thick black hair cut to her chin, tucked behind her ears. She wears a white Edwardian blouse, army pants, and a white-patterned kerchief knotted at her neck like a cowgirl. She looks much younger than she probably is. It must have taken her hours to get up here. She looks nervous. Her lovely thick Spanish accent makes it impossible to be angry.

Okay, okay. I wipe my hands on my shirt. You're here. You might as well come in. Would you like something to drink? Coffee?

Yes. Thanks. If it's not too much trouble, she says, following me through the screen door that slaps shut behind us. Will you go out in the field later? I was hoping to—

I've been back for hours, I say, not turning around. I like working when my shadow is ahead of me.

Sitting at the table, she aims the recorder toward me and says, When the red light goes on, if you could state your name, profession, location, date—

The kettle whistles. I get up to switch off the burner. Sunlight finds my hands as I pour the boiling water. The thick melodious screeches of parrot-infested trees outside. Willing my attention back toward her questioning.

Ivory Frame. Acoustic biologist. Outside of Las Pozas, near the village of Xilitla, Mexico. 1982. July. Not sure which day. I watch the familiar whorl, the needle bouncing to my voice— tape-recorded like all the other animals.

I am obsessed with language obsolescence. Threatened languages have a right to be protected. The Conservatory for Extinct Animals is affiliated with the university in Oslo and works in a number of areas, including habitat restoration, educating citizen scientists toward land management, analyzing data for shaping future conservation. And then there is my strange branch of bioacoustics and the dictionary.

When did it begin?

Well I acquired my first tape recorder in 1953 and have been recording animals ever since.

Why?

When the last speaker dies, it's as though the language never existed.

The project gave you agency.

What do you mean by agency?

There is the slow blink of the metal fan blades that Marisol will hear when she plays back the tape in her cramped apartment in Tribeca.

Why are you using cymatic imagery now?

It means I can work with a solid, reproducible image, not a

fleeting noise, which was all I went on before. I can see the imprint of the animal's sound on air, in water. It helps with deciphering their languages, like the low-pitched ruffle of a peacock's tail or the echolocating clicks of dolphins.

Can you explain cymatics?

It means wave in Greek. Founded by a Swiss scientist who was a disciple of biology's Nostradamus, Rudolph Steiner, famous for his 1923 bee lectures—*the hive is permeated by love.* He also wrote about the power of symmetrical images of sound waves. The patterns can be explained with classical physics, but it promises something else. A way of gaining a deeper understanding of communication—affirming the substance of the unseen.

Can you give me an example?

The forms of snowflakes and faces of flowers take on their shape because they are simply responding to sounds in nature.

She asks about all the usual things. We discuss endangered species, conservation, my fieldwork. She edges in closer, I see the flicker in her eyes. Do you ever feel you've had to sacrifice your personal life for your work?

Woman scientists who marry don't stand a chance. Men can get married. They can have children and go right on being scientists. Though this is not what I say. Instead I pick up her recorder, walk over to the window screen, and hold it. Through the cathedral-like, broad-leafed trees, the vociferous sounds of birds, frogs, and insects fill the room. The roar of bottle-green parrots like a waterfall.

I place the recorder back on the small table. These sounds are languages being communicated that we all might be able to learn from, they can show us a kind of cultural evolution. But most of the time we are not paying attention. We should be worried because unless we control our activities, we will lose all this, I say, gesturing outside. You ask about personal sacrifices, and I don't really know what to tell you. I know that love has a language that starts, and stops, but these languages. They ask for nothing. They fill you full of wonder. They hold you like a spell.

You've been cited as a protester because of your activism on certain issues. Does that bother you?

I prefer interventionist. Protesting is far too submissive a word. It implies that there is something to protest against. I'm the conservative here. I'm conserving. It's the radicals who are destroying the earth.

Marisol slips her shoes off her feet and perches on the chair, resting her chin on her knees. Her view of me has already shifted. She feels that any work that leads someone to a place like this, with its dangling charms, is worth the price. She has read of the nearby Las Pozas where the eccentric British aristocrat rumoured to be the illegitimate son of a king of England spent his fortune creating a surrealist Xanadu up here in the rainforest high in the Sierra Madre. He is half the time unaware that there are parrots perched on his head and arms as he races around conceiving and constructing. She had planned to spend time there before heading back to Xilitla, but feels the pull of the work, her subject. Her editor had told her that no one has ever got the biologist to speak about her past and thinks that Marisol, with her degree from the Sorbonne, her three languages, and her disarming approach, can.

On the third day Marisol is here, I feel more open and unaware of the recorder. I am enjoying her company. She has scrambled through the forest with surprising agility, scaling the steep slopes without complaint. I can see scratches up her arms, insect bites on her neck. Her quick intellect and curiosity are the virtues of a promising scientist, though she seems to know a lot about art. She spent time in Paris, going to galleries with her father. He took her to see the thick black paintings of Pierre Soulages. She tells me she was a tomboy who shoplifted books and wore an orange string around her neck for a whole year. We talk about our favourite places in Paris. I show her how to work the cymatics equipment and I watch her grow quiet when she sees the striking patterns of the green-blue macaws. She says she began in film, but found it deadly boring, all the downtime. She worked with a famous director whom she overheard saying that he was tired of making movies. Most of the people who work in film are uneducated, he said. In another time, they would be called carnies. She says she is possibly not cut out for journalism though it is the only way, so far, that she has been able to make money from writing. In a story meeting, she pitched an idea about an elderly somewhat obscure poet she loved who had just died. All her editor said was, Death is not a story. Now if it happens in a way that is unexpected, *that* is a story.

That night, we drink good tequila she brought with her and I play the only music cassettes that still work in all the damp— Sidney Bechet, Edith Piaf, Patsy Cline.

> *I've got your picture that you gave to me*
> *And it's signed "with love" just like it used to be*
> *The only thing different, the only thing new*
> *I've got your picture, she's got you*

The darkness falls to a sliver moon and all the glittering southern stars, and the rainforest pitches readjust. A slow seep of warmth, that familiar languid buzzing. Marisol's cheeks are flushed. The chair creaks loudly every time she shifts position. She tells me that most writers she knows in New York are odd.

They can be smart and charming and then while you are talking to them, they suddenly bolt out of the room, like a cat. She says that she finds dancing spiritual. Her hair falling into her face. She laughs and says, This place is a dump.

Well Marie Curie discovered radium in an unheated shed, I say.

I need to know all the facts. I leave tomorrow so early.

Fact? Nothing is a fact. I inadvertently let out a huge yawn.

Oh I'm keeping you up.

Well I go to sleep and wake up with the light. Like a chicken.

What's this one? she says, noticing a faint latticed coil of marks.

Monarch.

I love them, with their Halloween colouring. My mother always talked about the Day of the Dead celebrations in Mexico City. How millions of monarchs would fly, without fail, to the mountains on that day. They believe they are the souls of the dead returned.

That makes perfect sense, I say as she refills my glass. Psyche, the goddess of the soul in Greek mythology, is depicted as winged like a butterfly.

Ivory?

Yes?

Tell me about Lev Volkov.

I swallow. There is a pause. I hear the click of the fan blades. I don't talk about him.

When was the last time you saw him?

I fix my eyes ahead. Near the end of the war, I say dryly. Lisbon.

Was it war that separated you?

My body stiffens.

I read that you left him. But I also read that he became engaged.

Marisol. If you mention him again, I will have to ask you to leave.

This jolts her awake, shakes off the alcohol. She knows she's done the wrong thing. And she will continue to; when her editor asks her for the Paris details she will write in as much as she can find. The truth is, she interviewed Lev years ago for an art magazine out of Paris and found him impossible. She thought this was the sort of thing she would talk about with Ivory. They would grow serious and laugh and find the heart of it. But now she realizes she was mistaken. She knows not to mention it.

She rewinds the tape and presses play. Why the dictionary?

I breathe out. In the work, I am calm. Extinction, I say. If we ignore the past, we are bound to make the same mistakes over and over again. The work is a protest against forgetting.

Forgetting what?

The animals came in singing and now they are silent.

Can you explain this link, the notion of loss and extinction.

I once researched the explorers who travelled along a river in what is now Venezuela, in a place of astonishing linguistic diversity, as the tropics are. There were two warring tribes. The one tribe had recently wiped out the other. The explorers walked through the jungle in a cloud of phosphorus-green parrots that spoke an unintelligible language. When they asked the surviving tribe what language it was, they shrugged and said it was that of the tribe they had killed off. These had been their parrots. The tribe was dead, they said, and their language would die too with the last of their birds.

When I sit with the recording equipment the next morning, I have an odd intensity that sometimes happens the day after too much drink. The body more alive, more open, though there is a faint shrill pain under my skull. Marisol already on her plane has forgotten her notebook. I flip it open to see if there is a phone number or address.

FRAME PROFILE

Tropical rainforest high in the Sierra Madre.

The cabin is tiny, has crumbs around all the edges, filmy scraps of food on the floor, field books stacked, held together with rubber bands. Two buckets collect water that comes through the roof. Sand, recording equipment piled in every corner, stacks of cymatic images on letter paper — everything in a state of moisture.

The images are strange, compelling though — everything gets grouped in either EARTH/SKY/WATER. They read like a poem.

She seems to keep most of the information in her head.

She wears worn canvas pants and a blouse buttoned to the top, sleeves rolled to her elbows, old-timey lace-up boots. Magnificent mass of white hair in a loose Victorian bun. High cheekbones, deep eyes. Something startling about her looks. None of her pictures look like her. What is it? She always looks (in the photos) like something caught — prey (or is it just that she refuses to give parts of herself away?).

She often describes her body as having a buzzing almost mystic energy (she describes feelings as mystic) which she said a doctor tried to dismiss as a symptom from a parasite she picked up from contaminated water once.

She moves like a teenager through steep inclines of forest, I am breathing heavily, always behind her. Born in 1917. Sixty-six? (Check.)

Describes the jarring sound of a tropical bird (binomial Latin name, look up) as the sound of a child cutting a tooth.

The intensity of her gaze is almost impossible to withstand (where to put? beginning?).

Uses the word dazzle—as in, I have been drinking rosemary tea, hot water and herb, to dazzling effect.

Things she says that I'd like to use in a story: "uncommon energy," "its beauty hurt me."

She shows me her logs of recordings with field book marginalia. Ex: Lonesome elephant walking into a storm. Recording picks up wind rippling its ears like sails.

Times she withdrew from social contact altogether. She's sane though. Her mind moves faster than mine, finding it hard to keep up. She said she went mad. She said it exactly like that, and then nothing more. Must find record of this. Is there a record?

She plainly prefers the company of animals to people.

She has the self-sufficiency of an animal. She has no need
for society, the same as Volkov. What is the quote?
"People who choose to be alone are either an animal
or a god." (Kafka? Aristotle?)

When I showed her a photograph of a black Soulages
outrenoir painting, she said cryptically, "It was clearly
executed by someone who understands winter light."
(Find quote of when he was drawing black lines of ink
as a boy. Sister: What are you making? Pierre: Snow.)

Called artists aggressive competitive loners, but in the next
sentence said how much she— (I can't read this next line.)

Awkward coldness, nervous silence around anything
personal. She has developed a kind of carapace of
detachment.

Possessed.

Used to working without electricity. (Good with a
cookstove.)

There is something around the dictionary of animal
languages that she can neither explain nor control; it's as
though we are in the room with a live bird. She becomes
rapt (displacement/cessation/trance—the state of being
outside of oneself).

Her reverence for nature and animals borders on mystical.

When I ask her what her favourite animal recording is, she says, I don't answer those kinds of questions. (She later acknowledges that in a woman, this kind of remark comes off as rude.)

Sometimes her responses are confounding: e.g., Me: Can you talk about this duty to archive?

Her: Somebody once said that every atom of our bodies was once inside a star. Maybe that is why I am collecting these sounds. Like starlight they give light, despite the black.

Bangs at the sink washing dishes as I transcribe. I've said the wrong thing. Cold fury at the mention of Volkov—after all this time. I don't tell her about my interview with him in Paris. I mistakenly thought I would. She is careful. Her life is concealed. Even to her.

She is like a piece of lightning. Or an old saint. Wounded and then healed.

Crow

Undersong rambling, improvised, coarse.
Nose-diving, full glitter, into the blanks
between clouds.

IN THE DARK I see his wild eyes, though he wears them like a secret. After all this time I think I have bits of his body wrong only it is not my mind but his body that has changed. Thinner, harder, like a knife. He won't talk about what happened. He won't say. His spirit is untouched, unaltered as it has always been.

Without clothes, his ribs sharply outlined. A cage that surrounds his heart. I take him in, so stunned I cannot move or talk. Understanding that for now, in this moment, he is here.

He kisses my mouth, the skin by my ear, my throat. His hand on my chest holding me against the wall, and then pressing me into his arms.

I think of how I would have been at this hour, alone in my room. How I might gaze out at the cold streets or paint or fall into a state of lassitude. How when I switch on a desklight I move through the room as though he watches me. I write these unanswered letters full of their parched little questions and longing. All the feeling that I try to contain within two pages of white paper disguised by neutral tones, strictly practical language. The word love is never written. Though it's not a word he would ever use. People love cake, he says coldly. And for me, it is only that words never seem to match what I feel. They read them, I'm told. But there needs to be something, two points in time that connect us. To know that suffering has witness. I take it as a form of punishment. Letters being proof of separate geographies.

He sees all I have done, the work inhabiting the space, the smell of turpentine, notebook bloated with scribbled pages. An output that twins his own. This long arduous distance, the not-knowing. Separate, we have conducted ourselves in exactly the same way, but I wonder if he sees that alone, I have the strength and spirit to give myself to my work in a way that cannot happen in his presence.

He shows me a dark circle on a background, thick and white and illuminated, like a moon or sun, his images like something anticipating photography. His cramped, French handwriting below.

Little by little the sky is clearing. It alone.

His eyes focus on the canvas set on my easel.

That is the bird in this painting, I say. Though in my book of sound I wrote out the voices, in different parts, like a symphony. The notes like mysterious symbols on the stiff white sheets, some of them only half-filled, the little black rounds sitting on the thin lines like tiny crows on telegraph wires.

Against the silver sky, I saw from my studio window a crow catch itself on wires, then fall to the ground, electrocuted. They can only be electrocuted if they spread their wings to touch two wires, the current passing through a vital part of their body. The bird lay in the alley where a large group of crows gathered around it, all at the same time. They dotted the trees, assembled on the pavement, feathered the cars, and began to caw, a deafening, cacophonous noise, and then fell completely silent. This repeated every day, with the numbers of the group slowly dwindling. The body eventually disappeared, and the gathered cawing crows fell to a single crow. This solitary bird returned at the same time every day for months to the spot where the crow had fallen dead.

You are right, he says, looking at the painting. I wait for what he might say about the work. But after a lengthy silence he says, Crows have funerals.

I pour wine into chipped goblets I found on the street and pass him one. It is small in his hand. It fills me with a sudden dread. That he can just disappear and reappear, and I can stare at his hands, sometimes real, sometimes imagined.

I hear the rhythmic rise and fall of his chest, audible within the quiet walls. This small triumph. I see ink up the inside of his forearms, hieroglyphs on skin. Bouts of suffering, for him, have always been a source from which he draws. Suffering being a choice, whereas pain is not. The idea of creation that gets him through. And for the first time, I realize that it is possible that the same is true for me.

When we first met, Lev said that he always sensed he was doomed, predicting a short but intense life. And I said no, my fingers on his jawbone. There is no death in this face. Though now we would never say such things.

It is moonless and cold when I hear Lev's voice in the night.

Ivory, I want to tell you about my wife.

I say nothing. The word deadly, like air in a vein.

Aglaya. I have read that in Greek, this means beautiful. I do not want to know if the Russians ascribe the same definition. I try to remember what Mme. Tissaud says. That jealousy is the sharpest emotion because it is love and hate at the same time.

Aglaya is not from Vislok, the village in Ukraine where I am from, he says. She grew up in Moscow, though spent much time at her family dacha where she eventually stayed after her father died. In school she was forced to recite what would become Party-approved lines of Pushkin and Turgenev from memory.

My father was Russian, my mother Ukrainian, but we lived in a village claimed by the Habsburg Empire. So when I was nineteen, my brother Metro and I were forced into the Austrian army. For six months they taught us the arts of war. They transferred us to Peremyshl on the border of Ukraine and Poland, and then sent us to the Russian front. We were stationed in the Voluska province that had formerly been part of Ukraine. It was a bitter experience. The winter was severe. We stayed on a flat windswept plain and had to dig a trench two metres deep and two kilometres long to the kitchen. The cook rode a flea-bitten mare to deliver our food, along the sunken highway that became slick with mud from all the snow. Each soldier was given one chunk of cold meat, served raw in the middle of the night to avoid detection by the Russians. We were there for seven months until we marched on foot to Chernivtsi, a small town near Romania. When the Cossacks attacked the army we retreated again across field, forests, and streams until we came to a province in southern Ukraine near the River Prut. The Russians broke through the lines and surrounded us at such close range that I was struck from behind with a rifle. When I turned around, all I could see were Russian troops. I dropped my gun. My brother did the same. We were immediately taken prisoner. We were indebted to the soldier for sparing our lives. He could have shot us on the spot. It would have been easier for him. Even though we were part Russian, even though we spoke their language, we became their prisoners.

We were taken to the Russian province of Peskovsko where large land-owning barons began selecting us in groups of ten for service on their estates. At that time we had an old woman as the cook, who for every single meal made a fish soup. The soup contained not only the body of the fish but the head, eyes and all. We could hardly bear to look at it. At last, one day, we refused to eat the soup. The foreman called our baron, who summoned his wife. She came out to the fields brandishing a wooden spoon, in a great rage, and scolded us. You Ukrainians don't even have corn bread to eat and yet you refuse to eat our soup! But they did, after that, stop serving the soup at every meal.

Metro befriended one of them and traded his beloved pocket watch for paper and charcoal for me. I had always needed to draw, and once hoped to study art in Petersburg. Still, I never stopped drawing even where there was nothing. I had read of Japanese calligraphists keeping a diary in water on stone. Everything evaporates, they say, but if you drink with your eyes, you remain full.

We never even met our baron. Instead it was his foreman, who made us call him sire and every day would wake us up at three in the morning by kicking our straw mattresses on the floor, yelling, Get up, you miserable living corpses!

It was a bleak winter. Because everything was done by hand, wheat was cut in stages, and went well into winter. We would haul the sheaves from the fields in a sleigh and pile them in the second floor of a granary. Upstairs was very hot by a stove that a worker kept burning all night. This was the way they dried the grain. We would then toss sheaves down from the second floor. The millwheels smelled like wet wheat husk. It was so hot on the upper floor that when we finished late at night we were soaked with perspiration. On the walk back in the dark, our clothes would freeze to our bodies.

After some time, the neighbouring farmer invited us to a village dance. We were reluctant to accept the invitation because we were dressed in the shabby clothes of prisoners of war. When we told the wife of the oldest brother why we weren't going, she proceeded to lend us suits that belonged to the youngest brother, who was at the German front.

Dressed in these suits we eventually went to one of the dances. Women wore embroidered dresses and fur-collared coats. In stark contrast to the life we were living. Eventually a young woman came up to me. She stood for a long time in front of me and then I saw something well up in her. Her face graven. Then full of fury. Her mouth breaking up the words into sharp syllables. She was, I discovered, the fiancée of the man whose suit I was wearing.

It was there we first met Aglaya. She had pale gold hair down to her waist. She was small but strong. Though she now lived in a cottage, she had once known a different Russia. As a girl she had heard of parties where swans of ice had been encrusted with caviar. Cut glass dripped from the ceilings. All the gleaming, opulent things that can make a person mad with greed.

After her father died she moved to the dacha with her aunt, who then caught pneumonia that severe winter and died, leaving her orphaned. The house had wooden soffits and shutters carved in intricate patterns of animals and flowers, like something from a fairy tale. There were birch groves and high yellow flowers in summer. She felt safer at the dacha, though alone, away from the political turmoil of Moscow. She knew the name of every plant that grew near her. After the winter thawed into spring, there was always a scent of bruised herbs she'd picked from the tangle of wild plants around her house. When food became scarce, she would confect large meals foraged from the woods and crack on top of each dish a stolen egg. Salads and stews made of thick weeds. After what we'd been starved of and then fed as prisoners of war, their simple elegance was almost sacred.

Aglaya stood at the doorway to the dance. Striking in her heavy dark velvet coat, with snow-dusted hair. It wasn't just beauty. It was inward and outward. When she left the snow filled in her footsteps, making me question if she'd ever even been there.

After a meeting of the kulaks, the well-off farmers, they determined we were to cut wood in the forests that belonged to the nobility. The woods were thick with small-leafed trees bold enough to grow in the cold. Then, Metro and I went to cut wood in the lord's forest. For three solid weeks, we cut wood and piled them into cords.

Because they weren't feeding us, Aglaya prepared meals and brought them to us, carrying with her a hoe so that if caught, she could say she was going to dig potatoes, then still being pulled from the cold earth. Because we feared for her safety, we told her not to come.

When we returned in our sleighs to carry the wood, the lord appeared with his shotgun. You have no right to this wood! he yelled. He proceeded to tell us that a large German army had invaded Russia and decided that all civilians were to be restored their former rights. And so we returned home with empty sleighs. The German authorities announced that all prisoners of war had to report to German army headquarters for return by train to Ukraine.

Metro and I were immediately conscripted as machine gunners and then sent out to the Italian front. Though the war had ended, our commanding officer neglected to inform us. For some reason, he thought it would save our weapons and equipment by having us eventually return them to Austria via Italy. But when the Italian army caught up with us at Trieste we were disarmed, because our commander ordered us not to fire on the Italians. They marched us back into Italy as prisoners of war.

We were punished by our captors. They did not feed us, and kept us marching for eight straight days. We were made to sleep in fields without any cover, through rain, sleet, and snow. Many of our soldiers became very ill.

I remember those eight days walking. They made us go through the same villages and towns that Austrian armies had ravaged during the war. They threw things at us. Rotten food, metal scraps, scalding hot water as we passed under bridges. One of the nights, sleeping in a field in the sleet, Metro said he had something to tell me.

Aglaya and I were secretly married, he told me. We wanted to avoid harm or suspicion, so we told no one, not even you. Then he said, She is to have our child.

On the eighth day of a forced march, one starved soldier crossed into a field to pick some hard corn right off the stalk and was immediately shot. When Metro attempted to come to his aid, on the spot, he too was shot. Lev pauses.

I couldn't even go to him, lying on the ground. He died where he fell. I felt blood in my throat.

They buried him right there in a field with a few sticks on which they hung his hat to mark his grave.

Lev recounts this in such a controlled manner. He is numb, unwavering.

When she received news of my brother's death, Aglaya became perfectly still. The loss of him made her think and move with the gravest economy. She then took her father's shotgun kept by the side door of the house they would never live in together, and tested the metal on her mouth. She counted in her heart the minutes between losing him and returning to him again. She remembers hearing mosquitoes coming through the open window. The offbeat tick of the clock. The distant bark of a dog belonging to the peaceable brothers two fields over. She then turned slowly and purposefully, and shot a hole right through the clock. She shot the time right out of it. She wanted to remind herself of the precise moment when her life, as she'd known it, ended.

And then she felt a flutter. The baby moved. It brought her back to the world. It made her understand that even in the most desolate moment, she was part of it still.

I don't remember being loaded into a boxcar to a prisoners' camp at Caserta Casino in northern Italy. But I woke up there, lying on a cot. Like many of the Ukrainian prisoners, I contracted typhus. Drifting in and out of consciousness, I wondered if I too had died. My heart felt like a stone on top of my chest. My lungs were dry as leather. I had the feeling that the cot I was on was cursed, that too many people had died on it, but nothing came out of my mouth when I tried to speak. I remember the elderly Italian doctor entering the barracks with his nose and ears stuffed with cotton batting in order to keep out the stench. He would enter the room carrying a long cane that he used to point out the sick who were to receive the daily fare of an egg and a glass of milk. The food was severely rationed. A cup of soup and a piece of bread was usually all we could expect for the whole day.

All the prisoners from all parts of the Austrian Empire were repatriated, except the seven hundred Ukrainians who had no country to repatriate to. The national boundaries were redrawn and the western part of Ukraine where I was from no longer existed. For two years they held me prisoner in Italy because they had no idea what country to return me to. A Russian father, a Ukrainian mother. Nothing mattered except the ground you were standing on. It was the only thing that determined who you fought for. I ended up finding my way back to Peskovsko, to Aglaya. If I had returned to Vislok I would have been conscripted into the Polish army, which was then fighting the Russians. I'd had enough of the army, of the fighting. The borders and enemies changing, half the Ukrainians Russians, the other half Austro-Hungarians, fighting each other. The fields split in half. The town I grew up in was not on a map. I was from nowhere. I did not exist. I felt a great remoteness, like an ember in space.

The villagers considered Aglaya a fallen woman. Pregnant, no husband. When I first saw her, on what was to be our wedding day, she was an apparition. Her once-beautiful hair was matted. She was in filthy rags and lace, dirt-caked boots, her pale face drawn and cracked, eyes like craters, carrying wilted violets. Drained and absent.

I had written to her telling her to wait, and that I would come to marry her. But while I was in Italy the baby had been born early, sickly, and was incapable of drinking her milk. She tied the cord that bound them both with string and cut it with a kitchen knife. It was hard as bone, she said. He died a week later. Because she was unmarried with an unchristened child, the baby was denied burial in the church-consecrated cemetery. She wrapped it in her shawl and buried it by the river, digging at the hard mud with her own hands. She had named him Metro.

Overnight, she'd gone to the side of angels. She said there was no reason to marry her now, but I would never agree. There was no dowry except for an aged white cow and the dacha that had survived her father's death but would soon have to be given over to the state. Remnants of a ruined kingdom.

I found a job digging sugar beets, loading them onto wagons and hauling them into town where they were processed into sugar at a nearby factory. I painted at night, by kerosene lamplight, while she constantly touched her apron pocket where she kept a worn-edged bible. She stopped eating. She did not want to be a woman. She continued to lose all contact with the real world, only with God would she speak.

Unclean, unclean. I am a sepulchre. I do not belong here.

She was only bones, and unfocused eyes. When I came back from the fields one day, the house was empty. I later found that she had walked in rain, on her small bare feet, for eight days. She begged with grace for entry into the Novodevichy Convent in Moscow where the nuns were from noble families. And though she appeared in rags, she was accepted and sheltered.

I wrote to the abbess, who said Aglaya would not see me. She was a child of God now, they said. *Pozhaluysta.* Do not come back.

The woman who was once my brother's wife and now my own, disappearing beneath the golden domes of Novodevichy.

I would leave for France, paying for my passage by painting a portrait of a party leader who would later be stripped of everything and sent to a gulag for a casual remark made at a cocktail party. My accepting money from him did not go unobserved. But I understood that my departure from Russia was the departure from my life as I knew it. I wanted to find the life I had intended to live.

We lie in each other's arms, the tick of the leaves from the wind through the window. How improbable that it was just this morning when I crossed the courtyard of the Sorbonne to deliver a set of commissioned biological illustrations, snails, birds, a sphinx moth, handing them to the collector, M. Barbary. In his office he flicked through the folder, nodded, and passed me the agreed payment. Outside his cramped office window, there was the wind, the same ticking leaves I hear now, bracketing the brief drastic events that can occur in a day.

Songbird

Territory tenure is related to song-sharing
with neighbours, but not to repertoire size.
Ornithologists say that if you play or sing
to the birds, they sing back.

HE INSTRUCTS ME to pack one bag. We will meet the next morning. The door shuts behind him as though he was never here. I drag the valise from under my bed. The click of the brass latches, its shiny red viscera exposed in the middle of the floor. I am reminded how near to escape we always are. A woollen cape from Mme. Tissaud, two white dresses, underclothes, pencils, inks, notebooks, rolls of paper.

He has returned alive, unbroken. All the fears, the silences about his past he himself has dispelled. I never asked him why, with all my might I hesitated. What disturbed me most were his silences. But tragedy can be told only by someone who is ready to tell. It is almost perverse to be offered up this piece of small happiness that has come at such a cost. My pleasure predicated on someone else's pain.

In the morning I say his name, its strong syllable filling the room. It takes on an unreal air. Everything is different. He has spoken. A part of his past parcelled out, carefully, like an offering. I had begun to see his mystery as a way of lying but he is not an adulterer in the way everyone thinks. Colour drains back. I am elated, full of certainty.

I walk out onto the street. Its cool grey curve. The people tilt their watches and click along the cobblestones. The leaves move in the wind. The clouds like high wet feathers, the kind that don't mean rain. I look on this scene with detachment knowing that I am already gone. The arithmetic: he is here. I am gone.

But I don't see him.

The morning is starting to slip.

There is no way of trusting that fear isn't founded. That all the things that could happen haven't happened. Our plans suddenly seem too big, too sure for what surrounds us. I've lost the ability of interpretation. It has only been minutes.

The morning widens. There are doves and the loud squeal of engines, and Mme. Tissaud about to walk to her back room and inspect her refrigerator for her black-market cream. She will make coffee and then raise the blinds and let the sun through the glass storefront.

He is there. Faceful of morning light. Blinding me. He is in a borrowed car, one that Istvan needs us to take to the south. I am not looking down. I have only ever walked with him. His body outlined against buildings.

Driving, the air softens. Hours later the earth gives in to red, and then the silver of olive groves. The leather seat burns hot through my thin dress. The ditches are red with poppies, there is the slow winding sound of cicadas, and villages stand tucked into the landscape as they always have, undisturbed. Church steeples rise from the hills.

Lev has never owned anything, but people always want to give him things. A dealer from Paris who has begun to champion his work told him to go south. He gave him keys to his family's old country house. It is derelict, full of dust, covered in vines, he says. He knows Lev has no money. He will charge nothing.

We open the enormous wooden shutters and light is thrown across the large rooms. The air inside is miraculously old. Crickets escape. The wind smells of lavender, just out, everything being ahead of Paris. The days are filled with sunlight, too bright. Disorienting and long, as when the clocks are changed.

The house is unearthed through scrubbing, painting, hacking through weeds and vines that have overtaken the stones. We plant a garden so that we will eat what we grow. The only sounds are wind, birds, the sizzle of sun on the fields. Night slowly comes.

These long days have a sprawling low rhythm so foreign to the concise pieces of time in Paris. Lev's capture has kept him put for now, there is a stillness. Don't speak of it, I think. He knows, as I do, that there is a shadow of threat here always, sweet and ripe. We are adept at drawing out the day. Footsteps through the sunlit leaves. I cannot believe Lev is not more burdened by it, but he moves fully and assuredly, the same looseness in his body.

He begins working on a series of paintings for the dealer that he packages and posts to Paris. I have started and abandoned canvases, nothing holding. But life is easier here. There is no need to spend francs on coal, or draw out expensive drinks at cafés, or eat prix fixe at restaurants. No jabs of hunger while passing the opulent displays in boulangerie windows. The property thickens. Leaves unfold. There is the sudden rush of skylark wings. The silver river out back crashes loudly against the smooth stones. My sound journal fills with entries. Eventually a pale blue envelope arrives with money. It is a relief. We have not eaten much, waiting for everything to ripen. Lev comes back from town with eau de vie, wine, bread, olives, and delicious little packages from the fromagerie. Thank god you have talent, I say, sucking an olive pit, or we would starve.

The sun is hot enough in the day that we swim in the nearby stream, without clothes, which causes a flurry among the villagers. Right away we are met with narrow looks. Leonor, who is now living two villages over, tells us what they say. His accent is foreign. What is on his arms? That young woman's hair is too untidy, she may be a bit mad.

But the evenings are cool and we work by lamplight. We swallow eau de vie and wait for its truculent burn. Hand-rolled cigarettes to stay awake, the shadows flickering on the stone walls. On these walls we appear giant-sized in the night. I look at Lev's face.

Why sadness? I can see something in your eyes.

I don't trust this.

Trust what?

He looks at me.

Happiness.

For the first time it occurs to me that happiness can be a burden.

We consume black coffee and pick berries and herbs and fruit beginning from the trees studded with dusty-necked birds. A bounty amid the rations in the city. Lev scrabbles and unearths. He can make anything from nothing, wild watercress, leeks, mushrooms that he finds in the forest floor. His pockets full of lichen and roots and seeds. He has fallen in love with the weeds, in part because they remind him of his childhood. Even the sunflowers, he tells me. Ukraine is full of them. Soon there are cherries and white peaches soaked in Lillet then lit on fire, and apricots, the nectar sticky on our mouths. His hands on my neck and shoulders when I kneel in the violets. We fall asleep, Lev reciting Mallarmé, *Et notre sang, épris de qui le va saisir / Coule pour tout l'essaim éternel du désir*, a faded red and white quilt rumpled and warm beneath us.

Everything is thick and old and smells of roses and sun. The stream rushes loudly, and there are fat buzzing bumblebees and wingbeats and white caves and the open blue sky. Our skin grows darker, fingernails bleached from sun. We separate and work and walk alone. The paintings collect.

Lev tells me that his father kept bees in Ukraine. He would receive the queen in a box by post. He spoke tenderly to her, he says, as though she was a woman. The queen is the only sensual life form in the hive. Everything his father did was measured by the sun. Twenty-one days is what it takes for the sun to revolve on its own axis. It is exactly the amount of time a worker bee needs to develop. Then there's the sex act. It occurs in full daylight, he says, lining up equal-sized wooden panels against the wall. The queen flies as close to the sun as possible. The drone that flies the highest gets the queen, up there in the air. And then the strangest thing happens. The workers begin to feel so loyal to the old queen that their tiny eyes, the eyes that are never exposed to the external workings of the sun, suddenly feel the sunlight. Somehow they sense that a new queen is born from the sun. They cannot endure the light of her. It translates as fear. French apiarists call the emotion that takes hold of the queen the first time she creeps out of her cell and visits the flowers *soleil d'artifice.* The sun of disquiet. Joy undercut by terror.

At night he is tormented by nightmares, yelling and writhing. It is in one of these terrifying moments that he confesses the escape that presented itself on a quiet evening errand, with a cellmate poet who, it turns out, could not swim. He becomes a gleaming lumpen weight to be carried across streams. Moving through hills, hiding in barns, avoiding roads, towns. Bridges are the worst, he says. They are guarded at both ends. When he wakes, he says he cannot shake the feeling that he is being watched.

I had feared this freedom was self-made. It reminds me that these days are miracles, in part because they contain the possibility of the death of future ones. A small metal clock ticks in the house by the front door. Even when he leaves for a few hours, I note it. Waiting for his return. Aware of how when he is gone there is no present, only the promise of one.

Come with me, Lev says, walking into the house after a long day's absence.

I follow him along a narrow path high above the river. We sit on the edge of a jagged cliff and watch as the light illuminates the strip of land between us and the far hills, usually bleached as bone. We wait, and then it comes. The entire band of land glows and fills with the profusion of songbirds melodically chattering in a single continuum of expression. Lev and I are stilled into separate spheres of wonder, each of us filling with equal parts of sublime weight and joy from the singing, twining into one sublime weight and joy. And I think, Does what happens on the inside show on the outside? When I look at Lev I know that he feels the same. That the sound seems to be coming from inside. I could do anything, my life could be emptied of everything, I could even fall off the edge of this cliff and die, and every single thing that led up to this would have been worth it just to experience this one immeasurable moment.

We walk back to the house in silence.

Should we go out tonight? Lev says, unexpectedly referring to an earlier invitation that had reached us. A party. I can tell by the way he asks that he wants to go. Artists and writers gathering in an opulent house two villages over.

I've got nothing to wear, I say, half-jokingly. But what I really want to say is, I have no desire to leave this.

You don't need anything, he says, brushing his mouth on my bare shoulder.

Leonor's house glitters gold, ancestral diamonds. Luminaries from Paris fill the tall rooms like a network of tinkling glass. There are more people emptying down to the south. It is safer. Leonor seems exuberant in fur and feathers—flanked by her two lovers—she prizes visceral experiences above any other, especially emotional ones. She has dyed her dark Spanish hair platinum. It glints under the chandeliers. I have been told that Lev has been with her in the past but now they joke and tease each other, like siblings. Lev is quickly encircled by everyone wanting to hear about capture and escape, but he doesn't tell. For the first time we feel like conspirators. I am bolstered by it. When Leonor says, Cherie, let me take your, and pauses to find the word for the black velvet draped around me, I shake my head and she hands me a glass of champagne. The pricked bubbles loosen my head, tight with ideas and twitches of sound. Heels on the tiled floors, Leonor's pack of cats clawing and darting throughout the house, the metallic chime of silverware, corks popping, bursts of laughter, dry coughs, the offtime skip of Stravinsky muffled on the gramophone.

I begin to talk with a group of women, one dressed as a man, the others in silk dresses that up close are exquisitely battered, tiny holes, fraying at the seams. They are so animated, talking and laughing, cigarette filters red with lipstick. My mind is elsewhere. I see Lev talking to two women across the room. One of them moves closer to him. He looks over at me and touches the blue flower I threaded in the buttonhole of his jacket before we got in the car. A man with rolled shirtsleeves takes him by the arm outside. I am filled with an extraordinary sense of being, this secret joy. Beside me a woman has scissors in one hand as she kneels on the floor. I realize that what is really unacceptable here is something as bourgeois and staid as romantic love.

Leonor comes over. One of the women leans in and lights the cigarette between her lips, it glows in her mouth. Leonor exhales and turns to me saying loudly, Doesn't everyone look so much better when they are being fucked? She puts her arm around me. The women laugh. I shake my head at her, though I am smiling. She faces me and says quietly, resolutely, Desire is not a light thing. And, really, what else does one live for? And then she walks toward three new guests who have just arrived. I look around at her house full of people, of priceless carpets covered in cat hair, of the art she's started safekeeping, hung in clusters in the vast rooms, voices floating up the plaster.

I turn and ask the manwoman, a writer whom I recognize from Paris, what she is working on. She tilts up her head, exhaling smoke. My exit visa.

One of the silk-dress women, the one kneeling, is cutting up a piece of paper and writing questions on them. She has been handing out blank squares for answers and then begins randomly pairing them and reading them out.

What is equality? A hierarchy like any other.

What is the military? The sound of a lamp switching off.
What is reason? —

I decide at this moment to drop the velvet from my shoulders.

Everything stops. The men. The music, the conversation, all the surroundings are drained to an abrupt silence. Leonor winks at me from the door. I laugh, the sound spreading over the room in a confusion. Lev whisks me out.

What? I say, still laughing but serious-eyed. My heel jags some of the falling black velvet and makes a high-pitched rip. He runs his hand across the fabric, it bends under his fingers. He smiles, shaking his head.

You said—

He looks at me.

I can't believe skin could have such an effect, I say, rolling down the window of the car, resting my arm on the cool door as we drive away. Times really are troubled. No one usually reacts to such things at these parties. I feel bold, fully myself in the presence of him. All else is frivolous, make-believe. It provokes daring. An act that could be humiliating is just an exit, otherwise we might have stayed until dawn. What I want is privacy, I think. To be alone with him. But what I also feel is the secret dazzle of power.

Lev's voice above the shift of gears in what I think sounds like, the little satin parts.

No one laughed.

A beautiful naked woman is not funny, he says neutrally.

Why isn't it? Everyone laughed at Félix.

Men's bodies are funny.

Why?

I don't know. He shifts into fourth gear. Gravity.

Peacock

Bird of Hera, wife of Zeus. Immortal.
Tail feathers spread silently, all those
eyes gazing, marked by the sun.

I HAVE AN IDEA, I say. It is gold, morning.

Tell me.

First, you must pay me a compliment, I joke.

I think he will say something facetious but he stops and then says seriously, You have the rare gift of looking into the hearts of all living things.

I do?

You do, he says, taking my hand and brushing his mouth along my knuckles.

You have slept with one eye open since you can remember, I say. You must become the thing that pursues you so mercilessly in the night. You must confront the wolves. There is a Japanese legend about people who draw their nightmares and then throw them into the sea. But the sea grows unpredictable and it causes great sorrow for these people who fish and live off the ocean's riches.

And what do they do?

They draw their nightmares and then cut them to pieces and throw them into the wind. That's how we got kites. This is what you should do, I say.

We sit on the stone steps of the house drinking coffee in the sun. We spend days painting and then sculpting, Lev in the studio out back and me outside. We take breaks and bathe in the river, our fingers slippery as fishes from wet clay. One night while we drink wine, barefoot in the grass, we realize that we have surrounded ourselves in totems. Huge reliefs thrust out of roofs and walls that will occupy this house long after we go.

At night we exchange arms and legs, twined in sleep. Nothing is close enough. But the nightmares continue. I tell him I will watch him when he sleeps. What I do not tell him is that looking on terrifies me. It scares me to encounter him so unprotected. All that movement and terror in every fold of skin, the world growing eyeteeth around him. At night, asleep, is the only time he can be pulled under. In daylight he is untouchable, self-possessed, dangerous. A middle-distance animal that comes close only if it chooses.

Lev draws from nature but you would never know. He sees other things. Not the things I see.

His work is singular and clear and I know that it is good. I am conflicted. I am surrounded by my unfinished drawings, abandoned paintings. The desire for production, but nothing holding.

The bad paintings must be painted too, Ivory.

What if it's not a painting? I say in frustration. What if the path I'm taking is not right?

There is no such thing as a wrong path.

I think I'm losing faith.

In what?

Humans.

You can take that, he says, to somewhere else. I see what you do. Are already doing. You despise hierarchy and so you are creating a democracy.

His eyes glint.

A world where humans, animals, plants, and inanimate objects are of equal value.

Tacita said the same thing. I like that.

Then make it so.

I feel unequipped.

How? he says, though I wonder if he means why.

Birds, for example. Painting feathers seems insufficient when they have such an ancient language. And like other ancient forms of speech it is elliptical. Little is said but much is meant.

Then work on voices, not feathers.

There is a message in the voices. A warning. If only we could learn them. Understand them so they would not retreat. Or appear when they shouldn't, like the great black birds that come out during air raids.

As if on cue, a blast from the neighbouring farm. The shrieks of cawing crows.

What are they shooting? I ask, horrified.

Farmers protecting their cherry trees from nesting birds, Lev says, tying his boot.

When I draw Lev, it is my hand. There is something of me, my projection of him. It is almost impossible to capture him properly. There is always something missing. The blackness. Shimmers, but nothing whole.

While he paints out back, I record the animals in my sound notebook. The trembling of leaves. The laced wind. The vibrating drone of honeybees. The silky flip of the skylark's wings. It is the first time I sit down and really write. I drink sweet-tasting well water, deep in the pleasure of my work, and conceal my excitement.

I spend an entire afternoon gathering berries for ink. When I meet Lev, it is his sleeve red, my sleeve red. It bleeds through our clothes, and when we take them off the berries have stained our skin. There is sticky juice and dark purple everywhere, Lev licking. Stomach, fingers. We eventually find our way to the river. He grabs both my wrists with one hand and I bite his neck. We emerge from the water gleaming, like royalty. Peacocks, flickers of iridescent blue, hearts beating coming into full light. Laughing and dripping we walk back to the stone house.

The next few weeks are consumed by gathering. Elderberries, cornflowers, roses, walnut hulls. The colours burning the retina from this red earth. There are more parties, and gatherings in the nearby village that is on such a hill that coffee spills off the café tables.

When one day I return from the river, the door to the house is wide open. My limbs grow limp. Outside, for almost the first time since we have been here, there are sounds of rain. It falls shyly, and then becomes hard. The kind the farmers want.

Papers are scattered everywhere. Lev's drawings and paintings are gone. My sound notebook is gone. Lev, too, gone.

Lev. My voice not at all reflecting the desolation within. I stand raw, again, the skin off the wound. Standing for what might be a long time. Stunned. I search through every shelf, every drawer. What am I looking for? I flail around the room but there is nowhere to go to get away from my head. The room is sinking. I sit down at the table to keep from falling. The room grows black as night and I light candles. I pour the eau de vie, like bullets to the throat, burning the hollow of my stomach. Another glass. I want to feel something. Another. Until there is nothing left and the room blurs, candles flickering. I find a bottle of vodka. Everything else is dark and complicated, but the liquor the Russians consume is simple and clear. I pour a large glass as though it is water, the way they do, and am surprised by its severe, astringent taste. And when I pour another, the bottle slips from my shaking hands and crashes on the stone floor. I step on one of the shards trying to pick up the pieces and blood streams from my foot, mixing with vodka. It pools away from the front door, the floor tilted toward the back of the house.

I want to be injured. I want to divert the pain that I feel in my chest. There are tears now I think. I put my hand to my face and it slips across my skin from the wet. With tragedy there is repetition. It is never once, like the beginning of a fairy tale.

Night comes quickly, the blackest clot. I somehow manage sleep in the early hours, like falling into a dark rainsplashed hole. Fear staccatos my breathing. I find rags and clean up the blood that never dried. A pale pink layer of liquid sloshes on top of the stone dip. I inspect the gash. It is wide and red with raised ridges on either side. I bandage it and then sit down and steady myself. My head pounds. My eyes are swollen. My throat thick and dry. Swallowing is difficult. I put my shoes on, wincing, and walk slowly to the village, past the whispering children gathered on the winding dirt road, and begin to ask if anyone saw what happened. Yesterday afternoon.

The adults look at me, heads shaking, *Non. Non plus*. In their eyes the scorn has been leavened with pity, warmth even.

I try to be neutral, biting my lip to stop the tears. But still, they fall. I swallow rusted metal. A deep rumble of hunger and nausea jab at the same time, knocking the wind out of me.

There is a young girl with long blond plaits flicking over her blue shawl. They reach down her back, touching the top of her gathered skirt. I can see a bit of her legs between the skirt and her boots. They are covered in purple scars, possibly from insect bites. A woman missing some teeth comes forward in a faded housedress, flowers that must've been bright once, jaw hingeing from side to side like a goat. I am almost angered that she can eat, as though nothing is wrong.

She says they came in a shiny black car. They were not in there for long. The man was led out, peaceably, almost.

Did he say anything? Did you hear anything? Did you see his face? The—

Ce n'est pas grave, cocotte, she says. But she knows that it is not all right. Despite her attempts at comfort, her eyes say that it is not all right.

When they last took him away there was brutality. I remember seeing—

You remember too much, the old woman says. The best thing you can do is to forget what you've seen.

I never forget anything, I say.

She shakes her head out of sympathy, not disapproval.

Les enfants se souviennent, she says. She hands me a *pain au raisin*. She thinks I'm a child.

My last vision of Lev. We agree to meet for dinner back at the house. He grabs bread in one hand, brushes splayed in his other like a fan. He turns to me, solemnly, closes his eyes. And then, at the last moment, he flashes a beautiful grin and ducks out the door.

There was no force this time. The lack of it, oddly, makes it seem worse.

There was a slapping noise of boots on wet stone. The rev of the engine as it skids away sending dirt and small grey stones into the air.

Now the rain is light, colourless and without hope. I walk along the path, the tall grasses wet and brushing my legs. I can see my limbs, moving along the path, as though they belong to someone else. I fill my pockets, heavy with rocks, and head to the river. Though this isn't what happens. The weight that sinks isn't the rocks. What is pulled beneath the water isn't the body.

I am found, gripping sharp elbows, skinned, nerves exposed. Their timing a stroke of luck. Coming to collect the car for two writers who must get to the port. They get quiet right away, disturb nothing. Swiftly get me out of there. She moves around me, takes me to the house and brings me warmed milk, normally repellent, but it is all that seems to stay down.

Tacita, I am filling, filling, half-deep inside with water.

She hugs me, her body warm against my cold skin, the fields blurring backward as we drive away.

Whale

Megaptera novaeangliae. Only males sing.
Cut out musical lines from a spectrograph,
analyze, overlap them over and over again.
Identify individual voices in a quartet and
write out the score.

MY HANDS GROPE for the switch, but everything is black. I hear the sound of footsteps in the house. I let out a scream, muffled and only part-sure. A man comes toward me and grips my arm.

The room sways and I sink into a chair, half in and half out of the world.

A man's voice. Heart palpitations. The hideous thump. Out of the chair. Ice cold, and retching as though seasick. I've lost my sense of time and space. Remain calm.

Oh, god.

My age swallows even an intruder's ability to scene steal. It is me who becomes the shocking thing. Narrowed eyes, heaving body, I see in the dark the outline.

It's me.

How did you find me?

He doesn't answer.

Do you want to sit down? He helps me onto the sofa and fills one of the American's plentiful drinking vessels full of tap water and finds an enamel basin and places it on my knees with lapidary precision.

It doesn't matter. I had to come. There's something we need to talk about.

I know, I manage to say.

How do you know?

My mind lurches. I am slipping away. I'm going to die. But my instinct is to rat-hole. I can't breathe. Like the old whales who have to keep one portion of their brains perpetually alert, night and day, to make sure they keep breathing by surfacing regularly. Sometimes when they are very old, they strand themselves on a shallow beach where they can die without drowning. Without having to think about drowning.

This is not how I wanted to see him again. Flickers of sharp reality cant into a deeper, dark space. My mind inaccessible.

I attempt focus through the blur.

How did you escape?

He lights a match, that beautiful striking sound, and brings it to his face.

Lev.

I try to hold still my perception. Hold on. But my control flickers. No. I retch again into the basin. Whirling eyes, hot flashing up my neck and face. I've not spoken Lev's name aloud, I have scissored him from my memory. A victim of my silence. But he reappears, my limbs turned to ash. This meaningless body. Every memory of him an assault.

Time does not heal, it medicates.

I look at this face in the blue light. Untamed. Hair thick and tangled and owling out in parts. Once, in Paris, looking for Lev, a woman described a man to me who wore his hair parted low to one side. But no, I realized, I would be incapable of being with such an exacting man.

Eyes flashing. Long fingers.

Lev? He says it out loud as a question.

Yes.

It's me.

My mind searches for his name, like a lost word, refusing to form in my mouth. I cannot think. An after-image of his face. A black wing. Cold country. Siberian eyes. His voice. Paris. Notes and sounds and enigmata drifting through.

I do not know who you are, I say, genuinely shocked at this. Knowing, at least, that I should be.

He registers fear.

He takes me by the shoulders. The conservatory. The Yukon. Wolves. Fuck. I mean, Please.

Skeet. The attack has passed, the floor levels. Cognition limps back in.

OfcourseSkeet.

I need to talk to you Frame.

How did you find me?

Jesus Frame. I track animals.

Well yes, I say, you do.

I'm so sorry, he says, looking into my eyes. I had no idea I would scare you like that. Are you all right?

I'm fine.

Did you receive a letter from the conservatory?

I have been waiting but no, it never came. What I received—

So she didn't mention anything about someone coming to interview you?

No.

He looks down and then directly into my eyes. The person to be dispatched is not from the university.

I don't understand. A consultant?

No. The outside person is not connected to the conservatory at all. They've ordered a psychiatrist from a clinic, dread slows his breath, an assessment. To see if you are not—all here.

I would never let such a person—

I know. She knows. That is why it is under the guise of your work. So he can gain full access to make his assessment.

What? How is it even possible when I am engaged in research for them?

That's the thing. He hesitates. I tried to explain a while ago, at Hotel du Nord. But I wasn't sure what was actually going on at the university and the conservatory. They think you—

Please don't say it, Skeet. For god's sake. Though I'm certain after what you just witnessed, you have your own doubts.

Jesus, Frame, why do you think I'm here?

Why *are* you here, Skeet? Shouldn't you be compiling the data? You have that big conference in Denmark.

There is no more work for me.

I don't understand.

They've cut the funding for your project, a lot of projects, he says, reaching for the basin and taking it away. They even hired a PR firm to smooth everything over. Some company out of Los Angeles that just helped a breakaway nation emerge. An entire country. One of the istans, he says. The pipes creak as he turns on the tap. Apparently one of the women is a Pulitzer Prize—winning journalist. Knows how to spin crap into gold.

Sanity isn't a question, until you are thought to be mad. This I know. If only there were some form of assurance, like the swing of a crucifix around the necks of European women who lean into their housework. But it's not like that. This addling. This passing change in perception.

Skeet has told me before about new research into aging. Techniques being engineered, attempting to reverse the wear on bodies by replacing lost cells in bones, in hearts.

But what if those cells are supposed to be lost? What if they contain the parts of our lives meant to disappear?

But who wouldn't choose the alternative, he says.

The body grows cold, Skeet. Hard as ice. A worn-out container. When I look out, there are only these eyes not attached to any particular skin, flensed, no particular body but something less than a body. But who cares about the body? By the time you are old you live in it so little, though still, it is all we are. The thing about growing old is its suddenness. One day you look up and find that you no longer recognize anything, not even your own face.

Skeet shifts uncomfortably, pale light coming through, daylight faintly suggested.

Skeet, I say quietly, attempting to remain calm, I would rather drink lighter fluid than go into one of those homes. Those places smell like death. All those people identical, locked away as though they have a communicable disease. Do you know what people become in these places? Their rheumy eyes clouded over like a jar of bacon fat kept under the sink. Women who have lost the use of some part of their body or mind. Mme. Tissaud used to say that the mind is like a mirror, it collects dust. The problem is to remove the dust. Each face confused with all the other faces. Attendant. As though they are awaiting final instructions. You know what it is? It is as though they have already died.

At convent school they forced us to pay visits to these places, which I considered a traumatic activity. I remembered them being decorated with horrid paintings by children with virtually no artistic talent. There was a tiny shrunken woman with white shiny skin thin as bible paper who refused to visit her daughter in the south because she believed her exotic lily was about to bloom. The thing was awful. It smelled like a corpse and looked like a phallus. It's a very rare plant, you know, the woman protested. I am already an old woman, she said, and if I leave now, I most surely will never see it bloom. And in fact the nurses overwatered it, and when they read up on it, realized that it could be decades before a bloom emerged, if ever. There was also a woman who clutched what looked like a jewellery box. What she carried in the box was her husband. She would thrust it toward me, pointing to what looked like seashells propped up in sand. His shoulder blades, she said in an odd tone that I realized was pride. Most of the people who work there are mannish women with mean little eyes that seem invigorated by the taunting. All that wordless suffering, like helpless creatures. And the thing that is so impossible Skeet, is that those people are us. That is me, and will be you someday, sooner than you can imagine.

He stares at me. He is too young for this to register. It probably isn't the time.

I have come here because— He stops. There are things you should know.

The post-vertigo has produced a hollow pit, a terrible hunger. Skeet, may we be civilized about this?

He is already moving in the kitchen, half complicit.

Any eggs in the coop, Frame?

Yes, I tell him. But he's not heard. Coffee, I say. I still get a prick of pleasure to think of the first cup. It remains one of the cheapest enjoyments in life.

Bread, fruit, cigarettes too, I say brightly, grateful to be holding on to this thin calm. The eggs are from the farmer's wife, the only ones I dare eat. Those hens are magnificently cared for. Though the activists would probably disown me if they knew I consumed animal byproducts. Skeet puts his hands over his ears. I feel a flood of affection for him, for his long limbs, his rustic charm, his clean way of moving through things. Maybe that is the ability of the young, obstacles are merely chimeric, whereas in age they are made of stone.

There is a great unfairness, Skeet.

In the conservatory?

In life. I hear the whump of the gas igniting.

We wait and wait, but by the time we are fledged we are already on the descent.

The eggs skitter and pop on the stovetop.

It makes me think of how my obsessive listening to the rawest most private noise has allowed me to hear rapture in everything. In recordings. Ravel. Arvo. Satie. In Sappho's rhythms. *Eros has shaken my wits, like a wind from the mountain falling on oaks.* This read in Toronto, everything licked clean. All the sound dreams when I first arrived. In one, I am huddled in burgundy ditches of dogwood surrounded by owls making their low rasping noises, scratchy and ethereal like the fragile 78 in Lev's studio. When I tried to transcribe it, everything fell silent and it was just a needle rhythmically hitting the centre of a record like a heartbeat. In another, I am startled by a fox who creeps up to me and begins speaking. There is no actual voice but I hear the words, We did not reveal this to you so that you would do nothing. The other animals sit watching, like a jury. I wake up panicked, remembering that Freud said that every dream is either a wish or a counter-wish.

Breton had asked in his manifesto, Why is it that we attach more importance to waking events than to those occurring in dreams?

Skylark

Alauda arvensis;
June 10 – Rose, sheet 9 a.m.
June 11 – Violet, forked and very grand, about 10:50 p.m.
June 12 – Blue and yellow, various, much sheet, about 11 p.m.
June 13 – Red, pale yellow and blue, sheet, distant storm, 11:30 p.m.
June 14 – Pink, sheet, 7:20 p.m., blue, sheet, at midnight.
June 16 – Yellowish, but on nearer approach, rose;
most vivid flash 7:26 p.m., violet.
June 17 – Pale yellow, forked, but not severe.
June 18 – Beautiful rose with a tinge of violet.
Thunderstorm about 4 p.m.
June 19 – 3:34 p.m. vivid bright yellow, 3:36, yellow,
3:37 pale yellow, 3:41 vivid pink, 3:51 vivid pink,
3:54 vivid pink, 3:55 vivid pink – the most beautiful
pink – so rich a colour I have never seen.

SKEET POURS THE COFFEE. The breeze is now warmed by the slow sun, this mystical light on clouded windows reminding me of such disparate things. At convent school, walking to the dining hall for breakfast, the elastic of my stockings loose, wool itching my legs. I could see my reflection in the glass, walking in, to what? What exactly had I done or said to the other girls? I have almost forgotten entirely, though I remember silence and the sparkling world cast by the sun alone. The same quality of light in Lev's studio. All the amorous mornings, profane acts in daylight that altered me, these memories now turned into something else. I am struck by how everything, the pain, the joy, the essence of it faded, leaving only traces of images, sounds, how the light fell. How so many memories lose their substance, what lies at the heart of them. Sometimes I wonder if I have forgotten Lev's face. I cannot determine whether this is an act of cruelty or kindness on the part of time. Whatever they say about time not being a straight line, life assuredly moves in one direction.

Frame?

Okay, I say, tell me.

He takes a sip of coffee and then searches through his large bag.

You know you should be in the company of some extravagantly sexy girl, I say, uninvited. An awkward silence.

Shit, his eyes say. She knows.

Okay, he says, completely ignoring me. Frame—he begins to empty out the contents of his bag—I'm on the run. Which means, well, it means that *we* are on the run.

Are you joking?

Negative.

Is it the university? The conservatory?

Sort of. Their board.

God. That sickly collection of men.

It seems they're concerned with, among other things. How should I put this—

Just say it Skeet, there is little that can shock me at this point.

They don't know what to do with your things.

That is absolutely not what I was expecting you to say. I need a cigarette.

He takes a pack of matches out of his pocket and strikes one on the stone wall.

Things? Meaning my work? My files? What?

They have a very valuable item of yours and they are not sure where it should go. Well. Okay. I think they want to sell it. It's huge for the conservatory given how strapped they are.

Skeet, there is something I'm not getting here. Shouldn't the valuable item of mine go to—I look him squarely in the eyes—me?

They think it's time you go to a facility. They think you are not—

I laugh. Of sound mind. It just occurs to me now, the pun.

And because they thought you had no survivors, they have hired a lawyer and are looking into power of attorney.

I drain my coffee cup and wipe my mouth with a napkin in an attempt at composure. Skeet?

Yes.

Why did you say *thought* I had no survivors?

I take the letter from my pocket and hand it to him. He opens it. Scans it. Runs his hand through his hair. Sits down. Something flickers across his face but he says something else. He knows. The museum contacted Valentina about where to find me. He already knows of the granddaughter.

The item. What is the item?

It is a painting, he says in a low tone I've never heard before.

A sudden flood of fear beats blood into my ears. I wonder whether he is speaking to me about things that have never happened. I only catch—bourgeois woman renovating her chateau in the south. She instructs her mason to repoint the stones, but no, at the last minute she decides she must replace them. He removes them carefully, holding the smaller ones in his palm, hingeing his arm up and down at his elbow as though attempting to determine a weight by feel. A corner of colour juts up from the stone. It is caught in the few centimetres of space between the wall and the fireplace. It must have fallen down. He carefully slides it up and out, and sees that it is dated. It is old. It is by that famous Russian artist. He is dead. Is he dead? That odd thing that happens with famous people from another era, you would be just as surprised to hear they were alive as to hear they were not.

Exit wound.

It was sent to Oslo by the woman because it was addressed to you, Skeet says. She looked you up and found you through the conservatory. They had it authenticated. Because a lot of his paintings from that time were destroyed, they say it's worth—a lot.

Why was I not notified?

It's all been—he clears his throat—recent.

The word recent doesn't actually mean anything. Did you know that?

I'm sorry Frame, he says.

It's monstrous. I don't know whether to laugh or cry. I feel like a child. Powerless. A quiver of anger. All this time spent protecting the present from the past. From what? Gravity. A space between two objects that was not supposed to let in a third. The same gaps that allow others to make decisions about my own life.

Skeet?

Yup.

Tell me what the painting is.

He looks at me and then to his bag and grins. You can see for yourself.

I appreciate a patient person. Professor Tapping was also like this. He would sit quietly for hours marking papers, discussing, at length, small ridiculous questions posed by his students.

At first I did not ask questions. I read, went to lectures, copied notes. The city looking presentable but dead, like a postcard. I lived between the university and the small room I'd rented, a few blocks between, lined with thin brick houses. There were no sidewalk cafés. Everything happened indoors. Another top floor of a house. An attic. Freezing in winter, broiling in summer, little else in between. I opened the windows, cleaned the room. It was Lev who taught me that you have to tell your story and then you must forget it. Each morning, below my window, a boy would toss the news and miss. I heard the *sssss* when it would hit the bushes. Before I arrived, before I was well, I was not. There are so many things, I'm unsure what was the worst. The loss of Tacita upon Lev felt like skin removed. There wasn't a day when I didn't think of him. Carrying his name everywhere. Unable to remove his presence. Everything having been gulped, flesh and bone, his utter calmness within it. Memory going back at every chance. And Tacita, who would tell me there was no choice, everything unfolded the way it must. We would draw and write and laugh, and sorrow would not control my days. That was the way my mind worked.

Tacita was the one who told me that friendships are acts of accumulation. And then what? It is almost too much to think of her now. I will never be able to listen to a Paris ambulance, its minor key, without a sickening feeling. Its dissonant tone, a bird in the house, every time it delivers the news that she is inside, covered in a white sheet.

When the gendarmes came to the door all Istvan could say was, She is dead? He is in utter shock though he remains perfectly still. Absolutely dead?

I remember feeling hardly more than a diagram of anatomy, skinless, strings of red and blue veins.

Il faut refaire ton vie, they said to Istvan. What they meant was, You can find another wife.

On her way home, rain had started again. She walked down a narrow street just off Rue du Bac not far from Deyrolle. She stopped to inspect something shining on the road. She was crouched when she was hit. The driver braked too late. It was the back right wheel that crushed Tacita's skull. Her brain seeped out on the wet cobblestones.

A single white rose dropped out of nowhere on the wet sidewalk in front of me just before I heard. My last unfinished painting dim against the noise of inadequacy of this act, the absurdity of it in the face of death. I feel no interest in what I have depicted, it seems superficial, ridiculous even. You can lie with other things, but you can't lie with drawing. Everything grows cold, as when the seasons change and the sun gives no heat. I will out of existence this tendency. Extinguish it. I lay my brushes carefully in a box, and give them all away. I give away all my paint and canvas rolls to young artists who are as I was when I first came here. Tacita had so many boxes, the stacks had grown bigger and bigger. And when I left, they sat there, like a flight cancelled. Istvan, alone and so distraught, offered himself up to his cause. With a small group of volunteers helped hide people in the south until they could be smuggled out. He managed to secure travel visas, arrange escorts for the more vulnerable, organize new crossing routes. It is the kind of behaviour that can get someone killed. Only in his case, it saved. It allowed movement where there wasn't any. Despite blocked borders. Despite passports infested with swastikas. But still he's left with Tacita's things, meaningless without her linking everything, fitting the world, all the little pieces, into one continuous dream.

I had agreed to leave only because Istvan told me to. I wanted to stay and help him. He said, Do it for her. It's what she'd wanted for you. And when I arrive on the coast, I have to speak a language I am not acquainted with. I find these words, these short foreign sentences useless. What is a language? *I am. You are.* Just sounds we make.

Everything smells of wet velvet. Life feels cheap, uncertain. My mind plays tricks. Tugging me under. There are days at the beginning, waiting for papers, when I don't wash. My stockings laddered. Dangling limbs. Body aching in a fever. Stomach turning, provoking unwanted appetites. Longing for Lev. A toothsome woman along the docks talks to me. She may be a prostitute but it is hard to tell. Most women here have dirty hair, worm-eaten coats, painted eyes looking for escape. She tells me I should take lovers. Sleep with men to see if I can feel anything. I am so empty I want to be filled. Their fingers, their mouths, everything thrusting until I feel I might break. With arousal, there is shame, hips moving under them. Sometimes I am dead. Lifeless. Sometimes it is rough and violent and I want this. Mostly I feel nothing. And all along there isn't a single part of my mind that is not horrified by my actions. The body separate from the self.

No one discusses her time at the clinic.

A biologist in a sweater-vest who rolled his own cigarettes

asked me to dinner months after I arrived in Toronto, and I was stunned. You can't tell, I think, how far I am from you. I am amazed you don't see that parts of me are missing.

Sometimes I could see Tacita's shining eyes, her fingers, her intentions so blinding that I think she is more alive than I am. I begin to wonder if maybe it was me who died, not her.

I soberly start to suspect that my work at the university might embody more than I'd hoped. There is a shift. It is possible to work when there is no joy, and this is what can lead you out. Symbols become equations that begin to write themselves overtop of my life. Prophecies that demand truths. At the university I was considered intelligent, austere, unsentimental, like a man. I remake my grey dress, I let my hair grow. I laugh. I have dinner every Sunday with Professor Tapping and his two sisters. There is only work now. My devotion to it singular. Gratifying. Whole. It is how I will begin to forget.

Skeet?

Yes?

What is the painting?

I had to take it wrapped. No one's seen it except Valentina, the appraiser, the board, I think.

Aren't you curious? What were you waiting for?

He clears his throat. You.

My heart beats into my ears, though I feel light and separate.

From the contents of his bag, he extracts a package. He tears into tape and cuts the plastic bubble wrap wound tightly with his fingers to reveal a single white canvas, no larger than a leaf of letter paper. He unfurls it delicately. It is brittle and thick with paint, now fissured like a cracked desert floor.

Silence.

He knows how to say nothing.

Oh my god. Skeet. I begin to laugh, looking at the canvas. I start to shake.

I was so entwined with him, we exchanged fingers, arms, parts of our mind. But that painting? I never saw that painting.

When I urge him to paint his nightmares I know there is nothing I can say to make him do anything he doesn't want to. He doesn't believe in advice or influence. His only obedience being to his own mind. I look at the painting in disbelief. It is not the thick white and pale grey geometry of familiar abstraction. He has abandoned his beloved non-objective world. The painting is covered in dense trees. There is sky and grass and jewelled light. It depicts a forest of wolves. Grey wolves encircling one wolf. The lone wolf looks upward to a branch where there is a single skylark, as though overseeing a ritual. On the bottom right corner, it is Lev's script. *Requiem for Continued Existence*. And then underneath: *For Ivory, composing*. I feel joy and sorrow at once. Thinking for the first time how a work of art contains the unknown thoughts of the artist, and how everyone looking at this work will never know what was in him when this was made. Even me.

In the south, Lev painted in a small stone building off the main house. There was one window to the north with the right kind of light, evenhanded. He often kept the door open and tied his shirt around his waist, because there was no breeze. Though it was cool and dark at night, lit with oil lamps. I rarely went out there. We worked separately. We knew how to keep our distances. He didn't like to talk about what he was painting and I never asked. Some days I would abandon the sound notebooks and find the sun on the side of the house by afternoon. Leonor would drop in when she was passing by. Once she came over with a new camera and was taking pictures while I lay back against the stone windowsill wearing Lev's shirt, opened to let the light of the sun warm my skin. Lev startled me, coming from behind. He kissed my neck and put his hands on my breasts. She said to him, What an idiot. Why have you not painted her? *Ta femme.*

And sell it to those men in Montmartre for pocket change? he joked. Never.

She gave me the photographs later. She said there is always a moment of truth in the darkroom, the image appears as your own face ripples back at you in the pan of water. There were shots of the arched stone walls covered in vines, the animal totems. And then the picture with Lev's hands on me, the edges of his shirt barely visible, the sun on my knees, his shirtsleeves rolled up, head resting on my head, eyes closed. I am struck by the expressions—his look of tenderness, mine of defiance. The man who had such little respect for most things gave such a pure kind of love, full of delicacy. I remember talking and laughing in the bright sun. What were we saying? I have no memory of the words. But I can see the kitchen, the table where I worked, the tilted floor. Getting up and walking to shake the numbness from my legs after hours of sitting. Or peeling potatoes by the sink, outside sounds fluttering in. The feeling I would get when he would come through the door. He would say, Don't move. I need to see everything that is essential about you. And I was helpless. I have remembered this moment so many times that the memory has become compressed into one sound—the abrupt metallic click of a doorhandle being turned.

It occurs to me that each moment in life, each thing we do, is a way of forgetting. I moved toward the group of artists to forget that my parents had abandoned me. To Tacita to forget that I was alone. To Lev to forget myself. To my work to forget Lev. He did it too. He came to me as a way of forgetting. Forgetting his past. Forgetting that he was being hunted. At first, in the south, he could hardly look at the linen curtains moving in the breeze, the stacks of books, the vase of wildflowers on the table, this peaceable domestic scene. He found it hard to know what to eat. I would suggest things, and he would murmur in my ear, Anything, hands lifting my dress. Only when he painted, or when he was with me, his need to constantly be inside me, could he forget.

I shake off all the images, but in truth, I don't know how to forget him. He saw me more clearly than anyone else could. It makes me realize how remote I have become. I suddenly have a longing for that version of me, feverish, ardent. That person has long vanished, that is clear. I feel how I looted my own life to come to this point of view. I made listening into a shelter. I turn and see Skeet, his long limbs and thousand-yard stare. Our eyes meet for a moment but we say nothing. Something tacitly is exchanged between us. It is as though I am only, finally, seeing things truly in this moment. This house, these caves white and high, and it strikes me as odd, really, to be here. The caves are mythical but dirty. Their shining purpose scarcely visible. Sonorities. Skeet hands Lev's painting to me. I feel my eyes well and blur, thinking of him. Remembering him so sharply as though he is standing here. His gait, the direct fullness of his response to everything, like no one I've ever known. Or will know. Where did it go? All of it. I am struck by all that is lost in life. By all the cruelties. The extremities of want. We were young and so sure of what could be discarded. With no idea how rare things actually are. All these memories, the weight of them suddenly displaced. Like space being made for space, as though someone has ripped off the sky. Why has all this come, at this completely inappropriate moment, I think, wiping my face. Blood banging into my ears, thinking of my grim resolve, the grave determination to remain afloat. The worked saved me. It got to the heart of things. Different heart. Different things. My hands trembling. I suddenly must set down the painting, like a live feather. I've held on to sorrow long enough. It ruptures the silence I have carefully walled around the past. In terms of history, silence is forgetting.

Horse

Snorting, jerking its head, tilted hooves clicking
on stones. Skin rippling, twitching off flies.
Its ears prick and pin back signalling
something else, something alive.

EVERYTHING IS BRIGHT and then there is nothing, only darkness even with eyes wide open. It causes me to collapse and fall. This time onto the sidewalk, knee split open, blood on the pavement. I see a physician, not one I know but one a stranger has led me to. A cold stethoscope, the prick of a needle. He asks me a series of questions, including the date. I know enough to know that this is what they ask people who are undone.

I have been to Lev's studio. Tacita took me straight there when I would not return to Mme. Tissaud's. There must be clues. I will take anything. I will gather up his work, all that weight of paint, and bury it in a field until he is released. I will read every book on his shelf. I will learn Russian. I will lie down on the floor with the paint and dirt and papers that I will guard until his return. But when we get there, arranged through the landlord, money has been exchanged, its beautiful squalor has been wiped away. No drying racks. No art. No letters. With no trace at all of Lev in particular. The only thing that is left is the bed, his desk, and his empty easel in the corner.

I want to stay here. It is the only way I know how to be close to him. I remain for days without leaving the room. His easel watches me like a dog. It is airless and I find only tins of sardines and bottles of alcohol. I am continually sick. When I feel anything, I feel it in my stomach. My skin is chalky and damp and feels like the skin of someone else. I am paralyzed. My mind sloshes, eyes sliding around the room calculating the dimensions of my own captivity. But I cannot bear it. They have already erased Lev's presence here, even for me. It is cleaner, tidier, their having gone through his things. It reminds me only of the absences. Of what cannot be changed. Eventually, out of hunger or despair I'm not sure which, I wander out into the bright, a night moth skittering toward light.

So when he comes out with it, I can scarcely breathe. The doctor's proclamation a stunning broadcast without mercy. My chest is suddenly weighted under a pile of bricks. I remember nothing except the overwhelming instinct to flee. But there is nowhere to go when it is your own body that has betrayed you.

I used to tell women there were three options, his voice deep and authoritarian. But now there is really only one. He clears his throat and needlessly shuffles papers in front of him. There is an ashtray made from a large pink seashell containing cigarette butts beside his lamp.

As you may know, one has been made punishable by death, the other, another throat clear, difficult in these times.

I will later hear that the laundress who helps dozens of desperate women will be sent to the guillotine for her actions. *La faiseuse d'anges*, they call her. Angel maker.

A middle-aged man in shirtsleeves who decorates his weekends with dinner parties and tennis lawns, whose framed university degrees look down on me from behind his head, delivers these words like little blows. As though they do not gut.

I cannot listen a moment longer. I leave, forgetting one glove, a blight on his tidy desk with its glinting pens angled in their granite holder, like bones stripped of meat. I think of what the doctor said. *Vous n'avez pas de chance.* You don't have luck.

I didn't pay, I realize. The doctor. The francs still folded in my coat pocket. His cologne draconian, still, impossibly, on my coat, blocks away from his office.

In the streets women stand in doorways muttering. Like me, they might live on fifty centimes a day, though dinner parties can contain lavish things bought on the black market. Most of the food is shipped to Germany. They have started handing out ration cards, soon people will grow hungry. The city is meant to look normal. The women still knit, the click of their needles in the gardens of the Palais Royal. What compels them to knit? What are they thinking? No one wears anything handknit here. The cafés are full, though two-thirds of the city fled in a slow-moving wave of panic. Mme. Tissaud says it is impossible to get leather for her books anymore. It all goes to their army boots, she says. They have hung their flag at the Arc de Triomphe and have concerts of Wagner in the Tuileries and have imposed a curfew that starts at nine o'clock. At night the streets are eerily empty of cars and people. The electric lights are no longer reliable at night. I can hear Mme. Tissaud striking match after match. There is almost no birdsong since they began dumping gasoline in the Seine estuary, wiping out most of the birds. Still, there are black bicycles and young couples holding hands. The city smells of chestnuts warmed by sunshine. *Se débrouiller.*

Unconsciously I have walked, with no memory, to Lev's street, Rue Jacob, like a homing pigeon. The wind is so strong, as if at sea. I have no idea where to go. Just seeing the handscrawled *Sept-Bis* sends the pain of missing Lev through me like a blade. I don't know whose handwriting it is. I have never noticed it before. It looks like the school-taught cursive of every French child with its hooded letters, capitals with curving tails. Lev's landlord's maybe. A man who reluctantly accepts artwork for rent. He is a pale, almost tubercular man of little imagination. The sort of man who determines whether he should eat by looking at his watch.

The window above is still full of sun, mid-afternoon warm, the steep coil of stairs behind the thick wooden door that does not open. I have left it, so it is now locked to me. But still this building, even without him inhabiting it, continues to have authority over me. His studio. The vast space of it. All the tubes of paint squeezed onto palettes. All the pots of paint now grown over with skins.

A woman named Joséphine would be bent over in her dull labour, washing the small black and white hexagons of tile in the front hall. Though she is a hunchback, she has the look of someone who was once beautiful. At some point, Lev said, she had married a titled person but now she was reduced to cleaning houses. Reduced. The landlord's word, not Lev's. I once spoke to her and she said she found cleaning satisfying. She did not need to answer to anyone. Left alone as she scrubbed the grooves that gently dipped in the middle of the wooden risers. Dust, she had said to Lev, is people. It's just everyone who once was here.

In the midst of fear there is still shape. She cleans. The landlord owns. The stores sell, though much less now.

The rip and crack of the laundry that hangs by a wooden stick from an upper window sounds like flags snapping. And I think, How violent flags are. Maybe it is the Russian woman who claims to be Polish. She says it is safer. The sound reminds me of Lev saying listen to nothing but the sound of your own heart beating when there is the nuptial flight of turtledoves high and circling, the whipcrack of their downward-flicked wings against the grey sky. These small miracles, he says. They make treachery bearable.

How quickly the unthinkable becomes normal. The people of this city have been so hungry they once did something so egregious, now commonplace—they ate their own horses. Something they keep up, even when the plenty comes back. They then dined on zoo animals, including a beloved pair of elephants. Though the line was drawn at monkeys. No matter the level of desperation, this makes even the creationists uneasy.

I have a moment of calm. Like a cool wind, it blows through me. Lev saying when he was born his father caught him in his own hands in the middle of the night. His mother had to wait until his father had delivered the horse and two cows first. He had to use an axe on the iced-over door to empty the contents of the enamel bowl into the splintering cold. The only time his mother was truly warm in that high house full of cracks was when she was giving birth.

There are uniformed men who surface here and there, like extras in a play. They drink coffee, watch ballets, wind their watches. Paris looks much the same despite the darkness rippling underneath. I see them posing in front of the Tour Eiffel. Perhaps they occupy it in this manner because, like everybody else, they just want to enjoy Paris.

I wear my hair the same way, plaited, though messily. I consider where to walk. Playing this role, the one where everything is fine.

Tacita says, Be careful. If you practise hard enough, you can forget who you are.

Before I know what I'm doing I've thrown a rock through the window of the woman's apartment with the laundry. The one who pretends to be Polish. I need to hear something break. A delicate web in the glass. There is shouting. I must get out of here. For a moment I've lost my French. This pain is stunningly clear. Like the cold that only people from the north know. It isn't about being numb, it is about being knocked awake. Stinging skin, a trickle from the skull, down the spine. The kind of cold that means you have to keep moving or you die.

Crustacean

*Dirty green. Noisy. Sounds produced by tapping,
scraping, bending, clicking, or rasping
parts of their exoskeleton.*

TIME DOESN'T BLUNT ALL MEMORIES. Some grow edges
sharp as knives. I thought I was past everything, out of
everything. But I find I have only sealed things off. A pain ripens
anytime these things come in uninvited, as they do, in the form
of a simple question, or rain falling at a certain angle, or the smell
of a solvent. Lev's painting alters the order of things. Realization
flickers through. Not the great sweeping kind, but the miracle of
this one small thing. The great revelation never comes, because
how could there ever be just one? It is all the things that strike,
unanticipated, defiantly outside of reason or emotion.

I now see why old people live in the past, I say to Skeet. It
saves you from surprises because it tricks you into counting on
what comes next.

But all the wisdom of age—

I see his brown hands, pale eyes. He is also someone who shook
off one life to find another, left mostly alone. I am certain he doesn't

subscribe to some cliché of a wise old woman, just as he wouldn't to an old rattled one, gathering frustration. There is a part of me that wishes none of this had ever surfaced. That he didn't know. It took so much effort to keep it away. I never wanted to be one of those women who cling to their past. To the sad, hard facts of war. You talk about work, they talk of hunger. You mention joy and they tell of hardship. They deny their lives by staying in the past. Their suffering asks for witness. And now they are almost all gone. I have avoided witness. It is almost funny. Someone who has spent life observing, to understand only now that a life, any life, needs witness. I remember how, in painting, you can only know what you've made once it has been contemplated by someone else. And now Lev's painting, here, sending the anguish through me all over again. It is too late, too messy, too fractured to be put back together, in this rented house, in the middle of these scorched fields.

Frame, he says, eyes down. I wait. Do you miss him?

There is no need to ask who he means. I wonder what Skeet must feel. He would never tell. Looking at him reminds me of the losses I must negotiate. Of fieldwork that I will never conduct again, Skeet and I staring quietly as the sun dropped, pink light washing over us. Packing up recorders, microphones, and walking back to the truck, senses quickened, ears pricked to every sound, for days after. Of all the work that will not be carried on. Skeet moves as though there is no clear truth or falseness in anything. He prefers questions over answers and always takes himself out of the equation, which, I see, is exactly what I do. Have always done.

I sit, thoughtful, for a moment. Every morning I wake, I smoke, I work. The sounds connect me to the world. And when I am in a state of pure discovery, when I am completely unaware of everything else, that's when I am most alive. I am not unlike the birds I've observed, who have their own private world. Their own sense of light, and comfort and purpose.

Yes, I finally say, I do.

Frame?

Skeet, I don't know how to tell. Essential things are too far inside to have an obvious language. I'm older, everyone gets older, but that doesn't necessarily mean you gain anything from it. Everything becomes more daily. More urgent. But at some point you have to be able to find the truth of the time you've taken up. All the living—the value of it.

What about the knowledge from the dictionary, from all this work. I mean, why do it? Why the compulsion to organize the unorganizable?

I place my cigarette, glowing, in the shiny ceramic ashtray. God. I never thought of it that way. As a compulsion to organize. Like Mother. I always think of it as documenting the present for the future. This is what art does. It allows for a continuous present. It encapsulates what cannot be known until something is lived. When Lev painted, I saw how he truly existed out of time. He was articulating what was beyond his own ability to know.

I want to show you something, I say to Skeet, getting up from the table, slowly, with difficulty.

Skeet picks up his bag and ducks his head under it, the leather strap across his chest like a newspaper boy, and takes my arm. We walk through the front door, the gravel making small rips underfoot, brush past the lavender down the stone steps and out through the archway. The cave walls gleam white. I see that one of my taped notes has fallen down. *Nine thousand years of protecting ourselves from nature, now we must protect nature from ourselves.* For the longest time I had a William Blake quotation above my desk. There is no difference between the whole thing and one thing, was what it said. It both made sense to me and confounded me intermittently. But seemed as sturdy a philosophy as any to live by. My pages weighted under stones. There is little breeze down here, and it is surprisingly arid. I wrap my shawl around me. The sight of all the work a small thrill that grazes me still.

Skeet's hands touch the pages, his eyes move around the space. I didn't picture it like this, he says, looking up. Eyeglints in the absence of light.

What did you picture?

I don't really know.

He looks at all the work, piles of papers, my drawings of parabolas translated into shapes, then mapped as expanding webs of glissandos. Writing pinned to the walls, digital recorders, a box of batteries, a stained teacup, pencils, huge stacks of vertical files, stiff large paper covered in symbols, crates of hard drives full of data, tapes, fieldbooks, several headphones, fieldnotes scrawled on slips of graph paper, broken-down recording equipment from various eras, empty packages of cigarettes, photographs, yellowed notes, spectrographs.

This— He stops. I forget how much you've seen, he says in a solemn voice that requires space around it.

First, I lost myself, I say to Skeet, and then I saw it clearly and began the conscious work of construction. And after all these years I see now that it comes from a devotion to life.

But where, he wants to know, does that devotion come from? Is it outside of you or inside of you?

It is bigger than me.

———

That night in the south of France, there were no more stars, the sky was black. There was a low rumble when the sun still shone. When I was out walking by the river. First there was a short rain. And after I went back to the house, after I saw that Lev was gone, the true rain began to fall. The earth calling for it. I stayed inside and listened to the sudden violet storm, counting the seconds between lightning flashes. I sat outside on the slippery stone steps. Lightning moving closer. Strike me.

There is no edge between the sorrow and the rain. I run out into the storm and feel its sullen chaos. Rain pricks my skull. Already this rain between us, erasing everything. Your dry footsteps. Sun glimmering through the spaces between every leaf, a cache of ancient gold. High larks filling the silverblue dawn. Ditches red like the first poppy you ever saw, dark-hearted and delicate. Your paintings so heavy I can't even hold them in one hand. It's all paint, you say, squinting in the sun. Paint upon paint, no money for new canvases. And they completely change. In the morning I wake up and everything that was dark is now white. Everything that was white is now black. You say that over time black on black becomes white on white. The edges are an archaeology of colour. The whip of white paint trailing along the foreground, the brush flicks from your hand like another perfect finger.

The truth is, no matter how close you get to another person, it will never be close enough.

We need the spaces in between, Lev says. The not-knowing. In between, the world is real.

But the most important thing is the thing we will never know.

I look around the large room. How an open door and upturned papers can contain violence. I oscillate between numbness and a wretchedness that comes in waves, the kind that can pull you under. I am vile and old. Cracked, dull, lined, hollowed. Though when I flash in the mirror as I move by the front door, dark as a crow, this is not what is reflected back. I am a rain-ruined figure, but it is only my eyes that look off. It is only the old who look older in tragedy.

I wanted to see Lev go. That he has vanished makes no sense. I understand now why people want to see the dead. The open casket, the body dressed in finery for the angel of death. Glasses on unseeing eyes, jewellery, a bloodless decoration outlasting skin. Hair combed—untidy is diabolical. We so obviously want to witness the goodbye. As though our observances will lessen the fact that people can just vanish. But where do they go? The child's question and the adult's question are the same.

Lev's cries in his sleep, warning calls. The one sound the recorder of sounds refuses to recognize. In rapture there is no room for anything else. Not even like a storm where there is calm in the eye. Rapture is a place where beauty rests entire. But I am reminded that everything is temporary. Nothing lasts. I try to picture his hands. I can see them perfectly. I know how he's boned. The things that cannot be led away without witness. Still, the rain falls.

What are you thinking about? Skeet asks.

Weather, I tell him.

We don't have a lot of time, he says. At the same moment we both realize how absurd this is. Like wrongly timed laughter that comes when moving furniture. Or at a funeral. Skeet's laugh is low and infectious and makes me laugh.

I've lost my sense of time.

Maybe that's a good thing.

I remember strange things, I say.

Like what?

I don't know. Ridiculous things, like houseflies buzz in the key of F. Crustaceans are instrumentalists. Or during social moments in unusual surroundings, seahorses turn bright colours. Then I think of my father, for instance. I never had much time with him as a child, but sometimes we would say the same thing at the exact same moment. Something uncommon like, Through the din.

There is a sound above. Hold that thought, he says.

EXTRACT OF INTERVIEW WITH
LEV ALEKSANDR VOLKOV,
PARIS, FRANCE, 1974

Q.

A. It's finding another shape or another myth,
something that tells us more.

Q.

A. Epiphanic chaos.

Q.

A. I think artists have a large capacity for
uncontrolled emotion.

Q.

A. No, it is deeply ordered. Though there are
accidental things.

Q.

A. I always try to take the work further, to move
closer to what I want.

Q.

A. The risk is that as you move nearer it is possible to lose the image completely.

Q.

A. I don't discuss my dreams.

Q.

A. I do not answer categorical questions.

Q.

A. Wrong question. Next question.

Q.

A. What is it that you want to know?

Q.

A. Not my wife, or my children.

Q.

A. Facts are just pinpricks. They are like the little dark holes that show where rain has hit.

Q.

A. There are no more facts when someone dies. There are things more vital.

Q.

A. Death made me grow up.

Q.

A. I have experienced extreme violence at close range. But I have also seen beauty.

Q.

A. Beauty. Does it have to be qualified?

Q.

A. Not beauty but unexpected outcomes.

Q.

A. Gypsum.

Q.

A. Tied to the end of a long stick.

Q.

A. Gravity.

Q.

A. Nature? No. I think it crass to merely copy what you see.

Q.

A. There comes a point when talking about a painting is beside the point.

Q.

A. The point being?

Q.

A. If I'd wanted to express through words I would be a writer.

Q.

A. No.

Q.

A. For the viewer? It is the residue of the activity. That fleeting moment and how they themselves interpret that moment.

Q.

A. Free it from the dead weight of the world.

Q.

A. Valéry said to give sensation without the boredom of its conveyance.

Q.

A. I've no idea. It is an act of impulse. Impulse that alters itself as I stand behind it.

Q.

A. The lure of pure feeling. Nothing more.

Seahorse

They greet each other with a dance every morning
to make sure the other is still alive, and then,
for the rest of the day, they float alone.

TIME IS MEASURED IN CENTIMETRES. One week, one centimetre. It makes me realize how unfair we are to children. Popping buttons, wrists sticking out below shirtsleeves. Pinched and accommodating in last year's shoes. Warmed and fed and nurtured while we pretend that they are not experiencing something as disturbing as changing size. The sheer panic of taking away what you know.

That anything could grow in these times is a miracle.

At first I could barely look at Tacita. A breach of contract. That I should be in this state, the one we agreed would not be ours. *Elle est tombée enceinte.* She fell. This is the part I hear. How soon it doesn't matter. Tacita remains the same. We conspire. We make a pact that despite everything, this will be a creative time.

It has given me new status among the artists. A small rebellion against the bourgeoisie whose eyes flit straight to the bare finger.

Wanton. *Pauvre cocotte*. But general scorn is nothing compared to the anguish from within.

I do what they say. I drink milk and sleep, deep lumbering sleeps where I am tugged under to blackness. There is nothing left to do but sleep. I am corpulent and raw and all desires are unmediated, like a child's, and I know that in this puerile state, with this calm body unwieldy and dense, is the promise of coming violence.

I return to the cocoon that is Mme. Tissaud's. Her ample arms around me, having swept my studio, a dustpan full of flaked paint, flung the window wide open to let in the autumn air. I tried staying with Tacita and Istvan but their apartment, with all its love and beauty, was weighted. I have unpacked my valise, the shiny lining funereal. Inside I find one of my dresses from the south, crumpled, forgotten. I hang it on the back of the door and iron out its wrinkles with the edge of my hand. The dress is white with small eyelets at the sleeve and hem. I notice a purple stain. Then the deadening sound of a plane overhead. All the planes. French or enemy. No one seems to know.

I sit still in my chair, waiting for inspiration to arrive. It comes, it doesn't come. The only thing I am able to do with consistency is record in my sound notebook. The comfort of its cool white pages. Mme. Tissaud gave me an alum-tawed book, one of the books meant for Angel's library, but she'd stitched the white cover with a faint red linen thread, and it seemed not right for him. She produced it, and I told her of the theft of mine, in that order. Everything with her is in that order.

Though the smell of solvents makes my stomach lurch, I start to paint again. I worry that parts of me are drifting away. My head feels stuffed thick with cotton. Painting holds me here the way I need it to. The work begins as a glimmer, a sense of something imagined. It slowly becomes something I can see. Then it becomes something I can do. It is a self-portrait. There is something about it that feels final. There are wooden floorboards and two walls that form an off-centre corner as though I am putting my subconscious on a quiet, anticipatory stage. I am seated on a chair, also off-centre, and am encircled by animals. A wolf, a white horse, a red fox, a deer, a raven, and other birds at my feet. I have a frontal gaze, eyes locked, unsmiling mouth, hair let loose and moving in an unsettling way. My clothing is earthy and male, with the exception of fine lace-up boots. Bright red slashes of paint alongside my arm show the chair beneath me. It would appear that I am holding court, communing with animals. Though this would be wrong. The index fingers of my right hand are extended in the sign that I have seen in Italian paintings. Extending or repelling evil. Bound in a pact. I spend too much time on the fingers, as they are the hardest to draw. I give everything delineated shadows. The one window is not painted perspectivally. There is a sense, as I paint, of suspended time, not controlled by a clock, where anything might happen. The stark contrast of inside and out. When I stand back, I see how wild I am. The animal in me stares back.

I sleep on the side my heart is on. I have listened to the heartbeat through a stethoscope. It sounds like horses at full gallop. Sometimes I am up for whole evenings. Tacita tells me that legend says when you cannot sleep you are awake in someone else's dream. There are days of working and eating bread and cheese and fruit. And then days of cigarettes and wine out with Tacita and the artists. I am reckless, I am chaste, I am dangerous, I am arch. I am sunk.

You know this is good, Tacita says. Other selves are good. It's nearly impossible to always be the same person.

I didn't want this. But I did nothing. I drifted, went blank.
And then it was too late. Tricked by my own body. But the body
alone achieves nothing. It pulled me in. Climbed inside my mind,
and silenced it. What began as dread became softer, sweeter,
sickening in its need. It washed over me with such force, filling
every crack. And I find myself startled to not only want it, but to
be protective of it. That someone who doesn't yet exist could
have the power to alter my way of being so profoundly is
chilling. I lose my grip. But in it, there are flashes of clarity, when
for a moment I remember who I am. A current rips through me.
I am no longer an inanimate object as all other adults are. The
mind floats, but the body is sure as metal.

It is a public act, this. Everyone has an opinion, all the
monologues that are regularly restrained now take on hard,
tangible sound. A stranger on the street places his hand on my
stomach, uninvited, and says he named his daughters after female
saints, and I wonder if the very young woman beside him is one
of the saints or his mistress. A woman says my arms are too thin.
Another says that God sees everything. She repeats this holding
her second and third fingers in a V below her eyes to accentuate,
in case I might need a visual aid for His eyeballs boring into my
corrupted flesh—reminding me of how much I dislike religion in
people. The uniformed men snicker. With their thin cold lips
they comment in their language, though it requires no translation.

The museums have closed. Their collections crated,
masterpieces wrapped in horse blankets and sent to the provinces.
The rarest animals in the zoos have been evacuated. Each week
another one gone. Tacita and I continue our project. We
document the disappearing animals. In a small notebook I record
their voices while she paints their portraits like royalty.
Classically styled, regal, catching their expressions through the

bars. It is a departure for both of us. We ask the zookeeper where they go. He tells us nothing.

Everything about this state is elaborate and held in place, not dramatic like dying. So when I climb the stairs with food procured from tickets and other machinations (I think of Lev's country, standing in line for onions and apples and matches), a sudden flood of water shocks me. It is warm and streams down my legs, making the wooden stairs slippery. A torrent. River water the faintest pink.

Like death, birth is too rapid. We wait and wait, but still it is a shock every time.

I walk slowly, full of purpose, a trail of water, leaking, forming streams, pooling, creating a visible trace of every movement. I place the bag of food on the wooden table. Even in terror, there is protocol. I feel the first stab of pain. I panic, and make an animal sound rapidly becoming a choking, terrified cry.

I don't want to do this alone.

I make my way down the stairs. Mme. Tissaud is out. I walk out zagging onto the sunlit street like a lunatic. In public, I think, nothing bad can happen. This is how unreliable my mind is.

What I remember flickers. A stranger's kind face. A dark car. The blur of arches and stone. And then white. I find myself with a stiff sheet over my legs, bright silver lights in my face creating a mosaic of tiny metallic glimmers like the eye of a fly. There is something wrong. Already everything is canted toward danger. I am a different, volatile version of myself. Combative. My limbs flashing and twisting. Fighting everything. What the nurses say when they can't find any veins. When they wrestle me into an ill-fitting gown and rubber pants like an incontinent child. Tell her, they command one of the doctors. Tell her she will slip and hurt herself in her own waters. Tell her she needs to listen to us.

I can hear my heart pounding in my ears. Black waves. I see for a moment, then black again. Pain comes with such force it threatens to rip in two and then it moves cleanly away without a mark, leaving stretches of nothingness. Unthreateningly pleasant, like cold water in a glass. In these moments I could paint, smoke a cigarette, kiss. But with the beginning of the stab is the memory of it right there, just below the surface. And when it comes, it comes so hard that it is impossible to do anything else, even breathe. It goes deeper each time. Primordial. Slicing through skin and nerves to underlying bone. Deeper than bone. A body ripping open for life is the closest you can get to your own death.

Something changes. I try to tell them that I can't breathe. Everything blurring and flashing, but nothing comes out. I cannot speak. It is like a bad dream where everything is wrong. The loss of voice and the movement of limbs. They are mistaken. I hear them say something. Blood pressure has bottomed out. There is a surgeon. Nurses grab my arms as I flail, and tie them down on either side, spread out like Christ. They say it's because the instinct is to grab out, to reach down for the baby.

This isn't how it is supposed to be. It doesn't match any of the prior slowness. The indolent growth. The scrimmed mind. The thick long days.

With other creatures, birth seems other, poetic even. Like seahorses, swimming in pairs linked by prehensile tails. I've read of complicated courtships that include full moons under which they make musical sounds. When the males give birth a few weeks later, out of a cloud, like magic, hundreds of fully formed seahorses appear.

———

I wake up in the dark. The air is stale. Used up. I am in a room and there are women in beds with iron bars coated with white paint. Bassinets on metal casters beside them. Small catlike cries of tiny pink-faced creatures that barely yet contain sound. I take a deep breath and exhale and realize that there is no knifing pain in my ribs. No sharp twisted muscles. No thick ropy feeling in my stomach. No pressing of hard head on bladder. No pinch and shift of internal organs. I feel open and bare and stretched, like an abandoned carcass. Big pieces of sky between each rib, stripped clean and gleaming. I touch my stomach and it is nothing but soft loose skin, not round and hard. My breathing comes rapid and shallow. All the months it took to get used to the steady growth and in one quick moment, everything gone. The mind does not work this way. This fast. The baby grows and slowly displaces you from your own body, and then tosses it back to you in an instant.

Beside my bed there is no bassinet. I feel husked. I panic, try to get up. A jolting pain in my stomach. I slide off the bed, attached to an IV, its heavy metal shackles. It isn't as light and smooth-rolling as I expected.

I wander through the hall, bare feet cool on the tiled floors, gown falling off my shoulder blade, bumps of vertebrae exposed, raining blows on all the doors. The astringent scent of floor cleaner presses through the halls. Madwoman, I can see this reflected in the nurses' little eyes like pins that fix a butterfly's wings.

There is a note on the door to the nursery. It is a schedule. *Fermé. Ouvert à huit heures*, it says.

I bang on the door. A nurse with undertaker makeup comes out and reprimands me. I should not be up. *Allez au lit!* she says harshly, as though I am a child.

Ou est mon enfant? I say, at first a quiet rumble and then louder, raging.

Revenir le matin, she says in a clipped, authoritative voice, pointing to the sign.

Revenir. Revenir le matin, I repeat catatonically. Tell me what happened. My words come out sounding like shavings on bone. I need to talk to someone. Where is the baby.

Sit down or you will rip your stitches moving like that.

Tell me, I scream. Tell me.

She directs me to my bed and snaps off the light.

Almost more painful than birth is when the milk comes in. The body gives a couple of days' respite and then suddenly there is filling, filling, chest hardened swollen, stretched raw, blue veins to the surface. Only there is no baby to alleviate this. Instead they come in, without consent, and in the night bind my chest so the milk will dry up, an act so painful I can scarcely breathe.

I am told that normally unwed mothers are segregated, but because of shortages we are all in the same ward. It is hard to believe we are anything but in the same ward, sanded down to sameness. At any given moment there are women in other rooms, pacing and groaning and bellowing like animals in a cage.

C'est à cause de la pleine lune, one of the nurses says. *Elle rend les gens fous*—she pauses, a sudden hard laugh slams out of her—*ou les accouchent.*

My eyes claw at the walls. Torn, aware in the stillness. But everywhere there are obstacles, the reluctance of my limbs, my mind.

Your baby died during the birth, a nurse comes in and tells me, though I'm not sure about when she comes, how many days later.

It is for the best, she says, then lowers her voice and adds, considering your situation. With no sense of the incomprehensible fact she has just delivered. She leaves me a tray of food that contains sausages and beans. As if this offering were perfectly normal following this news. The sausages are a whitish pink and shrunken in their casings. It reminds me of all the lost fingers, the men who have cut one off. A precaution, Lev told me, against conscription.

I hear a woman singing in a soft voice to a baby in the corridor and feel my own heart recoil. There is no lullaby capable of singing a baby who dies to rest. My body begins to shake. Each lurching sob sending a ripple of pain. Then the metal tray on the floor with a clatter. A child created and cancelled as though for my punishment alone.

There are sounds. There is a flurry of clicks on the tiles. My fists against the nurse. Another nurse. There is an injection and then a warm, slow seeping euphoria before the subterranean dark.

When I wake up I remember the dread each time, though each dread is nothing compared to the newest. I try to find the attending doctor. No one knows. No one seems to know. I am told nothing. I have moments of clear thinking and then others where I remember nothing. They have stopped the bleeding. The numbers have balanced and stabilized. I am made to sign a release form and then sent outside in a wheelchair that stops at the door, as though once this line is crossed you are fine.

And when I walk out, carefully moving into the cold morning, my body moves through the grey. Only now in the outside world, back in season, back in time, do I realize that life is not the same. As though a part of me was lowered in the grave with the baby. Though there is no baby. There is no grave.

So it will be born in February, an Aquarian. The stars hold something, Tacita does a chart. Birthflower: violets, she reads aloud. Birthstone— A graven-faced silence.

What, Tas?

Nothing. She says it in a way that I know it's not.

Tacita, what aren't you telling me? I ask laughing, reaching for the book. And then I see it. It says, amethyst.

The air is cold, and the instant it hits my skin I know that I must get out of here. I am told that my own tragedies are small against the greater tragedies that exist right now in the world. But tragedy doesn't calibrate that way, I want to say to the nurse. It isn't dwarfed by the whole. Tragedy is not general. How do we possibly compare tragedies? Instead, I am silent. I speak to no one.

I wish I lived in a different place. A place of opposites. Where it is night instead of day. This place is too old. Too complicated. A ruined holy city. I want green and plain. The outside air burns into my eyes. Everything spiritless. The entire city is a soft corpse, slack-necked, head lolling, open misaligned eyes. The streets, graves. The unnatural silence. The boarded-up shops. The blackened buildings. The dark uptwisting trees. The empty wet chairs in the Tuileries. The icy wind. I stand awkwardly. The pain in my body is present but fading, though I want it to stay. I want it to match what remains unbearable.

I am lost. Useless. The cobblestones grow slick with wet. The white snow turning to ash as soon as it touches the pavement. Throat twisted, I see black footprints behind, through the colourless slush. Proof I am still here. Three uniformed men observe me from a balcony. I smell concrete, its deep mildewed earth dragonish through all the holes. I walk blankly, fixedly. Though Tacita wears a bright red coat, ample and stylish, I do not see her, standing below.

Heron

Sheets of feathers, crackling of reeds,
waist-deep, dagger beak jacked to kill.

EVERYTHING HAS CHANGED in the way it happens in fairy tales when the whole kingdom falls asleep except for one person, the one cursed to remain awake. It makes me want to exist under another constellation, wake up in another time. I lie sluggish in bed for days. When I go out, for the first time I see the danger everywhere. It is busy, confusing. The sound of metal, the men in dark uniforms, the pained expressions, everyone fleeing. The deafening silence of Lev. That people can disappear. Whole populations can disappear. They can slide off the edge into nothingness.

He could be banished to Siberia, a woman in line at the post office says uninvited, scanning my envelopes, the thin pleas that go unanswered. Not as far north if accompanied by their wives, she adds, as though they are all polygamists.

It is a coarse wind slanting from the east. I walk to Tacita and Istvan's. Inside the apartment, the tinkling glass sound of Russian Orthodox church bells, and then a Stravinsky waltz. Russia engraves everything, even this Hungarian-occupied apartment in Paris.

Istvan is consumed with the idea of freedom. He works tirelessly, helping artists escape. There is an heiress with a house in the south. Special routes. Ways to get papers. Tacita and I have been helping too.

It would be so easy now to do nothing, Tacita says, squeezing my hand. But don't.

I look at her as though I cannot hear, concentrating on the human lips moving, the even tones, a look she possibly interprets as reassurance.

I think I need to get out of here. I look up at her, into the dark pools, her sloe eyes.

Yes. You must go, I, she says, looking over at Istvan. But he will not leave his work here yet. We will eventually book passage and set sail from Portugal too. We must get you a ride to the coast, I. You cannot stay here. You can sail to New York.

She looks at me and smiles. Then we will see each other on the other side.

I nod.

A flicker of possibility that, despite all the things I cannot change, there could be a way out of this. This rolling anguish that pulls me into its ripeness where extinguishing life seems perfect and near.

At the call of the whistle, Tacita picks up the kettle and pours into a mint green teapot. Steam rises. She puts her spoon in the jar of contraband honey, takes it out and carefully licks it.

When we meet again in New York, she says, we will have our exhibition based on the disappearing animals.

I begin making elaborate black line drawings, hunched in my coat. Fingerless gloves. Eating little. I am waiting to be taken to

Marseille, and from there I will go to Lisbon and join others, waiting like orphans, for escape. But something new is in me, something dark and not-mine. I notice that murder is everywhere. On these men's faces, their tight-lipped mouth holes. A fox that hangs around a woman's neck, the small claws dangling somewhere between her clavicle and her shoulder blade. All the skins furled like unopened lily-of-the-valley leaves pinholed with air in Mme. Tissaud's atelier. Pigs, calves, cows, dotted whorls of ostrich necks, goat stomachs. Though there are so few now, almost no leather anywhere. I begin to see things that make me unsure. I start to say things out loud as a test, to see what others will say.

Do the cries of animals make you uneasy? I say to Mme. Tissaud, motioning to the skins.

I hate nature, she laughs. It's so—vegetal. I find it vast, tedious. I am comforted by electric lights and music and the rose windows of Notre Dame. I would rather look at a Delacroix than a forest. I have no romantic attachment to nature, she says, lining up text blocks. It was severed when I was a child. I remember watching a mother duck gliding, trailed by three yellow ducklings on a summer day. A majestic heron flew over them for a moment and then disappeared. I watched the mother and her ducklings smoothly moving on the lake's surface and thought how serene they were. And then a flash of feathers. The heron landed and skewered them. One. Two. Three. It ate all three of the ducklings, gulping them down in front of the mother who swam around frantically, crazed, wings flapping in water.

I think I have been too close to the earth, she says and twirl-locks the cutter in place. Tilling soil, walking through wet fields, fingers rubbed raw from picking crops. We had livestock, and killed the animals we ate. We witnessed the savagery without spell. Animal skins are no different to me than cloth, other than how they perform in binding.

This clarifies nothing, I decide.

She wipes her hands on her coarse apron and I follow her back to the kitchen. She takes out a bag of dried bracts that sprout from the linden leaves and begins to pound them into paste, letting them rest in a sieve. She will use it to bake biscuits, flour now being scarce.

Ivory, Jean-Yves, my oldest son, is coming to take me to the Dordogne. You could come with me. After everything—

Everything?

You need to be careful, she says, mixing, crumbling more leaves in her fingers. It's not safe here.

Safe?

I am capable only of repeating what she says.

There are so many more of them here. And more people have been taken away. Just the other day I saw them drag a teenage boy to Gare d'Austerlitz and board him on one of those trains without a destination. His eye had been punched into a shiny purple circle. She stops. I can see her eyes filling up with emotion. She brushes off her fingers and puts them on my shoulders, looking directly at me. I can tell my eyes startle her. Their dullness, their remoteness. She says, Against change of fortune set a brave heart. Though for the first time her voice sounds scared, making it unclear whom she says this for.

And Lev. Silence, a new language that trickles between us like blood.

No one mentions his name. But, Tacita says, slowly parsing the words, don't underestimate him.

Tacita, I cannot talk about it. Though nothing I say matches the desolation within. I feel like something has been switched off.

I eat carefully, potatoes only, while incomprehensible events unfold in the outside world. All of it interests me very little. It increases, this encircling darkness, though nothing threatens me from outside. Strangely, I feel as though I am not destined to die. Living with this deep-hulled absence seems like a sentence, one that I will have to endure. Wondering whether or not it is a gift to survive. With only Tacita noticing that there are things not normal in me.

I sit down at my easel because it is what I know, but it is more a relic from a former self. I find narrative pointless. Why a story? Why now? But I squeeze the ends of tubes and mix colours, silverblue and icy grey with russet undertones. A vivid centre of colour, a mantle of fur depicted out-of-doors in a wintery landscape. There is a small bird offset in the left corner. The bird is slowly disappearing and can barely see its own reflection in the mirror that juts out from the snow. The figure in the mantle has a half-smile as though he carries a secret. The moon sits, immovable.

I hear a quiet knock on the door.

Come in.

Tacita's shoes tick across the floor. Oh, you're working, I. I can come back.

No, I say, not looking up. Stay.

She squints and comes close to the painting and then stands back. It seems to be a discovery, she says, no imperatives in her voice.

I keep painting while she walks and then sits on the bed. There is a long silence.

Ivory?

Hmm.

I'm scared.

I stop and put down my brush, walk over to her and sit beside her on the bed. She is shaking. What is it, Tas?

God, I wouldn't know, there are so many things, she says, fighting back the emotion.

Tell me.

I spend so much time standing in line for hours to collect some rotten scraps of food like a rat. All that time waiting gives my mind too much room. I am not thinking of the divine. I keep thinking, When there is no beauty, what exactly have we got? Have we got truth? And then my thoughts fill with all the things that are tightening, making me feel I cannot breathe. Everyone I see with plundered faces, yellow stars pinned to their coats. How quiet the streets are. So quiet you can forget your own life. I am a *chiffonier*, like the rag-pickers from the Belle Époque combing the streets for broken glass and dead animals to skin. There is nothing here. And I know that Istvan's work is essential, but it scares me. All the artists and writers he is getting to the house in the south. Then everywhere I look I see the soldiers, and am sure that they know. The awful prying eyes as I walk by our captors who live and multiply among us. I think I might be paranoid, but then something real happens, like coming home and the bath is drawn. Water right to the top. They are trying to tell us that we are being watched. And then I think, Where is Lev? She starts to cry. And where are you, I? Where are you?

I put my arm around her shoulder. Tas, I am here. It's— the world that has changed its shape.

Well that is why we must go, she says, wiping her cheek.

Tas—

Yes?

Tell me. Honestly. Do you think I might be a bit—mad?

She pauses for a long time. I think you are really, extraordinarily, awake.

But do you think by leaving we are fleeing the failure of civilization?

She takes in air. I think that we are not yet eaten away by our own cynicism. We have faith. She pauses again. Your making that painting proves it.

It does? I feel like everything is untrustworthy. This painting seems so absurd. Even language. *J'ai peur*. What does it even really convey of this experience? We are bound together in this, but we aren't. Not really. We have to go it alone. We have to live with ourselves. I feel like I'm drifting, Tas. My mind keeps playing tricks. I look at basic things, and I find I can't tell what they are anymore. At least not their purpose. We make sense of things by always relating them back to ourselves. I wonder what they've done to Lev. And it makes me want to—

She looks at me. Her eyes look worried.

Exist in something truthful, I say. Something full of grace.

Tacita lights a cigarette. You will, I. You are about to return to the larger-than-life forests, like you had in childhood. The wilderness that you love. I can see a thought flicker across, and then she smiles. You know it might be Mother Nature who is actually your real mother. Her eyes go to my laddered stockings. It's funny because childhood is so brief, but then you end up missing it for all the rest of the years.

You don't miss yours.

Some things.

I've spent my life running away from things.

You've spent your life running toward things. This is no different.

But I'm different, Tas.

I keep having dreams where I can taste dirt in my mouth. That I'm dead and that I have to negotiate my own body somehow, I say in a quiet voice.

Well, thank god, she says, uncrossing her legs, we don't have to undertake our own burials. She looks up and walks to the window; she still has her coat on. Everyone now lives with their coats on. The winter has been shatteringly cold. There is no coal. The electricity has been shut off. We shove newsprint between our sweaters and coats. People stay in bed for days just to keep warm. Outside the cold rain falls.

I can hear the wet slap of the tree branches against the side of the roof in the wind.

You know what scares me, Tas?

What?

That I'm getting used to it.

To what?

To everything.

People can get used to anything, she says and then adds, but that isn't always bad.

I don't know. I'm not sure what will survive. I can already feel the hardening of collective hearts. Of my heart.

Tacita is so serious when she turns on her heel and looks at me, though her eyes look large and tired. Ivory, don't you see? What lives on is this. She sweeps her hand across the air. Our day-to-day lives.

I look at her blankly.

Everything. This dust on the floorboards. Those dried silver teabags on your saucer. That plant with the browning leaves. Your tubes of paint dried at the openings. The bubbles in the glass of that window. The leafless branches of that tree that will blossom and leaf and scatter, over and over again. The matches that will be used to light those cigarettes. The stacks of books that you may or may not have read yet. All the stamps on all the unopened letters you have sent. Mme. Tissaud humming downstairs. This beautiful, unfinished painting. We have to hang on to it. All of it, because when we are gone, everything slips away and our time, these things—all these things will be gone.

Then we will hold on, I say.

What I don't tell her: I dream that I jump out my window in my sleep and wake on the way down.

And while we hug goodbye, outside, the rain falls.

Moth

Lunification.

THE THING IS—the clock moves an inch—there is something else.

What do you mean? Another tick.

There was a child born in Paris.

There is no child, I say flatly. The baby died.

Skeet looks into my eyes. A whole lifetime passes back and forth.

It didn't. I mean, she didn't. I have the hospital records the museum sent, he says, gesturing to his bag. This is what they would tell unmarried women, he says carefully, when in fact the child had been adopted. That the mother was often heavily drugged for days at a time. That there were always many families that wanted a baby. This child, this girl, was adopted by a childless couple who fled to the south and later settled back in Paris.

A daughter, I say, attempting to move past this word functionally, but agony grips my chest and forces it out, stilted. The horrible sound stuck in the walls.

283

But, before anything else, I have to tell you. He drops his head. She's gone now.

When I say nothing, he says, They called her Jeanne.

My heart heavy as water. I swallow several times to regain control of my voice. Oh god, Skeet. I have to just—

I'm sorry Frame. I'm so sorry. I just wanted—

I should be crying, soaking his shirtsleeve. But I am stunned. I had known, somewhere, that this is what the letter meant, but would not, for a moment, let myself think it. The pain I had kept tightly in the heart of my heart, stopped it filling my entire chest. All these years as though a sound, muffled offtime, stayed with me. Another heartbeat faintly beating behind my own. In order to forget one life, you need to live at least one other life. The young can withstand the shock of love because another life is still possible. It is only the old who die of heartbreak.

When the director came from the Volkov Museum, Skeet says, I heard Valentina say she would track you down, as though she hadn't just received sound files from you. In those deadly goddamn conservancy progress meetings, she began to imply that the dictionary was over, and that your single-mindedness around it was a sign that you really had gone crackers. When the painting sat in her office and she made no move to notify you, I began to wonder if it wasn't she who was crazy.

Skeet says he radiated with anger. He will confront Valentina. No, he will call the police. No. He will do neither. He once told me that everything he knows he stole. Only he didn't realize what he was getting into. And still, he couldn't stop. Not all of life is accumulation. Sometimes a single moment of a single day can determine a life.

He observed when Valentina took her coffee each morning in the small glassed-in eating area with smooth birch tables and a view of the treetops. She would sip from her mug with her notebook and files in her lap and read for a quarter of an hour, sun on her shoulders. He picked a bright cold morning, moved quietly, clicked the door shut. He knew he had only minutes. His heart beat wildly but he was oddly focused. He took the pin from between his teeth. It slipped in his damp fingers as he twisted it into the lock of the drawer underneath her desk. After an excruciating minute of frantic precise movements, it opened. He pulled out the letters and put them in his bag that also contained a hard drive of every single file from the dictionary he wiped clean from the sound lab. The documents and the painting were not where he remembered them in Valentina's office. He panicked. His eyes scanned the room, tidy and sharp. He opened the filing cabinet. There were steps at the door; he held his breath. His head chases the image of his mother painting her toenails on the metal steps of the fire escape with the glass bottle he had pocketed for her for the first time. He felt so odd because it had both made her happy and violated something. He was probably only six or seven. She saw him looking down at her. Why so glum chum? No harm, she paused. Done. The steps continued along the hall, and he let out air silently. He found the file folder containing faded records from a hospital in Paris, from Spain. There is a report from an internment camp, a pale blue telegram, adoption papers, a letter from an art appraiser. He takes the entire folder and puts it in his bag. His eye catches the edge of a padded grey envelope. He pulls it delicately, slips it under his shirt. The sharp corners prick his chest as he walks out the door and shuts it behind him. He slides his hand along the cool wall, perhaps to steady himself, or to remind himself of where he is, or both. He moves through the hall in long strides, his shoes are silent. He takes the stairs, and then holds his plastic security card underneath the thin red line of the scanner. Hurry, he thinks. No, stay still. Nothing happens. Finally, there is a beep. The turnstile opens and he walks through the doors. The sun flickers onto his face, his back to the building. After all the years spent there, all the hours with Ivory in the sound lab, he understands that he will never see it again. He doesn't turn around.

Do you want some water Frame?

Thank you. No. Skeet. There is some sherry on the kitchen shelf.

I'll get it. He stands up, his legs carrying him toward the house.

I sit huddled in this cave, little animal that I am. I had never thought ahead to what would happen once the baby was born. Lev was unreachable. There was, eventually, no post. No news, good or bad. He knew nothing of me. He was dead in the eyes of everyone.

Skeet comes back in what seems like an instant. Youth. The distinct thud of his gait, sun-swung into the cave carrying a bottle and glasses. He pours the sherry into a cheap tumbler and passes it to me, putting the bottle down on my desk. He hesitates—it is morning still, or perhaps because it is a woman's liquor—and then pours a glass for himself.

We sit, joined in thinned silence.

How, I finally say, did she die, Skeet?

He braces himself, sitting up higher on his elbows. It said— He chooses the word carefully, letting all the other ones fall away. Fire.

But Frame, she too had— He shifts so quickly on the desk edge that he spills his glass.

Jeanne had a daughter, he announces slowly. Lou. He pauses.

Feeling the need to add something, says, She lives in New York.

Loup? I say in disbelief.

Lou. No "p."

History shifts underfoot. Unreliable ground. I've no idea where to take refuge. Everything built around love ruptured, a child who died. This information trips up my plodding rhythm. Like the composers who insert a scherzo two-thirds into a piece. A joke. But here it comes out dark and heavy, savage almost.

There is a roar of an engine swinging into the drive. I am filling with pain and exhaustion. The physical miseries setting in as they reliably do. I can tell by the urgency and economy of Skeet's movements that he thinks it is to do with the conservatory.

We hear the crunching of gravel up above. Skeet and I sit huddled in pitch-black silence. He folds his hands behind his skull, his frame long against the rounded walls. With his arcane knowledge and renegade bloodline, it strikes me that he makes the perfect criminal. He told me once that when he was small, he had seen his mother take a bottle from the shelf at the liquor store and put it under her coat. She told him it isn't stealing if you really don't have the money to pay. He said he realized in that moment that thieves are never made later in life. It only comes easy when you have always done it. He won scholarships that were never quite enough to live on. He told me when we first met that he was so broke at university he'd sold his blood for a doughnut. And now here he is with me. And I think, As with animals, association with anything weaker foreshadows doom. Lawlessness demands synchronous agility of mind and body. Like that French-Algerian writer and her lover who broke the same bone in their foot escaping from different prisons.

The gravity of the situation just now flickers through. I've had grief and joy in my life but nothing like this.

I don't know who I am, I say.

I've said it out loud. Everything dislocated in my mind. What a person does is who they are. The work accesses the deepest part of me. Which is not a part.

Skeet, I say slowly, it's just— I've survived such a long time. It can't end with a witless falling-off.

Then don't let it.

Dread fills the space.

You've never spoken about Lev. About your past.

You might be the only one who knew not to ask.

It is there. It is always there. Offered up on these delicate documents thin as cigarette paper. Documents with signatures and stamps that have crossed vast spaces. It is all recorded. It is not a mystery. Things don't just slip away.

He hands me the file, but I have no need for these coloured papers, pale and small, covered in elegant script and silver type, beautiful and inaccurate. Written out in languages I do and do not speak. How could something so neat and thin possibly tell of life, so huge and hard and wild.

Prénoms: Jeanne Albertine. Sexe: Feminin. Née à l'Hôpital Saint-Vincent-de-Paul, le 10 février 1941. Mère naturelle: Ivory Frame. Père naturel: Inconnu. Parents adoptifs: Gilles et Marie Archimbault du Souillac, France.

Nombre: Ivory Frame. Género: Femenino. Años: Aproximadamente veinte. Cabello: Marrón. Ojos: Marrón. Altura: 170 centímetros. Peso: 43 kilogramos. Nacionalidad: Británica. Observaciones: Rechazó el examen físico. No responde a castigos por parte de las

enfermeras. Es incapaz de caminar en línea recta.
Es incapaz de subir escaleras. No come. No puede
dormir por la noche. Su sentido moral es cuestionable.
Solitaria. Delirios: 1. Cree que la institución es
'Un Inframundo'. 2. Asegura que puede comunicarse
con animales. Diagnosis: posible psicosis, delirios,
reacciones de ansiedad.

Lev Aleksander Volkov. Feind ukrainischer Herkunft.
Camp des Milles. Entkommen, April 1940. Nähere
Umstände unbekannt. Verhaftet und inhaftiert, August
1941. Ausweispapiere: nicht vorhanden. Einweisung
in Drancy 11.Juni.1942. Morgenappell bei Gewitter:
Häftling abwesend. Flucht des Häftling bestätigt,
14 Uhr. Nähere Umstände unbekannt.

When Lev escaped to Paris, no one was there. It seemed the city had been boarded up, emptied out. Their flags snapped overhead. The streets quiet, dark, and foul-smelling as though there had been an epidemic. He didn't know of anything. He didn't know that Istvan had moved to work out of the south. That Tacita was gone. That I had gone. That somewhere along the way to the coast, I broke. Was given drugs, injected into my spine, that created such terror the doctors thought they could shake me sane.

In the clinic, I had gone to hell. At least that is what I felt. Food administered through a tube in my arm. The door in my room has bars. I feel like a wild animal caught. I don't know where I am or why I am here. There is a mattress scarcely covering the slats on my cot like a whale skeleton.

Starched-collared nurses with their clanging keys and coloured pills, thin lips telling me I am here for a rest, their voices moving at terrifying speeds, never looking at me, instead picking up the chart at the end of the cot. Reduced to a white rectangle. I am given one dirty sheet and a pencil. There is the smack of the little explosion of the gas lamps turning on. The milky light. The smell of blood and urine and ammonia coming from the black and white diamond tiles. Long empty days full of terror for simply being somewhere where no one else is.

At night, I twist in my sheet. I examine the details of my captivity: the cheap varnished wardrobe, the objects they eventually give back to me—a jar of face cream, centimes, a small mirror. I hold them carefully. In my hands, they bristle with meaning. I arrange them as though they might contain the answer to escape but when I wake up each morning nothing is coming off them. They have lost their significance. One day, through a window in the hall, I hear the click of horse hooves on the stones, followed by the low call of a pigeon on the grubby windowpane. Glimmers of sound that make me desperate for the outside world. I catch my mind looking for Lev's face and feel such sharp pain I erase the memory of him. My mind is not right. I am not yet well. There is a doctor who offers to help, occasionally putting his cigarette in my mouth, but when he slides his hand up my thigh, I understand what kind of help.

Eventually they give me books but I have no interest in them, no desire to read. The head nurse is often followed by a black dog. Medium-sized, soft-hearted, with wiry hair and large wet eyes. I feel desperate to read his inner resources. I can hear vibrations of beings and feel no need to communicate in the normal way. Spanish words bullet off the walls, needing no translation. My body is always burning hot. I wipe it with the nightdress worn all day, all night, and far too large. There is no monthly bleeding because I am neither woman nor person, just eyes and skin and organs. But when asleep in the windowless room, I am in my body. I dream I am pregnant. When I wake there is no stomach, no baby. Foolishly alone. I sink into a deep panic. Lying on my narrow mattress, I become the child. I stretch my arms or move my fingers, and, for a moment, I feel I am the baby. The one robbed of childhood, never to experience its sorrow or its magic. I wonder if dying is harder than being dead. I can't seem to walk properly. My mind tries desperately to unite with my body, but everything is jammed.

After a stretch of silent weeks, I see parts of myself flicker in, all my senses quickened. A moth flutters into my room, its wings jerk and catch the light from the exposed bulb and flash bright and precise as paper. There is an inch of hope. The wings say: tragedy will be burned, nothing more can die.

I discover that I am not in a mysterious place. It is a madhouse. I draw maps of escape and then one day, miraculously, I do. My parents want me further away so as not to bring further disgrace. It puts an end to speculation as to how I got here. The institution isn't what they object to. It's the other things I have done. They send their housekeeper to take me to a new clinic. We drive along the highway beside a lorry crammed with sheep. Their braying is fierce. But my mind feels clear and sharp in the outside air, enlivened at leaving behind the dirty, sordid world of the institution. The feeling of moving toward a precise, mathematical existence. In town, we stop to eat at a restaurant. The housekeeper eyes me nervously. I realize that she is hesitating to give me a knife, which suddenly strikes me as uncontrollably funny though I don't dare laugh. I excuse myself, go to the washroom, and am thankful I have calculated correctly. I crawl out the window and eventually make my way to the port. I wait and wait for passage.

Months later, on the street in Lisbon, I see a figure in the distance. A man walks toward me. The man is Lev.

Mourning Dove

Fast flight, bullet-straight vector.
Wings make sharp whistling noise.
One of the most hunted species.

WE BOTH HAVE TICKETS in our pockets. My ship, his plane. We don't know how to greet each other. Nothing is as I had imagined. I am frailer, wilder. He is toughened. We are fallen. But when we move closer to each other it is the same. Parched hearts, earth-struck, everything gold. He takes my hand and kisses the ends of my fingers. A welter of heat in my insides. I have been so numb, it makes me aware of how much my body suffered, separate from him. I am reminded how remarkable his movements are. His mesmerizing eyes, their mad quick glitter. How they knife into you. I am immediately brought back to the agony of him. The touch of him is all. It slices my past from me. It is hopeless to try to recover my sense of what is happening, the surface of my mind slips. This moment will never play out slow enough. His presence so sharp I feel it in my teeth. His cool skin. He smells like the forest. This history of skin. Every organ in slow articulation. A list of hungers. The pull and click, the honesty of shameless coarse desire. My obedience to it. Shoulder, mouth, wrist, neck. How quickly he alters me. My mind burns. When someone is killed. When a baby dies. When someone returns from the dead. When death is woven into every single thing. It seems ridiculous to give up anything, however imperfect. To not simply dwell in the miracle of the body—it is stronger than anyone thinks. He touches my face, my hair, blown and knotted as though I am at sea. I wonder if he sees that I have lost my youth. He would never say it, but it would be true. Of all the death. Of everyone vanished. All this weight that came suddenly, the burden of it. And then, he stands here in full tide. Alive. It is so surprising, that we insisted, it seems, on living. We hold each other with sounds of gears shifting, shoes on cobblestones, and voices speaking in a different languages all around us. He kisses me, gravely, sensually. Everything goes silent for the length of a single breath. My heart deepens its beat. That familiar feeling of being both hollowed out and then completely filled, with what I am never sure. My mind filled with a thousand things I cannot tell. He says he thought he would never find me. I say I thought he was dead. He looked for me in Paris, but I had left. Taking nothing. He hadn't, at first, accepted this as an explanation. I notice he has new clothes, but this isn't what creates difference. I see that something else has changed. He carries himself differently. His world caught. His movements unfamiliar. A buoyancy lost. But then I understand it is not he who has changed but me. That he has always had the knowledge that life evades. That we grasp it only for a moment. It is what makes him untouchable, yet oddly more alive.

I am engaged.

His voice like the centre of a flame.

My heart snaps in two.

I see the dark beginning to unwhorl. I try to think of when I last was looking at him. Time is so different, I think, when we are in pain, when we suffer.

An American, he says. She will get me to New York.

My body grows so cold it feels like burning.

She helped with my papers.

My hands tremble. A jolting pain like a nick to the arteries.

She is wealthy.

My eyes rip the pavement below his feet. Trying to comprehend what he says though I am still taking him in, I am still with him, the image of him. Stunned that he can announce he is leaving, as though he is an ordinary man with an ordinary fiancée.

He is held back by torment. Ivory. His eyes search my eyes. They contain all we cannot alter. He says, The only person I have ever loved is you.

And I think, That is a lie that tells the truth.

The only way I know how to express myself is to offer him my body. From the top of my skull downward a scalding pain. He knows what I think. That too much has passed between us. Too many things, and how would you begin to tell? But we are forced to go on as people do.

I can't find my pitch. I'm gone. Everything in me that was you is gone. Lev. Can't you see? But this is not what I say. Instead I walk back with him to my rented room like an animal dragging a trap. It is bright with the last available light. The tree out the window, with its good practical leaves like a memorized poem. Each of us with so much to say, but acutely aware that words so often say nothing. They strike the wrong spot. They force you to give up. Maybe this is why we use the same two dozen words for everything. And the truth is, you could search your entire life and you would never find a phrase that would even remotely fit this moment. I know Lev doesn't feel this way. He says words can be as precise as an arrow.

He tells me he hasn't painted in so long it feels like injury.

I gave away all my art supplies, I say. Everything.

It is possible to begin again.

His words are pressed, lasting. He is right. This notion of what must be moved toward is inside me like a separate person. I know, I say. What I want is to tell him everything, but there is no translation. And what good would it be, if we were able to tell all there is to tell?

Ivory. Where are you? You seem. Separate.

We are silent.

I learned it from you.

Nothing can keep me from you.

You, the one who has never needed anyone.

His voice splinters in the altercation at street level below. Shouts, the crush of metal. Everything neither real nor unreal. I am reminded of how he is not bound by common standards of love or morality. He brings beauty to the room, as he always has. I love him for this alone.

His hands on my ribs. Impossible to stop. Burrowing my whole body toward him. Our hands, our feet. Engraving bodies to bone. His body is so close to mine, I can almost forget him. I am used to getting silent quickly with him. There is no need for me to alter anything now, he is worth the torment. Everything vanished in this moment alone. We lie in each other's arms.

Lev. You must know, I tell him, heart shaking, when we first enter my room, that I can never see you again. Promise me.

I move my eyes to the cracks in the wall. His head on my thigh. How odd that the sun should be shining and mourning doves singing. Receiving their songs, silver and necessary. The source of light high above this room. The sun's light down the length of his back. He knows how to love. He has a talent for it. There is a woman on the other side of town who waits for him across this blue distance, in an extravagant hotel room. There is no order to this. It is not possible to love completely and not lose your identity. I have shattered once. I will not do it again.

He watches me dress. I pull on my stockings and sit on the edge of the bed, reach over and touch his scars. New ones. Two on his shoulders. Shining, unknowable. I move toward the window, my hand shading my eyes, his eyes on the line of my body through the thin dress.

I will make it right, he says. Let me.

You don't understand, I say. He knows how to make anything, I think, but how could anyone fix something like this?

What don't I understand?

He looks at me, his eyes filling with emotion. He knows everything. He knows nothing.

I foundered. I am just barely back into being. I unclasped my heart. You had every part. What has happened fixes us to this outwardness, to a place where neither of us now are.

All I say is, I am someone else. What I don't say is that I do not altogether know who I am.

He gets up and walks toward me. I rest my face against his chest. He speaks to me but I do not answer, shaking my head.

Sounds collect below. Here there are electric lights, food, shopping. People at parties. Prostitutes along docks and alleys where the mist rolls in after dark. Filthy men. Crooked agents. Aristocrats gambling at the casinos. Money dwindling at cafés and restaurants from all the waiting. Thin-armed women hollowed out from hunger, hipbones like axeheads. Bribes for tickets to get on the crowded filthy ships. One visa expiring while waiting for another. They are running out of rooms.

Is she an artist? I finally say.

No. A collector.

Good. That will be good for your work.

He takes my face in his hands. None of it matters.

He looks at me. Immemorial. Say something.

Your taxi is here.

He says he will tell the woman that we have seen each other. I imagine her tilting her head when she receives the news. They will speak in low tones. They have their own serious conversations. This thought alone inflicting injury. I make a pact to extinguish any further thoughts of him. Anguish inlaid with intention. We don't even say goodbye. He just walks out the door and closes it behind him. I marvel at how simple it is. This precise gesture. A door closing. I listen to the sound of him walking down the stairs, slowly growing faint. Abandonment is not enough, I think. You must stay gone.

He will tell me that the woman who has been waiting is pained. She feels ridiculous, like something cancelled. But she offers to buy me a plane ticket, which I think noble, though I say no. Thank you. I will take the ship. Set sail. We will see each other on the other side, he says. And I think, If there is one word for Lev, I know what it would be. It would be survivor.

The light jerks in my eyes. Love makes space. Love takes it away. Though I have witnessed everything going, and too soon, I still feel bound to him. With him, I discovered what people were capable of. Without knowing it, he brought me closer to the world.

Why didn't you—

I shake my head.

But you could have—

I could never have been anything if I remained with him. Don't you see? Who wants to be a helper, merely? But I don't say this. It sounds cold when in fact the opposite is true. He eclipsed everything. I handed myself over to him and he lived in me. I found it almost impossible to do anything in his presence. It occurs to me, only now, what he gave me by not saying he loved me. My solitude. He wanted what was at the heart of me to remain my own. Being with him required all my thinking and loving and force, all the time. Everything I had. It was not pure awe, because somehow it oddly gave me strength. To see into the centre of him and then into the centre of me. But now I think, Why centre?

And after all this time, I say at last, I'm not sure if I never mourned him, or if I'm mourning him still.

Butterfly

Asterope, a butterfly genus. Asterope,
a main-belt asteroid. AsteRope, a pair of
parallel circumferential tethers circling an asteroid
to enable improved extra-vehicular activity.

THROUGH THE OPENING of the cave, Skeet can see a man's legs step out of a car. There is a dangerous flicker of energy to him, his sharp, impatient movements, though when he gets to the front door his knock is quiet, polite. He says my name several times and then gives up and tries the name of the American. His accent, I recognize it. Is it American? I whisper to Skeet. I can't see him.

No.

We both say nothing. Do nothing, frozen like deer, and eventually the knocking stops. We hear the car door slam. The tires rip at the gravel as the car pulls away.

God, Frame, how did you, his voice low across the cave, recover?

How does anyone? You remake yourself. The studying, the learning, it filled me with certainty. My work. I shift on the stones. The animals becoming the part of my heart that he did not have. The part that allowed me to become myself. I stop. And then something passed through me.

But even things that pass clean through leave a mark, he says.

The silence is broken by a high whip of wind. I look up. Motion is part of listening. In the forest, sounds last for a long time. In most places there is so much other noise that sounds all end up dying young. Cities are obituaries of sound, I say. Did you know that urban noise complaints go back as far as ancient Rome?

Skeet stares ahead.

I know what you're thinking, Skeet. That these sounds we are recording are obituaries too.

He looks up and squints, as though in the sun.

This whole work, the entire dictionary of animal languages, evolved out of an art project, begun with a friend who is now dead. And now it is, I realize, almost an art project again. I stop to consider. This idea like an undersong. You know, I say, if you have a point to make, I wonder if maybe art is the better route.

What the hell kind of question is that.

There is a live spark in it that few things can touch. It forces you to really look at things, and I think that really looking at things is never time wasted. You would never know until you reach an age like mine that small experiences could possibly occupy equal ground, alongside everything, even gratifying accomplishments. Even love.

Lev would often say that artists are the sum of their risks. I had once posed a question when we were walking under a chestnut tree in spring, its pale blossoms dervishes, shedding onto the pavement below. The tiny woman with a twig-ended broom sweeping them up would have been right out of a fairy tale had she not been shaking her fist at the tree, shouting expletives.

Va-t'en! Dégueulasse! Still, they fluttered down.

A wedding in the air, Lev observed aloud.

Why, I asked him, do we need art?

Because the world is terrifying. He looked up. And beautiful.

And?

And not sayable.

But all my experiments, the sketchbooks, the canvases, the sound notebooks—they all led to this. I didn't want to paint, or interpret nature, I wanted to record it so that it could be itself.

Skeet leans back, resting his head against the wall.

You know, I've always felt that my work contains death and love at the same time.

If you're talking about the conservatory, it doesn't matter. You can take your work elsewhere. I know activists who could help.

No it's the whole project, Skeet. Don't you see? It came out of the wisdom of grief. If you can call it that.

He looks up.

I have learned that you must not wait for death in order to grieve for something. You must grieve for it while it is still alive. My friend Tacita tried to tell me this, but I didn't understand what she was saying until much later. The animals whose languages we are recording. I feel connected to them. They carry a kind of disappearing inheritance. But I don't think it's negative as I once did. If you revere things while there is still life in them, there remains only the revelation of being.

I don't know if I'd say *only* the revelation of being. I would consider the revelation of being everything.

Well exactly. What you come to know is that grief isn't about understanding anything. You go it alone.

Skeet turns one of the smooth stones from the cave floor over in his fingers.

My friend who started the project with me was hit by a car. It was raining. They said it was an accident. Nobody knew for sure. Her husband worked for the Resistance. Accidents in those times were not always accidents.

Skeet looks so attentive, as though he's listening to me from the kind of depth that can be accessed only from instinct.

She died, I say. And I grew old. My whole generation, gone. I suddenly realize that there will never again be anyone like us. But of course no one is like anyone else, regardless of era.

I shift on the cold ground. Sometimes I wonder if I've become so obsessed with pieces of sound that I've overlooked the value of silence. Silence does not betray experience, words do. There is a composer who wrote a piece of music interspersed with fifty-three quotations of poetry from Hölderlin meant to be sung silently during the performance. To achieve what the poet calls The Delicate Harmony of Inner Life. He even wrote notes to his performers also taken from Hölderlin:

A more secret world / in rich silence / born from ether / in the eternal silent light / emerging into air and light.

But once you are observing silence, he says, you are no longer in it. It loses its purpose.

I think it gives you a kind of spiritual power. Being able to regard yourself abstractly. I catch glimpses. The out-of-doors childhood, the musical ear, the feeling of really being in a painting, the orientation of cells. Instead of being overwhelmed by the details of an individual life, you can hold on to the patterns, the tones, the sensations of everything. I've seen enough to know that death always comes before the end of your story.

Frame, isn't it you who always says that ninety-five percent of your time is spent watching animals sleep? The rest of the time they chew and spit and fuck. And that you have to really wait around if you want to witness death?

But it does come if one is patient enough. The waiting, it occurs to me, is something I have practised my entire life. First with Lev, then in the field. All for that one perfect moment to declare itself.

Skeet?

Yup, he says, not smiling.

Around the same time the vertigo spells started, I started to experience stunning, incomprehensible moments of well-being I've not mentioned to anyone. Experiencing things the way you do as a child, with nothing between you and the moment. Not "I am listening to this" or "I am seeing that," but actually seeing and hearing outside of everything. As though I have direct access to all things. And in these moments I am full of such rapture, amazed at everything.

Skeet gives me a look hard to interpret.

God. Do you think it means I am about to die?

Well you can't die now, he says, standing up and banging the dust off his legs. That would just be unacceptable.

So many people at the end of their life tire of all the vastly complex but banal upkeep it requires to be human. What Beckett called The Mess. All the vile little things that rattle on. They want to be done with all of it. They make their life so unlivable they actually die from it. It's just—

What? Skeet says.

I look to the bundle of pages tied with twine. This boundless sheaf of messages. It has the look of a parcel waiting to be sent, optimistic but with an odd intensity. Like Lev's painting, it contains the promise of something else. Whatever the differences, whatever the hardships, we both had the essential luck of being able to make things.

Curiosity glints through. It readjusts everything. Jeanne. Lou. This idea of dying when the world is in such turmoil means you can't help worrying that you will miss something surprising that might actually happen. That maybe there is no end to life.

This dictionary—you can continue the work, I tell him. Take any part of it and go to the end of it. Think of the next step and take it in that direction. Maybe you will need new materials, new technologies. It takes so much strength to reject rejection, but you must do it without them. You must get it all back from the conservatory, I say, referencing his other skill.

Skeet is thinking of Lou. He wants to be the one to bring her to Ivory. He tracked her down from the museum's contact, sent a message to her, and a message came back. Timorous. He felt it was impossible to know where to begin, what to say, so he sent her the fragile recordings of the man who said he could sing the sun, the ones he hummed to Ivory when they first met. She sends back an image of star fields, lunar dust written in spreading rays of light, she calls *99 Other Names for God*. It feels like something scratching faintly at the invisible. Something in her note smells of resin. He feels the weight of his body and has to sit down. The response is almost an erotic experience.

Stripes of light lengthen on the gravel floor.

Skeet finishes his drink and wipes his mouth with his sleeve.

You must go to Lou, I tell him. This painting is now for her. You must give it to her.

I have written her, he offers delicately.

Good, I say, looking at him with a sudden, abrupt wonder. His extraordinary honesty and wholeheartedness with everything that comes his way. The wide magnificent sweep of his brain. Aloof, to be sure. But I see that I can open something in him. That he can open something in me. He, too, has given himself over to science. But science is strange. You can get quiet in it. Unassimilated. I remained alone so no one would know who I was. I wonder now if I took it too far.

But she will come to see you.

I'm not sure there is time, I say.

He closes his eyes and opens them.

Receive the sounds quietly, as in a dream. My chest tightens with a spray of pain. Hearing has the most power. I swallow and then whisper, Don't let them vanish.

His eyes meet my eyes. They are full of intensity.

Skeet, please. Don't. I'm someone who has studied extinction for a long time. You can't think I haven't learned something of it.

I tell him to follow me.

The crunch of tires on gravel stops us.

He sees my alarm. All that I know. All that he keeps from me still. Skeet's look says, as he stands stock-still, that he is relieved. I know what he thinks. He thinks panic means there is still something to lose. Maybe that's the fear of dying, I say to Skeet. The simple notion of losing the only thing we really ever have.

We only ever understand things when they are truly lost, he says, tenderness flooding his voice.

Nothing we love is ever truly lost.

Low voices brush the walls of the cave. There are at least two.

The activists, Skeet hopes, with their beatific energy. He has given them the entire dictionary now. And Lou, who tells him about changing the relationship between an object and its shadow. How the scale of the work means it is experienced by the body before it settles in the mind. This back and forth between presence and absence. She says she likes anything that loops, especially time. She has been handed a history. The immeasurable space of passing time entering through a once-closed window. He wants to bring her to Ivory, but he also knows about estrangement and invitation and what happens when they assemble too quickly. He can taste the cheap sherry, sweet and rotten at the back of his throat. He almost feels a bit drunk. He understands there has been too much history for a single encounter.

Voices tunnel down the staircase, stilled in mid-air. A panic flickers between us.

If there is a word all animals are thinking, that word is run.

My body jammed stiff but my memory freed. A shock. A reminder that another story is always possible. It has the quality of being inside a perfect dream.

Follow me, Skeet. Skeet, the only child I've ever known. This thought coming to me like blood back to the fingers. I will sleep, immediately after. I promise him. We walk slowly, purposefully, following the contours of the cave through a small passage that recedes at the back, until it is open overhead, as though walking through a dry riverbed, wild and twisting. And the light flashes in and out, the sides of the caves licking up skyward, darkening. Not the kind of dark that gives light but as though we are walking into a shadow without end. Though instead of dread, I am suddenly overcome by the desire for more. That even now, I want more. That there is more than what fades and suddenly disappears. That there is more to us than what is actually lived.

And then, in the air, is held the thinnest sound. A sound so singular it makes everything else seem deserted. It startles. It is resonant like the last syllable of a last word. Flapping. All the wings, flapping. They pour out from the cracks, rolling out, ribbons of black. Clouds and clouds of butterflies with small black wings. Beating and glittering and thick in the light. They keep streaming out. They form a flapping shape, its luminous ruin, a widening fragile beauty. A stampede to freedom. Filling space, creating space. Bright and brave like a beautiful secret, they go.

Acknowledgements

Gratitude to the Toronto Arts Council, Ontario Arts Council, Canada Council, The Banff Centre for the Arts, and to Alana Wilcox at Coach House Books for the Writer's Reserve Grant— for giving me the space and time to write this book. As well as to Dave and Claire Cameron for the jewel in the woods.

I wish to thank my agent, Jane Finigan, for her heroic support and invaluable advice. To my editor, Nick Garrison at Penguin Random House, whose immeasurable insights have made this a far better book. I owe you at least one good bottle of scotch. And to Philip Gwyn Jones at Scribe UK, for wisdom and belief.

Thank you to Ani Castillo, Julie Gagné, Deborah Kirshner, Lisa Markon, Rahul Parekh, Lizabeth Ronk, Martin Spreer, Kevin Temple, and Camille Watts. To Alisha Piercy, Natalie Matutchovsky, and to Leonora Carrington, who let us into her house in Mexico City where a tree grew through it, for two magical afternoons. And whose astonishing mind and rebellious life helped this story take wing.

I am deeply grateful to Suzanne Sopinka, for lifelong love and support, and for being an example of how to live. And to Nick

Sopinka, steadfast and true, my first editor, and the person I hold accountable for my problem with books. To Metro Sopinka, whose memoirs informed parts of this story. To Zoe McCready, Amy Sopinka, and Steve Sopinka—the best constellation. And to Claudia Dey, whose exquisite thinking and sistership have been integral in the writing of this book and beyond.

Thank you to Kes Lake, Soren Penn, and Winter Violet, who came into the world during the various stages of this book, and who compel me to want to make every single moment of this rare, wild life count. And to the inspired women, including Jill Connell, Kerri MacLellan, and Gabrielle MacLellan, who took care of them so well when I wrote. Lastly, thank you Jason Logan, for your extraordinary eye and brain and heart, and to whom this book is dedicated.